W9-CEO-947

Dragon Teeth

ALSO BY MICHAEL CRICHTON

FICTION

The Andromeda Strain

The Terminal Man

The Great Train Robbery

Eaters of the Dead

Congo

Sphere

Jurassic Park

Rising Sun

Disclosure

The Lost World

Airframe

Timeline

Prey

State of Fear

Next

Pirate Latitudes

Micro

NONFICTION

Five Patients

Jasper Johns

Electronic Life

Travels

Dragon Teeth

A Novel

Michael Crichton

An Imprint of HarperCollinsPublishers

This book is a work of fiction. References to real people, events, establishments, organizations, or locales are intended only to provide a sense of authenticity, and are used fictitiously. All other characters, and all incidents and dialogue, are drawn from the author's imagination and are not to be construed as real.

HarperCollins books may be purchased for educational, business, or sales promotional use. For information please e-mail the Special Markets Department at SPsales@harpercollins.com.

FIRST HARPERLUXE EDITION

ISBN: 978-0-06-267421-0

HarperLuxe™ is a trademark of HarperCollins Publishers.

Library of Congress Cataloging-in-Publication Data is available upon request.

17 18 19 20 21   ID/LSC   10 9 8 7 6 5 4 3 2 1

Introduction

As he appears in an early photograph, William Johnson is a handsome young man with a crooked smile and a naive grin. A study in slouching indifference, he lounges against a Gothic building. He is a tall fellow, but his height appears irrelevant to his presentation of himself. The photograph is dated "New Haven, 1875," and was apparently taken after he had left home to begin studies as an undergraduate at Yale College.

A later photograph, marked "Cheyenne, Wyoming, 1876," shows Johnson quite differently. His mouth is framed by a full mustache; his body is harder and enlarged by use; his jaw is set; he stands confidently with shoulders squared and feet wide—and ankle-deep in mud. Clearly visible is a peculiar scar on his upper lip, which in later years he claimed was the result of an Indian attack.

The following story tells what happened between the two pictures.

For the journals and notebooks of William Johnson, I am indebted to the estate of W. J. T. Johnson, and particularly to Johnson's great-niece, Emily Silliman, who permitted me to quote extensively from the unpublished material. (Much of the factual contents of Johnson's accounts found their way into print in 1890, during the fierce battles for priority between Cope and Marsh, which finally involved the U.S. government. But the text itself, or even excerpts, was never published, until now.)

PART I

The Field Trip West

Young Johnson Joins the Field Trip West

William Jason Tertullius Johnson, the elder son of Philadelphia shipbuilder Silas Johnson, entered Yale College in the fall of 1875. According to his headmaster at Exeter, Johnson was "gifted, attractive, athletic and able." But the headmaster added that Johnson was "headstrong, indolent and badly spoilt, with a notable indifference to any motive save his own pleasures. Unless he finds a purpose to his life, he risks unseemly decline into indolence and vice."

Those words could have served as the description of a thousand young men in late nineteenth-century America, young men with intimidating, dynamic fathers, large quantities of money, and no particular way to pass the time.

William Johnson fulfilled his headmaster's prediction during his first year at Yale. He was placed on probation in November for gambling, and again in February after an incident involving heavy drinking and the smashing of a New Haven merchant's window. Silas Johnson paid the bill. Despite such reckless behavior, Johnson remained courtly and even shy with women of his own age, for he had yet to have any luck with them. For their part, they found reason to seek his attention, their formal upbringings notwithstanding. In all other respects, however, he remained unrepentant. Early that spring, on a sunny afternoon, Johnson wrecked his roommate's yacht, running it aground on Long Island Sound. The boat sank within minutes; Johnson was rescued by a passing trawler; asked what happened, he admitted to the incredulous fishermen that he did not know how to sail because it would be "so utterly tedious to learn. And anyway, it looks simple enough." Confronted by his roommate, Johnson admitted he had not asked permission to use the yacht because "it was such bother to find you."

Faced with the bill for the lost yacht, Johnson's father complained to his friends that "the cost of educating a young gentleman at Yale these days is ruinously expensive." His father was the serious son of a Scottish immigrant, and took some pains to conceal the excesses of his offspring; in his letters, he repeatedly urged William to find a purpose in life. But William seemed content with his spoiled frivolity, and when he announced his intention to spend the coming summer in Europe, "the prospect," said his father, "fills me with direst fiscal dread."

Thus his family was surprised when William Johnson abruptly decided to go west during the summer of 1876. Johnson never publically explained why he had changed his mind. But those close to him at Yale knew the reason. He had decided to go west because of a bet.

In his own words, from the journal he scrupulously kept:

Every young man probably has an arch-rival at some point in his life, and in my first year at Yale, I had mine. Harold Hannibal Marlin was my own age, eighteen. He was handsome, athletic, well-spoken, soaking rich, and he was from New York, which he considered superior to Philadelphia in every respect. I found him insufferable. The sentiment was returned in kind.

Marlin and I competed in every arena—in the classroom, on the playing-field, in the undergraduate pranks of the night. Nothing would exist but that we would compete over it. We argued incessantly, always taking the opposing view from the other.

One night at dinner he said that the future of America lay in the developing West. I said it didn't, that the future of our great nation could hardly rest on a vast desert populated by savage aboriginal tribes.

He replied I didn't know what I was talking about, because I hadn't been there. This was a sore point—Marlin had actually been to the West, at least as far as Kansas City, where his brother lived, and he never failed to express his superiority in this matter of travel.

I had never succeeded in neutralizing it.

"Going west is no shakes. Any fool can go," I said.

"But all fools haven't gone—at least you haven't."

"I've never had the least desire to go," I said.

"I'll tell you what I think," Hannibal Marlin replied, checking to see that the others were listening. "I think you're afraid."

"That's absurd."

"Oh yes. A nice trip to Europe's more your way of things."

"Europe? Europe is for old people and dusty scholars."

"Mark my word, you'll tour Europe this summer, perhaps with a parasol."

"And if I do go, that doesn't mean—"

"Ah hah! You see?" Marlin turned to address the assembled table. "Afraid. Afraid." He smiled in a knowing, patronizing way that made me hate him and left me no choice.

"As a matter of fact," I said coolly, "I am already determined on a trip in the West this summer."

That caught him by surprise; the smug smile froze on his face. "Oh?"

"Yes," I said. "I am going with Professor Marsh. He takes a group of students with him each summer." There had been an advertisement in the paper the previous week; I vaguely remembered it.

"What? Fat old Marsh? The bone professor?"

"That's right."

"You're going with Marsh? Accommodations for his group are Spartan, and they say he works the boys unmercifully. It doesn't seem your line of things at all." His eyes narrowed. "When do you leave?"

"He hasn't told us the date yet."

Marlin smiled. "You've never laid eyes on Professor Marsh, and you'll never go with him."

"I will."

"You won't."

"I tell you, it's already decided."

Marlin sighed in his patronizing way. "I have a thousand dollars that says you will not go."

Marlin had been losing the attention of the table, but he got it back with that one. A thousand dollars was a great deal of money in 1876, even from one rich boy to another.

"A thousand dollars says you won't go west with Marsh this summer," Marlin repeated.

"You, sir, have made a wager," I replied. And in that moment I realized that, through no fault of my own, I would now spend the entire summer in some ghastly hot desert in the company of a known lunatic, digging up old bones.

Marsh

Professor Marsh kept offices in the Peabody Museum on the Yale campus. A heavy green door with large white lettering read PROF. O. C. MARSH. VISITORS BY WRITTEN APPOINTMENT ONLY.

Johnson knocked. There was no reply, so he knocked again.

"Go away."

Johnson knocked a third time.

A small panel opened in the center of the door, and an eye squinted out. "What is it?"

"I want to see Professor Marsh."

"But does he want to see you?" demanded the eye. "I doubt it."

"I am replying to his notice." Johnson held up the newspaper advertisement from the week before.

"Sorry. Too late. Positions all filled." The door panel snapped shut.

Johnson was not accustomed to being denied anything, particularly a silly trip he did not want in the first place. Angrily, he kicked the door. He stared at the buggy traffic on Whitney Avenue. But with his pride, and a thousand dollars, hanging in the balance, he got control of himself, and knocked politely once more. "I'm sorry, Professor Marsh, but I really must go west with you."

"Young man, the only place you must go is away. Go away."

"Please, Professor Marsh. Please let me join your expedition." The thought of his humiliation before Marlin was awful to Johnson. His voice choked; his eyes watered. "Please hear me out, sir. I'll do whatever you say, I'll even provide my own equipment."

The panel snapped open again. "Young man, everyone provides their own equipment, and everyone does whatever I say, except you. You are presenting an unmanly spectacle." The eye peered out. "Now go away."

"Please, sir, you have to take me."

"If you wanted to come you should have answered the advertisement last week. Everyone else did. We had thirty candidates to choose from last week. Now we have selected everyone except— You're not, by any chance, a photographer?"

Johnson saw his chance and leapt at it. "A photographer? Yes, sir, I am! I am indeed."

"Well! You should have said so at once. Come in." The door swung open wide, and Johnson had his first full look at the heavy, powerful, solemn figure of Othniel C. Marsh, Yale's first professor of paleontology. Of medium height, he appeared to enjoy a fleshy, robust health.

Marsh led him back into the interior of the museum. The air was chalky and shafts of sunlight pierced it like a cathedral. In a vast cavernous space, Johnson saw men in white lab coats bent over great slabs of rock, chipping bones free with small chisels. They worked carefully, he saw, and used small brushes to clean their work. In the far corner, a gigantic skeleton was being assembled, the framework of bones rising to the ceiling.

"*Giganthopus marshiensis*, my crowning achievement," Marsh said, nodding toward the looming beast of bones. "To date, that is. Discovered her in '74, in the Wyoming Territory. I always think of her as her. What is your name?"

"William Johnson, sir."

"What does your father do?"

"My father is in shipping, sir." Chalky dust hung in the air; Johnson coughed.

Marsh looked suspicious. "Are you unwell, Johnson?"

"No, sir, perfectly well."

"I cannot abide sickness around me."

"My health is excellent, sir."

Marsh appeared unconvinced. "How old are you, Johnson?"

"Eighteen, sir."

"And how long have you been a photographer?"

"A photographer? Oh, uh—from my youth, sir. My, uh—my father took pictures and I learned from him, sir."

"You have your own equipment?"

"Yes—uh, no, sir—but I can obtain it. From my father, sir."

"You are nervous, Johnson. Why is that?"

"I'm just eager to go with you, sir."

"Are you." Marsh stared at him, as if Johnson were a curious anatomical specimen himself.

Uneasy under that stare, Johnson attempted a compliment. "I've heard so many exciting things about you, sir."

"Indeed? What have you heard?"

Johnson hesitated. In truth, he had heard only that Marsh was an obsessive, driven man who owed his college position to his monomaniacal interest in fossil bones, and to his uncle, the famous philanthropist George Peabody, who had provided the funding for the Peabody Museum, for Marsh's professorship, and for Marsh's annual field trips to the West.

"Only that students have found it a privilege and an adventure to accompany you, sir."

Marsh was silent for a moment. Finally, he said, "I dislike compliments and idle flattery. I don't like to be called 'sir.' You may refer to me as 'Professor.' As for privilege and adventure, I offer damned hard work and plenty of it. But I'll say this: all my students have come back alive and well. Now then—why do you want to go so much?"

"Personal reasons, si— Professor."

"All reasons are personal reasons, Johnson. I'm asking yours."

"Well, Professor, I am interested in the study of fossils."

"You are interested? You say you are interested? Young man, these fossils"—his hand swept wide, gesturing to the room—"these fossils do not invite interest. They invite passionate commitment, they invite religious fervor and scientific speculation, they invite heated discourse and argument, but they do not thrive on mere interest. No, no. I am sorry. No, no, indeed."

Johnson feared he had lost his opportunity with his chance remark, but in another swift change, Marsh smiled and said, "Never mind, I need a photographer and you are welcome to come." He extended his hand, and Johnson shook it. "Where are you from, Johnson?"

"Philadelphia."

The name had an extraordinary effect on Marsh. He dropped Johnson's hand, and took a step back. "Philadelphia! You—you—you are from Philadelphia?"

"Yes, sir, is there something wrong with Philadelphia?"

"Don't call me 'sir'! And your father is in shipping?"

"Yes, he is."

Marsh's face turned purple; his body shook with rage. "And I suppose you are a Quaker, too? Hmmm? A Quaker from Philadelphia?"

"No, Methodist, actually."

"Isn't that very close to Quaker?"

"I don't think so."

"But you live in the same city that he does."

"That who does?"

Marsh fell silent, frowning, staring at the floor, and then he made another of his abrupt turns, shifting his bulk. For a large man he was surprisingly agile and athletic.

"Never mind," he said, smiling once again. "I've no quarrel with any resident of the City of Brotherly Love, whatever they may say. And yet I imagine you are wondering where my expedition is going this summer, to look for fossils?"

The question had never crossed Johnson's mind, but to show proper interest, he replied, "I am a bit curious, yes."

"I imagine you are. Yes. I imagine you are. Well, it is a secret," Marsh said, leaning close to Johnson's face and hissing the words. "Do you understand me? A secret. And it will remain a secret, known only to me, until we are on the train headed west. Is that completely understood?"

Johnson backed away under the vehemence of the words. "Yes, Professor."

"Good. If your family desires to know your destination, tell them Colorado. It isn't true, for we won't go to Colorado this year, but that doesn't matter because you'll be out of touch anyway, and Colorado is a delightful place not to be. Understood?"

"Yes, Professor."

"Good. Now then, we depart June 14, from Grand Central Depot in New York. Returning no later than September 1 to the same station. See the museum sec-

retary tomorrow and he will give you a list of provisions you are to provide—in addition, in your case, to
your photographic equipment. You will allow supplies
sufficient for a hundred photographs. Any questions?"

"No, sir. No, Professor."

"Then I will see you at the platform on June 14,
Mr. Johnson." They shook hands briefly. Marsh's hand
was damp and cold.

"Thank you, Professor." Johnson turned and headed
toward the door.

"Ah, ah, ah. Where do you think you are going?"

"To leave."

"By yourself?"

"I can find my way—"

"No one, Johnson, is permitted unescorted movement through this office. I am not a fool, I know there
are spies eager to look at the latest drafts of my papers,
or the latest bones to emerge from the rock. My assistant Mr. Gall will see you out." At the mention of his
name, a thin, pinched man in a lab coat put down his
chisel and walked with Johnson to the door.

"Is he always like this?" Johnson whispered.

"Lovely weather," Gall said, and smiled. "Good day
to you, sir."

And William Johnson was back out on the street.

Learning Photography

Johnson wanted nothing more than to escape the terms of his wager and this impending expedition. Marsh was obviously a lunatic of the first order, and conceivably dangerous as well. He fixed on having another meal with Marlin, and somehow extricating himself from the bet.

Yet that evening, to his horror, he learned that the wager had become notorious. It was now known broadly throughout the College, and all during dinner people came to his table to talk about it, to make some small comment or joke. Backing out now was inconceivable.

He realized then he was doomed.

The following day he went to the shop of Mr. Carlton Lewis, a local photographer, who offered twenty lessons in his craft for the outrageous sum of fifty dollars. Mr. Lewis was amused with this new pupil; photography was not a rich man's pursuit, but rather a shifty business for people who lacked the capital to embark on a more prestigious livelihood. Even Mathew Brady, the most famous photographer of his day, the chronicler of the Civil War, the man who photographed statesmen and presidents, had never been treated as anything but a servant by the eminent subjects who sat for him.

But Johnson was adamant, and over a period of weeks he learned the skills behind this method of recording, introduced from France forty years earlier by the telegrapher Samuel Morse.

The process then in vogue was the "wet plate" photographic technique; in a darkened room or tent, fresh chemicals were mixed on the spot, and sheets of glass coated with a sticky, light-sensitive emulsion. The newly made wet plates were then rushed to the camera and exposed to the scene while still wet. Considerable skill was required to prepare an evenly coated plate, and then to expose it before the plate dried; later development was easy by comparison.

Johnson learned with difficulty. He could not carry out the steps fast enough, with the easy rhythms of his teacher; his early emulsions were too thick or too thin, too wet or too dry; his plates had bubbles and dripped.

densities that made his pictures amateurish. He hated the confined tent, the darkness, and the smelly chemicals that irritated his eyes, stained his fingers, and burned his clothes. Most of all he hated the fact that he couldn't master the craft easily. And he hated Mr. Lewis, who tended to philosophize.

"You expect everything to be easy because you are rich," Lewis would chuckle, watching him fumble and swear. "But the plate doesn't care how rich you are. The chemicals don't care how rich you are. The lens doesn't care how rich you are. You must first learn patience, if you wish to learn anything at all."

"Damn you," Johnson would say, irritated. The man was nothing but an uneducated shopkeeper putting on airs.

"I am not the problem," Lewis would reply, taking no offense. "You are the problem. Now come: try again."

Johnson ground his teeth and swore under his breath.

But as the weeks passed, he did improve. By late April his plates were uniform in density, and he was working swiftly enough to make good exposures. His plates were crisp and sharp, and he was pleased as he showed them to his teacher.

"What are you pleased about?" Mr. Lewis asked. "These pictures are wretched."

"Wretched? They are perfect."

"They are technically perfect," Lewis said, shrugging. "It means merely that you know enough to begin to learn about photography. I believe that is why you came to me in the first place."

Lewis taught him now the details of exposure, the vagaries of f-stop, focal length, depth of field. Johnson despaired, for there was so much more to learn: "Shoot portraits wide open with short exposures, because the wide-open lens has a soft quality that flatters the subject." And again, "Shoot landscapes stopped down with long exposures, because people wish to see a landscape sharp both close and at a distance." He learned to vary contrast by changing exposure and subsequent development time. He learned to position his subjects in the light, to change the composition of his emulsions on bright and dull days. Johnson worked hard and kept detailed notes in his journal—but also complaints.

"I despise this little man," observes one characteristic entry, "and yet I desperately want to hear him say what he will not: that I have learned this skill." Yet even in his complaint one notices a change from the haughty young man who a few months earlier could not be bothered to learn to sail. He wanted to excel at his task.

In early May, Lewis held a plate up to the light, then inspected it with a magnifying glass. He finally turned to Johnson. "This work is almost acceptable," he allowed. "You have done well."

Johnson was elated. In his journal he wrote: "Almost acceptable! Almost acceptable! Nothing said to me was ever so sweet to my ears!"

Other aspects of Johnson's demeanor were changing as well: despite himself he was beginning to look forward to the trip.

I still regard three months in the West in much the same way I would three months forced attendance at the German Opera. But I have to admit a pleasurable, growing excitement as the fateful departure approaches. I have acquired everything on the list of the Museum Secretary, including a Bowie knife, a Smith & Wesson six-shot revolver, a .50 caliber rifle, sturdy cavalry boots, and a geologist's hammer. With each purchase, my excitement grows. I have mastered my photographic techniques passably well; I have acquired the eighty pounds of chemicals and equipment, and the hundred glass plates; I am, in short, ready to go.

Only one major obstacle now stands between me and departure: my family. I must return to Philadelphia, and tell them.

Philadelphia

Philadelphia was the busiest city in America that May, nearly bursting with the vast crowds that flocked to attend the Centennial Exposition of 1876. The excitement that surrounded this celebration of the nation's hundredth anniversary was nearly palpable. Wandering the soaring exhibition halls, Johnson saw the wonders that astonished all the world—the great Corliss steam engine, the exhibits of plant and agriculture from the states and territories of America, and the new inventions that were all the rage.

The prospect of harnessing the power of electricity was the newest subject: there was even talk of making electrical light, to illuminate city streets at night; everyone said Edison would have a solution within a year. Meanwhile there were other electrical wonders to puzzle over, particularly the curious device of the tele-phone.

Everyone who attended the exposition saw this oddity, although few considered it of any value. Johnson was among the majority when he noted in his journal, "We already have the telegraph, providing communications for all who desire it. The added virtues of voice communication at a distance are unclear. Perhaps in the future, some people will wish to hear the voice of another far away, but there cannot be many. For myself, I think Mr. Bell's tele-phone is a doomed curiosity with no real purpose."

Despite the splendid buildings and enormous crowds, all was not entirely well in the nation. This was an election year, with much talk of politics. President Ulysses S. Grant had opened the Centennial Exposition, but the little general was no longer popular; scandal and corruption characterized his administration, and the excesses of financial speculators had finally plunged the nation into one of the most severe depressions in its history. Thousands of investors had been ruined on Wall Street; Western farmers were destroyed by the sharp decline in prices, as well as by harsh winters and plagues of grasshoppers; the resurgent Indian Wars in the Montana, Dakota, and Wyoming Territories provided an unsavory aspect, at least to the Eastern press, and both

Democratic and Republican parties promised in this year's campaign to focus on reform.

But to a young man, particularly a rich one, all this news—both good and bad—merely formed an exciting backdrop on the eve of his great adventure. "I relished the wonders of this Exposition," Johnson wrote, "but in truth I found it wearingly civilized. My eyes looked to the future, and to the Great Plains that would soon be my destination. If my family agreed to let me go."

The Johnsons resided in one of the ornate mansions that fronted Philadelphia's Rittenhouse Square. It was the only home William had ever known—lavish furnishings, mannered elegance, and servants behind every door. He decided to tell his family one morning at breakfast. In retrospect, he found their reactions absolutely predictable.

"Oh, darling! Why ever would you want to go out there?" asked his mother, buttering her toast.

"I think it's a capital idea," said his father. "Excellent."

"But do you think it's wise, William?" asked his mother. "There's all that trouble with the Indians, you know."

"It's good that he's going, maybe they'll scalp him," announced his younger brother, Edward, who was fourteen. He said things like that all the time and no one paid any attention.

"I don't understand the appeal," his mother said again, an edge of worry in her voice. "Why do you want to go? It doesn't make any sense. Why not go to Europe instead? Someplace culturally stimulating and safe."

"I'm sure he'll be safe," his father said. "Only today the *Inquirer* reports on the Sioux uprising in the Dakotas. They've sent Custer himself to put it down. He'll make short work of them."

"I hate to think of you eaten," said his mother.

"Scalped, Mother," Edward corrected her. "They cut off all the hair right around the head, after they club you to death, of course. Except sometimes you're not completely dead and you can feel the knife cutting off the skin and hair right down to the eyebrows—"

"Not at breakfast, Edward."

"You're disgusting, Edward," said his sister, Eliza, who was ten. "You make me puke."

"Eliza!"

"Well, he does, Mother. He is a revolting creature."

"Where exactly will you go with Professor Marsh, son?" his father asked.

"To Colorado."

"Isn't that near the Dakotas?" asked his mother.

"Not very."

"Oh, Mother, don't you know anything?" said Edward.

"Are there Indians in Colorado?"

"There are Indians everywhere, Mother."

"I wasn't asking you, Edward."

"I believe no hostile Indians reside in Colorado," his father said. "They say it's a lovely place. Very dry."

"They say it's a desert," said his mother. "And dreadfully inhospitable. What sort of hotel will you stay in?"

"We'll be camping, mostly."

"Good," his father said. "Plenty of fresh air and exertion. Invigorating."

"You sleep on the ground with all the snakes and animals and insects? It sounds horrific," his mother said.

"Summer in the out-of-doors, good for a young man," his father said. "After all, many sickly boys go for the 'camp cure' nowadays."

"I suppose . . ." said his mother. "But William isn't sickly. Why do you want to go, William?"

"I think it's time I made something of myself," William told her, surprised by his own honesty.

"Well said!" said his father, pounding the table.

In the end his mother gave her consent, although she continued to look genuinely worried. He thought she was being maternal and foolish; the fears she expressed only made him feel all the more puffed-up, brave, and determined to go.

He might have felt differently, had he known that by late summer, she would be informed that her firstborn son was dead.

"Ready to Dig for Yale?"

The train left at eight o'clock in the evening from the cavernous interior of the Grand Central Depot in New York. Finding his way through the station, Johnson passed several attractive young women accompanied by their families, but could not quite bring himself to meet their curious eyes. Meanwhile, he told himself, he needed to find his party. Altogether, twelve Yale students would accompany Professor Marsh and his staff of two, Mr. Gall and Mr. Bellows.

Marsh was there early, walking down the line of cars, greeting everyone the same way: "Hello, young fellow, ready to dig for Yale?" Ordinarily taciturn and suspicious, Marsh was here outgoing and friendly. Marsh had handpicked his students from socially prominent and wealthy families, and these families had come to see their boys off.

Marsh was well aware that he was serving as a tour guide to the scions of the rich, who might later be properly grateful for his part in turning their young boys into men. He understood further that since many prominent ministers and theologians explicitly denounced ungodly paleontological research, all research money in his field came from private patrons, among them his financier uncle, George Peabody. Here in New York, the new American Museum of Natural History in Central Park had just been chartered by other self-made men such as Andrew Carnegie, J. Pierpont Morgan, and Marshall Field.

For as eagerly as religious men sought to discredit the doctrine of evolution, so wealthy men sought to promote it. In the principle of the survival of the fittest they saw a new, scientific justification for their own rise to prominence, and their own often unscrupulous way of life. After all, no less an authority than the great Charles Lyell, friend and forerunner of Charles Darwin, had insisted again and again, "In the universal struggle for existence, the right of the strongest eventually prevails."

Here Marsh found himself surrounded by the children of the strongest. Marsh privately maintained to

Bellows that "the New York send-off is the most productive part of the field trip," and his thinking was firmly in mind when he greeted Johnson with his usual "Hello, young man, ready to dig for Yale?"

Johnson was surrounded by a cluster of porters who loaded his bulky photographic equipment aboard. Marsh looked about, then frowned. "Where is your family?"

"In Philadelphia, si— Professor."

"Your father did not come to see you off?" Marsh recalled that Johnson's father was in shipping. Marsh did not know much about shipping, but it was undoubtedly lucrative and full of sharp practices. Fortunes were made daily in shipping.

"My father saw me off in Philadelphia."

"Really? Most families wish to meet me personally, to get a sense of the expedition . . ."

"Yes, I am sure, but you see, they felt to come here would strain—my mother—who does not completely approve."

"Your mother does not approve?" Marsh could not conceal the distress in his voice. "Does not approve of what? Surely not of me . . ."

"Oh no. It's the Indians, Professor. She disapproves of my going west, because she is afraid of the Indians."

Marsh huffed. "She obviously knows nothing of my background. I am widely respected as the intimate friend of the red man. We'll have no trouble with Indians, I promise you."

But the situation was altogether unsatisfactory for Marsh, who later muttered to Bellows that Johnson "looks older than the others," and hinted darkly that "perhaps he is not a student at all. And his father is in shipping. I think nothing more need be said."

The whistle blew, there were final kisses and waves for the students, and the train pulled out of the station.

Marsh had arranged for them to travel in a private car, provided by none other than Commodore Vanderbilt himself, now a whitened eighty-two-year-old tucked into his sickbed. It was the first of many agreeable comforts that Marsh had arranged for the trip through his extensive connections with the army, the government, and captains of industry such as Vanderbilt.

In his prime, the crusty Commodore, a hulking figure in a fur coat worn winter and summer, had been admired by all New York. With ruthless and aggressive instincts, as well as a sharply profane tongue, this uneducated Staten Island Ferry boy, the son of Dutch peasants, had come to control shipping lines from New York to San Francisco; later he took an interest in railroads, extending his mighty New York Central from the heart of New York all the way to burgeoning Chicago. He was always good copy, even in defeat; when the secretive Jay Gould bested him for control of the Erie railway, he announced, "This Erie war has taught me that it never pays to kick a skunk." And on another occasion, his complaint to his lawyers—"What do I care for the law? Haint I got the power?"—had made him a legend.

In later years Vanderbilt became increasingly eccentric, given to fraternizing with clairvoyants and mesmerists, communing with the dead, often on pressing business matters; and though he patronized outrageous feminists such as Victoria Woodhull, he still chased girls a quarter of his age.

Some days before, New York newspaper headlines had proclaimed "VANDERBILT DYING!," which had roused the old man out of bed to bellow at reporters: "I am not dying! Even if I was dying I should have vigor enough to knock this abuse down your lying throats!" At least, this was what the journalists reported, though everyone in America knew the Commodore's language was considerably saltier.

Vanderbilt's railway car was the last word in elegance and modernity; there were Tiffany lamps, china and crystal service, as well as the clever new sleeper beds invented by George Pullman. By now, Johnson had met the other students, and noted in his journal they were "a bit tedious and spoiled, but all in all, an adventure-seeking lot. Yet we all share a common fear—of Professor Marsh."

It was clear, seeing Marsh stride commandingly about the railway car, now sinking into the plush banquette seats to smoke a cigar, now snapping his fingers for the servant to bring him an iced drink, that he imagined himself as suited to these surroundings. And indeed, the newspapers sometimes referred to him as the "Baron of Bones," just as Carnegie was the Baron of Steel, and Rockefeller the Baron of Oil.

Like these other great figures, Marsh was self-made. The son of a New York farmer, he had early shown an interest in fossils and learning. Despite the ridicule of his family, he had attended Phillips Academy Andover, graduating at the age of twenty-nine with high honors and the nickname "Daddy Marsh." From Andover he went to Yale, and from Yale to England to plead support from his philanthropic uncle, George Peabody. His uncle admired learning in all forms, and was pleased to see a member of his family taking up an academic life. He gave Othniel Marsh the funds to start the Peabody Museum at Yale. The only catch was that Peabody later gave a similar sum to Harvard, to start another Peabody Museum there. This was because Marsh espoused Darwinism, and George Peabody disapproved of such irreligious sentiments. Harvard was the home of Louis Agassiz, an eminent zoology professor who opposed Darwin's ideas, and was thus a stronghold of the anti-evolutionists—Harvard would provide a useful corrective to the excesses of his nephew, Peabody felt. All this Johnson learned in whispered conversation in the rocking Pullman bunks that night, before the excited students dropped off to sleep.

By morning they were in Rochester, by midday in Buffalo, waiting expectantly for a look at Niagara Falls. Unfortunately, their one glimpse, from a bridge some distance downstream, was anticlimactic. But their disappointment quickly vanished when they were informed that Professor Marsh expected to see them all in his private stateroom at once.

Marsh peered up and down the hallway, closed the door, and locked it from the inside. Though the afternoon was warm, he closed all the windows and locked them, too. Only then did he turn to the twelve waiting students.

"You have undoubtedly wondered where we are going," he said. "But it is too early to inform you yet; I will tell you after Chicago. In the meantime, I caution you to avoid contact with strangers, and to say nothing of our plans. He has spies everywhere."

Tentatively, one student said, "Who does?"

"Cope, of course!" Marsh snapped.

Hearing this unfamiliar name, the students looked blankly at each other, but Marsh did not notice; he was off on a tirade. "Gentlemen, I cannot warn you against him too strongly. Professor Edward Drinker Cope may pretend to be a scientist, but in fact he is little better than a common thief and keyhole-peeper. I have never known him to obtain by fair labor what he could steal instead. The man is a despicable liar and sneak. Be on your guard."

Marsh was puffing, as if exerted. He glared around the room. "Any questions?"

There were none.

"All right," Marsh said. "I merely want the record straight. You will hear more after Chicago. Meantime, keep to yourselves."

Bewildered, the students filed out of the compartment.

One young man named Winslow knew who Cope was. "He is another professor of paleontology, I believe at Haverford College in Pennsylvania. He and Marsh were once friends, but are now the most steadfast enemies. As I heard it, Cope tried to steal credit for the professor's first fossil discoveries, and there has been bad feeling between them ever since. And Cope apparently pursued a woman Marsh wanted to marry, and discredited her, or at least sullied her reputation. Cope's father was a wealthy Quaker merchant, left him millions, I was told. So Cope does as he pleases. It seems he is a bit of a rogue and charlatan. There's no end of sly tricks he will pull to steal from Marsh what is rightfully his. That's why Marsh is so suspicious—he is ever on the watch for Cope and his agents."

"I knew nothing of this," Johnson said.

"Well, you know now," Winslow responded. He stared out the window at rolling green cornfields. The train had left New York State, passed through Pennsylvania, and was in Ohio. "Speaking for myself," he said, "I don't know why you are on this expedition. I'd never go except my family made me. My father insists that a summer in the West will 'put hair on my chest.'" He shook his head in wonder. "God. All I can think of is, three months of bad food and bad water and bad insects. And no girls. No fun. God."

Still curious about Cope, Johnson asked Marsh's assistant Bellows, a pinch-faced zoology instructor. Bellows immediately became suspicious. "Why do you ask?"

"I am simply curious."

"But why do you, particularly, ask? None of the other students have asked."

"Perhaps they are not interested."

"Perhaps they have no reason to be interested."

"That amounts to the same thing," Johnson said.

"Does it?" Bellows asked, with a meaningful look. "I ask you, does it really?"

"Well, I think so," Johnson said, "although I'm not sure, the conversation has become so convoluted."

"Don't patronize me, young man," Bellows said. "You may think I am a fool—you may think we are all fools—but I assure you we are not."

And he walked off, leaving Johnson more curious than ever.

Marsh's diary entry:

Bellows reports student W.J. has asked about Cope! The audacity, the nerve! He must think we are fools! Am very angry! Angry! Angry!!!!

Our suspicions about W.J. obviously confirmed. Phila. background—the shipping background, etc.—Only too clear. Will speak with W.J. tomorrow, and set the stage for later developments. I will see that this young man causes us no trouble.

———

The farmlands of Indiana raced past the window, mile after mile, hour after hour, lulling Johnson to a sense of monotony. With his chin propped on his hand, he was drifting off to sleep when Marsh said, "What exactly do you know about Cope?"

Johnson sat up abruptly. "Nothing, Professor."

"Well, I'll tell you some things that perhaps you don't know. He killed his own father to get his inheritance. Did you know that?"

"No, Professor."

"Not six months ago, he killed him. And he cheats on his wife, an invalided woman who has never harmed him in the least way—worships him, in fact, that's how deluded the poor creature is."

"He sounds a complete criminal."

Marsh shot him a look. "You don't believe me?"

"I believe you, Professor."

"Also, personal hygiene is not his strong point. The man is odiferous and unsanitary. But I've no wish to be personal."

"No, Professor."

"The fact is he is unscrupulous and untrustworthy in the extreme. There was a landgrab and mineral rights scandal. That's why he was kicked out of the Geological Survey."

"He was kicked out of the Geological Survey?"

"Years ago. You don't believe me?"

"I believe you, Professor."

"Well, you don't look like you believe me."

"I believe you," Johnson insisted. "I believe you."

There was a silence. The train clattered on. Marsh cleared his throat. "Do you know Professor Cope, by any chance?"

"No, I don't."

"I thought perhaps you did."

"No, Professor."

"If you did know him, you would feel better if you told me all about it now," Marsh said. "Instead of waiting."

"If I did, Professor," Johnson said, "I would. But I do not know the man."

"Yes," Marsh said, studying Johnson's face. "Hmmm."

Later that day, Johnson met a painfully thin young man making notes in a small leather-bound book. He was from Scotland and said his name was Louis Stevenson.

"How far are you going?" Johnson asked.

"All the way to the end. California," Stevenson said, lighting another cigarette. He smoked continually; his long, delicate fingers were stained dark brown. He coughed a great deal, and in general did not look like the sort of robust person who seeks a journey west, and Johnson asked him why he was doing so.

"I am in love," Stevenson said simply. "She is in California."

And then he made more notes, and seemed to forget Johnson for a time. Johnson went off in search of more congenial company, and came across Marsh.

"That young man there," Marsh said, nodding across the carriage.

"What about him?"

"You were talking to him."

"His name is Stevenson."

"I don't trust a man who makes notes," Marsh said. "What did you talk about?"

"He's from Scotland and he is going to California to find a woman he is in love with."

"How romantic. And did he ask you where you were going?"

"No, he wasn't the least interested."

Marsh squinted at him. "So he says."

I have made inquiries about that Stevenson fellow," Marsh announced to the group later. "He's from Scotland, on his way to California to find a woman. His health is poor. Apparently he fancies himself a writer, that's why he makes all those notes."

Johnson said nothing.

"Just thought you would be interested to know," Marsh said. "Personally, I think he smokes too much."

Marsh looked out the window. "Ah, the lake," he said. "We will soon be in Chicago."

Chicago

C hicago was the fastest-growing city in the world, both in population and in commercial importance. From a prairie village of four thousand in 1840, it had exploded into a metropolis of half a million, and was now doubling in size every five years. Known as "Slabtown" and "The Mud Hole of the Prairie," the city now extended across thirty-five square miles along Lake Michigan, and boasted paved streets and sidewalks, broad thoroughfares with streetcars, elegant mansions, fine shops, hotels, art galleries, and theaters. And this despite the fact that most of the city had been razed in a terrible fire just five years before.

Chicago's success owed nothing to climate and locale; the shores of Lake Michigan were swampy; most of the early buildings had sunk into the mud until they were jacked up by the brilliant young Chicago engineer George Pullman. Water was so polluted that visitors often found small fish in their drinking water—there were even minnows in dairy milk. And the weather was abhorrent: hot in summer, brutally cold in winter, and windy in all seasons.

Chicago owed its success to its geographical position in the heartland of the country, to its importance as a rail and shipping center, and most particularly to its preeminence in the handling of prodigious tonnages of beef and pork.

"I like to turn bristles, blood, and the inside and outside of pigs and bullocks into revenue," said Philip Armour, one of the founders of the gigantic Chicago stockyards. Along with fellow meatpacking magnate Gustavus Swift, Armour ruled an industry that dispatched a million head of cattle and four million pigs each year—and which employed one-sixth of the population of the city. With their centralized distribution, mechanized slaughter, and refrigerated railroad cars, the barons of Chicago were creating a whole new industry—food processing.

The Chicago stockyards were the largest in the world, and many visitors went to see them. One of the Yale students was the nephew of Swift, and they went off to tour the yards, which Johnson regarded as a dubious tourist attraction. But Marsh was not stopping in Chicago for tourism. He was there on business.

From the magnificent Lake Shore Railroad Depot, he took his charges to the nearby Grand Pacific Hotel. Here the students were awed by one of the largest and most elegant hotels in the world. As everywhere, Marsh had arranged special accommodations for his party, and there were newspapermen waiting to interview him.

Othniel Marsh was always good copy. The year before, in 1875, he had uncovered a scandal in the Indian Bureau, whereby bureau officers were not dispensing food and funds to the reservations, but were instead keeping the proceeds for themselves, while Indians literally starved. Marsh had been informed of this by Red Cloud himself, the legendary Sioux chief, and had revealed the evidence in Washington, severely embarrassing the Grant presidency in the eyes of the liberal Eastern establishment. Marsh was a good friend of Red Cloud, and thus reporters wanted to talk to him about the Sioux Wars now raging. "It is a terrible conflict," Marsh said, "but there are no easy answers to the Indian question."

Then, too, Chicago reporters never tired of repeating the story of Marsh's earliest public exploit, the affair of the Cardiff giant.

In 1869, the fossilized skeleton of a ten-foot giant was unearthed in Cardiff, New York, and quickly became a national phenomenon. It was generally agreed that the giant was one of a race of men who had been drowned in Noah's flood; Gordon Bennett of the *New York Herald* and a number of scholars had pronounced it genuine.

Marsh, in his capacity as the new paleontology professor from Yale, went to view the fossil and said, within earshot of a reporter, "Very remarkable."

"May I quote you?" said the reporter.

"Yes," said Marsh. "You may quote me as saying, 'A very remarkable fake.'"

It was later determined that the so-called giant originated as a block of gypsum, carved secretly in Chicago. But the incident brought national attention to Marsh—and he had been talking to reporters ever since.

"And what brings you to Chicago now?" one reporter asked.

"I am on my way west, to find more bones," Marsh said.

"And will you be seeing bones in Chicago?"

Marsh laughed. "No," he said, "in Chicago we will see General Sheridan, to arrange our army liaison."

Marsh took Johnson with him, because he wanted to be photographed with General Sheridan.

Little Phil Sheridan was a compact, energetic man of forty-five, with a fondness for plug tobacco and tart expression. He had assembled the army staff now waging the Indian War—Generals Crook, Terry, and Custer, all of whom were in the field, hunting out the Sioux. Sheridan was particularly fond of Armstrong Custer, and had risked the disapproval of President Grant by ordering Custer back into service along with Generals Crook and Terry in the Indian Wars.

"It's no easy campaign," Sheridan said. "And we need a man with Custer's dash. The Indians are being driven from their homes, whether we care to see it that way or not, and they'll fight us like devils. And the fact that the Indian agency supplies 'em with good rifles doesn't help, either. The main conflict promises to be in Montana and Wyoming."

"Wyoming," Marsh said. "Hmmm. Will there be problems for our group?" He did not seem the least perturbed, Johnson noticed.

"I can't see why," Sheridan said, spitting with remarkable accuracy at a metal basin across the room. "So long as you stay out of Wyoming and Montana, you'll be safe enough."

Marsh posed for a photograph, standing rigidly beside General Sheridan. He then obtained letters of introduction to the three generals, and to the post commanders at Fort Laramie and Cheyenne. Two hours later, they were back at the train station, ready to continue westward.

At the departure gate, a rough-looking man, very tall, with a peculiar slanting scar on his cheek, said to Johnson, "How far are you going?"

"I'm on my way to Wyoming." As soon as the words were out of his mouth, he remembered he should have said Colorado instead.

"Wyoming! Good luck to you then," the man said, and turned away.

Marsh was beside Johnson a moment later. "Who was that?"

"I've no idea."

"What did he want?"

"He asked how far I was going."

"Did he? And what did you say?"

"Wyoming."

Marsh frowned. "Did he believe you?"

"I've no idea."

"Did he seem to believe you?"

"Yes, Professor. I think so."

"You think so?"

"I am fairly sure, Professor."

Marsh stared off in the direction of the departed man. The station was still crowded and busy. The echoing din was loud, pierced by departure whistles.

"I have already warned you about talking to strangers," he said finally. "The man you spoke to was Cope's favorite foreman, Navy Joe Benedict. A brutal thug of a human specimen. But if you told him we were going to Wyoming, that is all right."

"You mean we are not going to Wyoming?"

"No," Marsh said. "We are going to Colorado."

"Colorado!"

"Of course," Marsh said. "Colorado is the best source of bones in the West, though you can't expect a fool like Cope to know it."

Going West

The Chicago and North Western Railway carried them across the Mississippi at Clinton, Iowa, over a twelve-span iron bridge nearly a mile long. The students were excited to cross the largest river in America, but once its great muddy expanse was behind them, their lethargy returned. Iowa was a region of rolling farmlands, with few landmarks and points of interest. Dry heat blew in through the windows, along with an occasional insect or butterfly. A dreary, perspiring tedium settled over the party.

Johnson hoped to glimpse Indians, but saw none. A passenger beside him laughed. "There haven't been Indians here for forty years, since the Black Hawk War. You want Indians, you have to go west."

"Isn't this the West?" Johnson asked.

"Not yet. 'Cross the Missouri."

"When do we cross the Missouri?"

"Other side of Cedar Rapids. Half a day on."

But already the open prairie, and the fact of having crossed the Mississippi, had an effect on passengers. At each station and refueling stop, men would step onto the platform and fire their pistols at prairie dogs and prairie fowl. The birds would go screeching into the air; the little rodents would dive for cover, chattering. Nobody ever hit anything.

"Yep," said one passenger. "They're feeling the wide-open spaces now."

Johnson found the wide-open spaces extraordinarily tedious. The students amused themselves as best they could with cards and dominoes, but it was a losing battle. For a while, they would get out at each station and walk around, but eventually even the stations became monotonously the same, and they usually remained inside.

At Cedar Rapids, the train stopped for two hours, and Johnson decided to stretch his legs. Rounding the corner of the tiny station, which stood at the edge of wheat fields, he saw Marsh talking quietly to the scarred man—Cope's man, Navy Joe Benedict. Their manner seemed familiar. After a time, Marsh reached in his pocket and handed something to Benedict; Johnson saw a flash of gold in the sunlight. He ducked behind the corner before being spotted and hurried back to the train.

When the train resumed, Johnson's perplexity increased as Marsh immediately came to sit beside him.

"I wonder where Cope will go this summer?" Marsh said, as if thinking aloud.

Johnson said nothing.

"I wonder where Cope will go?" Marsh said again.

"Very good question," Johnson said.

"I doubt that he, like us, is going to Colorado."

"I wouldn't know." Johnson was beginning to tire of this game, and allowed himself to stare directly into Marsh's eyes, holding his gaze.

"Of course not," Marsh said quickly. "Of course not."

They crossed the Missouri in early evening at Council Bluffs, the terminus for the Chicago and North Western Railway. Across the bridge, on the Omaha side, the Union Pacific Railroad took over and continued all the way to San Francisco. The Union Pacific depot was a great open shed, and it was packed with travelers of the rudest sort. Here were rugged men, painted women, border ruffians, pickpockets, soldiers, crying children, food vendors, barking dogs, thieves, grandparents, gunfighters—a great confused mass of humanity, all fairly glowing with the fever of speculation.

"Black Hillers," Marsh explained. "They outfit here before they go to Cheyenne and Fort Laramie, and from there travel northward to the Black Hills in search for gold."

The students, impatient for a taste of the "real West," were delighted, and imagined that they, too, had become more real themselves.

But despite the fevered excitement, Johnson found the sight sad. In his journal he recorded, "The hopes of humanity for wealth and fame, or at least for creature comfort, can delude them so easily! For surely only a handful of the people here will find what they are seeking. And the rest will meet with disappointment, hardship, sickness, and perhaps death from starvation, Indians, or marauding robbers who prey on the hopeful, questing pioneers."

And he added the ironic note: "I am most heartily glad that I am not going to the dangerous and uncertain Black Hills."

The West

Beyond Omaha the real West began, and aboard the train, everyone felt renewed excitement, tempered by the advice of older travelers. No, they would not see buffalo—in the seven years since the transcontinental rail lines opened, the buffalo had disappeared from view along the rail side, and indeed the legendary great herds of animals were fast disappearing altogether.

But then came the electrifying cry: "Indians!"

They ran to the opposite side of the car, pressed their faces to the glass. They saw three teepees in the distance, surrounded by a half dozen ponies and dark silhouetted figures, standing and watching the train go by. Then the Indians were gone, vanished behind a hill.

"What tribe are those?" Johnson asked. He was sitting next to Marsh's assistant Gall.

"Pawnee, probably," Gall said indifferently.

"Are they hostile?"

"Can be."

Johnson thought of his mother. "Will we see more Indians?"

"Oh yes," Gall said. "Lots of 'em where we're going."

"Really?"

"Yes, and probably riled up, too. There's going to be a full-on Sioux War over the Black Hills."

The federal government had signed a treaty with the Sioux in 1868, and as part of that treaty, the Dakota Sioux retained exclusive rights to the Black Hills, a landscape sacred to them. "That treaty was unnecessarily favorable to the Sioux," Gall said. "The government even agreed to remove all forts and army outposts in the region."

And it was a huge region, for in 1868, the Wyoming, Montana, and Dakota Territories still seemed distant and unapproachable wilderness. No one in Washington had understood how quickly the West would open up. Yet one year after the treaty had been signed, the transcontinental railroads began service, providing access in days to land that could previously be reached only by weeks of difficult overland travel.

Even so, the Sioux lands might have been respected had not Custer discovered gold during a routine survey in the Black Hills in 1874. News of gold fields, coming in the midst of a nationwide recession, was irresistible.

"Even in the best times, there's no way to keep men from gold," Gall said. "And that's a plain fact."

Although forbidden by the government, prospectors sneaked into the sacred Black Hills. The army mounted expeditions in '74 and '75 to chase them out, and the Sioux killed them whenever they found them. But still the prospectors came, in ever increasing numbers.

Believing the treaty had been broken, the Sioux went on the warpath. In May of 1876, the government ordered the army to quell the Sioux uprising.

"Then the Indians are in the right?" Johnson asked.

Gall shrugged. "You can't stop progress, and that's a plain fact."

"We will be near the Black Hills?"

Gall nodded. "Near enough."

Johnson's understanding of geography, always vague, allowed his imagination free rein. He stared out at the wide-stretching plains, which seemed suddenly more desolate and unappealing.

"How often do Indians attack white people?"

"Well, they're unpredictable," Gall said. "Like wild animals, you never know what they'll do, because they're savages."

West of Omaha the train climbed steadily and imperceptibly as it entered the high plains leading to the Rocky Mountains. They saw more animals now—prairie dogs, the occasional antelope, and coyotes loping in the distance near sunset. The towns became smaller, more desolate: Fremont, Kearney Junction, Alkali, Ogallala, Julesburg, and finally the notorious Sidney, where the conductor warned the students not to get off "if they valued their lives."

Of course they all got off to look.

What they saw was a line of wooden storefronts, a town composed, wrote Johnson, "almost entirely of outfitters, stables, and saloons, and doing a brisk commerce in all three. Sidney was the town nearest to the Black Hills, and it was filled with emigrants, most of whom found prices outrageously high. The town's reputation for murder and cut-throat life was not demonstrated to us, but then we had only stopped an hour."

But they were not long disappointed, because the Union Pacific train was now speeding them westward to a still more notorious locus of vice and crime: Cheyenne, Wyoming Territory.

Travelers loaded their six-shooters coming into Cheyenne. And the conductor took Marsh aside to recommend that his party hire a guard, to see them safely through the town.

"Such preliminaries," wrote Johnson, "gave us a most pleasurable nervous anticipation, for we imagined a lawless wild place which proved to be just that—a figment of our imaginations."

Cheyenne turned out to be a rather orderly and settled place, with many brick buildings among those of wood-frame construction, but it was not entirely peaceful. Cheyenne boasted one schoolhouse, two theaters, five churches, and twenty gambling saloons. A contemporary observer wrote that "gambling in Cheyenne, far from being merely an amusement or recreation, rises to the dignity of a legitimate occupation—the pursuit of nine-tenths of the population, both permanent and transient."

Gambling halls were open around the clock, and provided the major source of revenue to the town. Some indication of the business they did can be judged from the fact that the proprietors paid the city a license of $600 per year for each table, and each saloon had six to twelve green baize tables going at once.

The enthusiasm for gambling was not lost on the students, as they checked into the Inter-Ocean Hotel in Cheyenne, where Marsh had previously arranged a special rate. Although the best hotel in town, it was, noted Johnson, "a cockroach-infested dump, where the rats scurry up and down the walls, squeaking at all hours." Nevertheless, each student was given a private room, and after soaking in hot baths, they were ready for a night on the town.

A Night in Cheyenne

Timid, they set forth as a group—twelve earnest young down-Easters, still wearing their high collars and bowler hats, strolling from saloon to saloon with as much nonchalance as they could muster. For the town, which had appeared disappointingly tame by day, assumed a positively sinister aspect at night.

In the yellow light of the saloon windows, the boardwalk crowd of cowboys, gunmen, gamblers, and cutthroats looked at them with amusement. "These varmints'd kill you as soon as smile at you," said one student melodramatically. Feeling the unfamiliar weight of their new Smith & Wesson revolvers dragging at their hips, the students tugged at their guns, adjusting their weight.

One man stopped them. "You look like nice fellers," he told the group. "Take some friendly advice. In Cheyenne, don't touch your guns 'less you mean to use 'em. Round here, people don't look at your face, they look at your hands, and a great deal of drinking is done in these precincts at night."

There were not only gunfighters on the boardwalk. They passed several nymphs du pave, heavily painted, calling out teasingly to them from dark doorways. Altogether they found it exotic and thrilling, their first experience of the real West, the dangerous West they had been waiting for. They entered several saloons, sampled the harsh liquor, played hands of keno and 21. One student pulled out a pocket watch. "Nearly ten, and we haven't seen a shooting yet," he said, with a tinge of disappointment.

Within minutes, they saw a shooting.

"It happened astonishingly fast," Johnson noted.

One moment, angry shouts and curses; the next moment, chairs scraped back and men ducking away while the two principals snarled at each other, though they were just a few feet apart. They were both gamblers of the roughest sort. "Make your move, then," one said, and as the other went for his pistol, the first drew his gun and shot him right in his abdomen. There was a great cloud of black powder and the shot man was thrown back across the room by the impact, his clothes burning from the close shooting. He bled heavily, moaned indecipherably, twitched for a minute, then lay quite dead. Some of the others hustled the shooter out. The town marshal was summoned, but by the time he arrived, most of the gamblers had returned to their tables, to the games that had been so recently interrupted.

It was a cold-blooded display, and the students—no doubt in shock—were relieved when they heard the sound of music from the theater next door. When several gamblers left the tables to see the show, they followed hurriedly along to see this next attraction.

And here, unexpectedly, William Johnson fell in love.

The Pride De Paree Theater was a two-story triangular affair with the stage at the wide end, tables on the floor, and balconies mounted high on the walls at both sides. Balcony seats were the most expensive and desirable, though they were farthest from the stage, and so they bought those.

The show, observed Johnson, consisted of "singing, dancing, and petticoat flouncing, the rudest sort of entertainment, but the assembled patrons greeted it with such enthusiastic cheers that their pleasure infected our more discriminating tastes."

Soon enough they learned the value of balcony seats, for overhead were trapeze bars, on which swung comely young women in scanty costumes and mesh tights. As they arced back and forth, the men in the balconies reached out to tuck dollar bills into the folds of their costumes. The girls appeared to know many of the customers, and there was a deal of good-natured banter high in the air, the girls crying, "Watch them hands, Fred," and "Mighty big cigar you got there, Clem," and other endearments.

One student sniffed, "They are no better than prostitutes," but the others enjoyed the spectacle, shouting and tucking dollar bills with the rest, and the girls, seeing new faces and distinctive Eastern clothes, maneuvered their swings to come close to their balcony again and again.

It was all good fun, and then the girls overhead changed to a new set, and the swinging began again, and one of them came close to their balcony. Laughing, Johnson reached for another dollar bill, and then his eyes met those of the new girl, and the raucous sound of the theater faded away, and time seemed to stop, and he was aware of nothing but the dark intensity of her gaze and the pounding of his own heart.

Her name was Lucienne—"It's French," she explained, wiping the light sheen of perspiration from her shoulders.

They were downstairs, sitting at one of the floor tables, where the girls were allowed to have a drink with customers between shows. The other students had gone back to the hotel, but Johnson stayed, hoping Lucienne would come out, and she had. She had sashayed right to his table. "Buy me a drink?"

"Anything you want," Johnson said. She ordered whiskey, and he had one, too. And then he asked her name, and she told him.

"Lucienne," he repeated. "Lucienne. A lovely name."

"Lots of girls in Paris are named Lucienne," she announced, still wiping the perspiration. "What's yours?"

"William," he said. "William Johnson." Her skin glowed pink; her hair was jet-black, her eyes dark and dancing. He was entranced.

"You look a gent," she said, smiling. She had a way of smiling with her mouth closed, not revealing her teeth. It made her seem mysterious and self-contained. "Where're you from?"

"New Haven," he said. "Well, I grew up in Philadelphia."

"Back East? I thought you were different. I could tell from your clothes."

He worried that this might not find favor with her, and suddenly didn't know what to say.

"Do you have a sweetheart back East?" she asked innocently, helping the conversation along.

"I—" He stopped, then thought it best to tell her the truth. "I was awfully fond of a girl in Philadelphia a few years ago, but she didn't feel the same way about me." He looked into her eyes. "But that was—that was a long time ago."

She looked down and smiled softly and he told himself that he must think of something to say.

"Where are you from?" he asked. "You don't have a French accent." Perhaps she had come from France as a child.

"I'm from St. Louis. Lucienne's only my name de stage, see," she said cheerfully. "Mr. Barlow—the manager—Mr. Barlow wants everyone in the show to have a French name, because the theater is the Pride de Paree Theater, see. He's very nice, Mr. Barlow."

"Have you been in Cheyenne long?"

"Oh no," she said. "Before, I was in the theater in

Virginia City, where we did proper plays by English writers and such, but that closed with the typhoid last winter. I was going home to see my mother, see, but I only had money to get here."

She laughed, and he saw one of her front teeth was chipped. This little imperfection only made him love her more. She was obviously an independent young woman, making her own way in life.

"And you?" she asked. "You are going to the Black Hills? Looking for gold?"

He smiled. "No, I am with a group of scientists who are digging for fossils." Her face clouded. "Fossils. Old bones," he explained.

"Is there a good livelihood in that?"

"No, no. It's for science," he explained.

She placed a warm hand on his arm, and the touch electrified him. "I know you gold diggers have secrets," she said. "I won't tell."

"Really, I am searching for fossils."

She smiled again, content to drop the matter. "And how long are you in Cheyenne?"

"Alas, I am here for only one night. Tomorrow I leave to go farther west."

This thought already filled him with a delicious pain, but she did not seem to care one way or another. In her straightforward way, she said, "I must do another show in an hour, and stay with the customers another hour after that, but then I am free."

"I'll wait," he said. "I'll wait all night if you wish it."

She leaned over and kissed him lightly on the cheek. "Until then." And she swept away, across the crowded room, where other men awaited her company.

The rest of the evening passed as lightly as a dream. Johnson felt no fatigue, and he was happy to sit until she was finished with her performances. They met outside the theater. She had changed to a demure dress of dark cotton. She took his arm.

A man passed them on the sidewalk. In the darkness: "See you later, Lucy?"

"Not tonight, Ben," she laughed. Johnson turned to glare at the man, but she explained, "It's just my uncle. He looks after me. Where are you staying?"

"The Inter-Ocean Hotel."

"We can't go there," she said. "They're very strict about the rooms."

"I'll walk you home," Johnson said.

She gave him a funny look, and then smiled. "All right. That would be nice."

As they walked, she rested her head on his shoulder. "Tired?"

"Some."

The night was warm, the air pleasant. Johnson felt a wonderful peace descend over him.

"I'm going to miss you," he said.

"Oh, me, too."

"I'll be back, though."

"When?"

"Late August or so."

"August," she repeated softly. "August."

"I know it's a long time away—"

"Not so long—"

"But I'll have more time to spend then. I'll leave the party and stay with you, how does that sound?"

She relaxed against his shoulder. "That would be nice." They walked in silence. "You're nice, William. You're a nice boy."

And then she turned, and with complete naturalness kissed him on the mouth, right there in the warm Western darkness of Cheyenne, in a deep way he had never yet experienced. Johnson thought he would die with the pleasure of it all.

"I love you, Lucienne," he blurted. The words just came out, unbidden, unexpected. But it was the truth; he felt it through his whole body.

She stroked his cheek. "You are a nice boy."

He did not know how long they stayed like that, facing each other in the dark. They kissed again, and a third time. He was breathless.

"Shall we walk on?" he said finally.

She shook her head. "You go on home now. Back to the hotel."

"I'd better see you to your door."

"No," she said. "You have a train in the morning. You get your sleep."

He looked around at the street. "Are you sure you'll be all right?"

"I'll be fine."

"Promise?"

She smiled. "Promise."

He walked a few steps toward his hotel, turned, and looked back.

"Don't worry about me," she called, and blew him a kiss.

He blew a kiss back to her and walked on. At the end of the block he looked back once again, but she was gone.

At the hotel, the sleepy night clerk gave him his key. "Good evening, sir?" he asked.

"Wonderful," Johnson said. "Absolutely wonderful."

Morning in Cheyenne

Johnson awoke at eight, refreshed and excited. He looked out his window at the flat expanse of Cheyenne, boxy buildings stretching across the plains. By all accounts it was a dreary sight, but Johnson found it beautiful. And the day was lovely, clear and warm, with the fluffy high clouds peculiar to the West.

It was true that he would not see the beautiful Lucienne for many weeks until his return trip, but this fact added a delicious poignancy to his mood, and he was in excellent humor when he went downstairs to the dining room, where the Marsh party had been instructed to meet for breakfast, at nine.

No one was there.

A table had been set for a large group, but the dirty plates were being collected by a waiter.

"Where is everybody?" Johnson asked.

"Who do you mean?"

"Professor Marsh and his students."

"They're not here," the waiter said.

"Where are they?"

"Gone an hour or more."

The words sank in slowly. "The professor and the students are gone?"

"They went to catch the nine o'clock train."

"What nine o'clock train?"

The waiter looked at Johnson irritably. "I have a lot to do," he said, turning away, rattling the plates.

Their bags and expedition equipment had been stored in a large room on the ground floor of the hotel, behind the reception desk. The bellboy unlocked the door: the room was empty except for the crates containing Johnson's photographic equipment.

"They're gone!"

"Something of yours missing?" the bellboy said.

"No, not mine. But everyone else is gone."

"I just came on duty," the bell captain said apologetically. He was a boy of sixteen. "Perhaps you should ask at the desk."

"Oh yes, Mr. Johnson," said the man at the front desk. "Professor Marsh said not to wake you when they departed. He said you were leaving the expedition here in Cheyenne."

"He said what?"

"That you were leaving the expedition."

Johnson felt panic. "Why would he say that?"

"I really don't know, sir."

"What am I going to do now?" Johnson asked aloud.

The distress must have been apparent in his face and voice. The man at the front desk looked at him sympathetically.

"They're serving breakfast in the dining room for another half hour," he suggested.

He had no appetite, but he returned to the dining room and took a small table to one side. The waiter was still clearing dishes from the bare table; Johnson watched, imagining the group of Marsh and the students, imagining their excited voices, talking at once, ready to leave . . . Why had they left him behind? What possible reason could there be?

The bellboy approached him. "Are you with the Marsh expedition?"

"I am."

"The professor asked if he might join you for breakfast."

In an instant, Johnson realized that it was all a mistake

after all, that the professor had not gone, the hotel staff had merely misunderstood, everything was going to be all right.

With immense relief he said, "Of course he may join me."

A moment later, a clear, rather high voice said, "Mr. Johnson?"

Johnson faced a man he had never seen before—a wiry, fair-haired man with a mustache and goatee stood next to his table. He was tall, in his middle thirties, and rather formally dressed in stiff collar and frock coat. Although his clothes were expensive and well cut, he nevertheless gave the impression of an energetic indifference, even sloppiness. His eyes were bright and lively. He appeared amused. "May I join you?"

"Who are you?"

"Don't you know?" the man said, more amused than ever. He extended his hand. "I'm Professor Cope." Johnson noticed that his grip was firm and confident, and his fingers stained with ink.

Johnson stared, and leapt to his feet. Cope! Cope himself! Right here, in Cheyenne! Cope eased him back into his seat and beckoned to the waiter for coffee. "Don't be alarmed," he said. "I'm not the monster you have heard described. That particular monster exists only in the diseased imagination of Mr. Marsh. Yet another of his descriptions of nature is in error. You must have observed that the man is as paranoid and secretive as he is fat, and always imagines the worst in everybody. More coffee?"

Numbly, Johnson nodded; Cope poured more coffee.

"If you haven't ordered, I recommend the pork hash. I myself eat it daily. It is simple fare, but the cook has a feel for it."

Johnson mumbled he would have the hash. The waiter departed. Cope smiled at him.

He certainly didn't look like a monster, Johnson thought. Quick, energetic, even nervous—but no monster. On the contrary, there was a youthful, almost childish enthusiasm about him, yet also an air of determination and competence. He seemed like a man who got things done.

"What are your plans now?" Cope asked cheerfully, stirring a dollop of black molasses in his coffee.

"I'm not supposed to talk to you."

"That hardly seems necessary now that the old schemer has left you behind. What are your plans now?"

"I don't know. I have no plans." Johnson looked around the nearly empty dining room. "I seem to have been separated from my party."

"Separated? He abandoned you."

"Why would he do that?" Johnson asked.

"He thought you were a spy, of course."

"But I'm not a spy."

Cope smiled. "I know that, Mr. Johnson, and you know that. Everyone knows that except Mr. Marsh. It is just one of the many thousands of things he does not know, yet assumes he does."

Johnson was confused, and it must have shown on his face.

"Which fantasy did he tell you about me?" Cope asked, still cheerful. "Wife beater? Thief? Philanderer? Ax murderer?" The whole business seemed to amuse him.

"He doesn't have a high opinion of you."

Cope's inky fingers fluttered in the air, a dismissing gesture. "Marsh is a godless man, cut loose from all moorings. His mind is active and sick. I have known him for some time. In fact, we were friends once. We both studied in Germany during the Civil War. And later we dug fossils together in New Jersey, in fact. But that was a long time ago."

The food came. Johnson realized that he was hungry.

"That's better," Cope said, watching him eat. "Now, I understand that you are a photographer. I can use a photographer. I am on my way to the far West, to dig for dinosaur bones with a party of students from the University of Pennsylvania."

"Just like Professor Marsh," Johnson said.

"Not quite like Professor Marsh. We do not travel everywhere with special rates and government favors. And my students are not chosen for wealth and connection, but rather for their interest in science. Ours is not a self-aggrandizing publicity junket, but a serious expedition." Cope paused, studying Johnson's earnest attention. "We're a small party and it will be rough going, but you are welcome to come, if you care to."

And that was how William Johnson found himself, at noon, standing on the platform of the Cheyenne railroad station with his equipment stacked at his side, waiting for the train to carry him west, in the party of Edward Drinker Cope.

Cope's Expedition

It was immediately clear that Cope's party lacked the military precision that characterized Marsh's every undertaking. His group straggled into the station singly and in pairs: first Cope and his charming wife, Annie, who greeted Johnson warmly and would not be drawn to say anything against Marsh, despite the prompting of her husband.

Then a barrel-chested man of twenty-six named Charles H. Sternberg, a fossil hunter from Kansas who had worked for Cope the previous year. Charlie Sternberg walked with a limp, the result of a childhood accident; he could not shake hands because of a "felon," a fistula in his palm; and he was subject to occasional bouts of malaria, but he exuded an air of practical competence and wry humor.

Next, another young man, J.C. Isaac ("it just stands for J.C."), who was Indian shy; six weeks earlier, he had been among a party of friends attacked by Indians. The others had been shot down and scalped, and only Isaac escaped, leaving him with a deep fear, and a facial tic around the eyes.

There were three students: Leander "Toad" Davis, a puffy, asthmatic, bespectacled boy with protuberant eyes. Toad was particularly interested in Indian society, and seemed to know a lot about it. And George Morton, a sallow, silent young man from Yale who sketched constantly and announced that he intended to be an artist or a minister like his father; he wasn't sure yet. Morton was withdrawn, rather sullen, and Johnson did not care for him. And finally Harold Chapman from Pennsylvania, a brightly talkative young man with an interest in bones. After being introduced to Johnson he almost immediately wandered off to poke through some bleached buffalo bones stacked near the station platform.

Johnson's favorite of the group was the lovely Mrs. Cope, who was anything but the deluded invalid Marsh had claimed. She would accompany them only as far as Utah. Then the six men—with Johnson making seven—would set out for the Judith River basin of northern Montana Territory, to hunt for Cretaceous fossils.

"Montana!" Johnson said, remembering what Sheridan had said about staying away from Montana and Wyoming. "Do you really mean to go to Montana?"

"Yes, of course, it's tremendously exciting," Cope said, his face and manner radiating his enthusiasm. "No one has been there since Ferdinand Hayden discovered the area back in '55 and noted great quantities of fossils."

"What happened to Hayden?" Johnson asked.

"Oh, he was driven off by the Blackfeet," Cope said. "They made him run for his life."

And Cope laughed.

West with Cope

Johnson awoke in inky blackness, hearing the roar of the train. He fumbled for his pocket watch; it said ten o'clock. For a confused moment, he thought it was ten at night. Then the darkness broke with a shaft of brilliant light, and another, and flickering shafts illuminated his sleeping compartment: the train was thundering through long snow sheds as it crossed the Rocky Mountains. He saw fields of snow in late June, the brilliance so dazzling it hurt his eyes.

Ten o'clock! He threw on his clothes, hurried out of the compartment, and found Cope staring out the window, drumming his stained fingers impatiently on the sill. "I'm sorry I overslept, Professor, if only someone had awakened me, I—"

"Why?" Cope asked. "What difference does it make that you slept?"

"Well, I mean, I—it's so late—"

"We are still two hours from Salt Lake," Cope said. "And you slept because you were tired, an excellent reason for sleeping." Cope smiled. "Or did you think I would leave you, too?"

Confused, Johnson said nothing. Cope continued to smile. And then, after a moment, he bent over the sketch pad in his lap, took up his pen, and drew with his ink-stained fingers. Without looking up, he said, "I believe Mrs. Cope has arranged for a pot of coffee."

That night, Johnson recorded in his journal:

Cope spent the morning sketching, which he does with great rapidity and talent. I have learned a lot about him from the others. He was a child prodigy, who wrote his first scientific paper at the age of six, and he has now (I believe him to be 36) published some 1,000 papers. He is rumored to have had a love affair before his marriage that was broken off, and then, perhaps in despair, he traveled to Europe, where he met many of the great natural scientists of the day. He met Marsh in Berlin for the first time and shared correspondence, manuscripts, and photographs. He is also considered to be an expert on snakes, reptiles and amphibians in general, and fish. Sternberg and the students (except Morton) are devoted to him. He is a Quaker, and peace-loving to the core. He wears wooden false teeth, which are remarkably life-like; I wouldn't have known. In this way and nearly every other, he is utterly different from Marsh. Where Marsh is plodding, Cope is brilliant; where Marsh is scheming, Cope is honest; where Marsh is secretive, Cope is free. In all ways, Professor Cope shows greater humanity than his counterpart. Professor Marsh is a desperate, driven fanatic who makes his own life as miserable as the lives of those he commands. While Cope shows balance and restraint, and is altogether agreeable.

It would not be long before Johnson took a different view of Cope.

The train descended out of the Rocky Mountains to Great Salt Lake City, in the Territory of Utah.

Established thirty years before, Salt Lake City was a village of wood and brick houses, carefully laid out in a regular grid pattern, and dominated by the white facade of the Mormon Tabernacle, a building, Johnson wrote, "of such breathtaking ugliness that few edifices anywhere in America can hope to surpass it." This was a common view. Around the same time the journalist Charles Nordhoff called it "an admirably-arranged and very ugly building," and concluded that "Salt Lake need not hold any mere pleasure traveler more than a day."

Although Washington claimed this as the Territory of Utah, and therefore a part of the United States, it had been established as a Mormon theocracy, as the scale and importance of the religious buildings made clear. Cope's group visited the temple, the Tithing House, and the Lion House, where Brigham Young kept his multitudinous wives.

Cope then had an audience with President Young, and he took his own wife with him to meet the elderly patriarch. Johnson asked what he was like. "Gracious man, gentle and calculating. For forty years, the Mormons were hounded and persecuted in every state of the Union; now they make their own state, and persecute the Gentiles in turn." Cope shook his head. "You would think that people who had experienced injustice would be loath to inflict it on others, and yet they do so with alacrity. The victims become the victimizers with a chilling righteousness. This is the nature of fanaticism, to attract and provoke extremes of behavior. And this is why fanatics are all the same, whatever specific form their fanaticism takes."

"Are you saying Mormons are fanatics?" asked Morton, the minister's son.

"I am saying their religion has made a state that does not halt injustice, but rather institutionalizes it. They feel superior to others who have different beliefs. They feel only they possess the right way."

"I don't see how you can say—" began Morton, but the others jumped in. Morton and Cope were always at loggerheads on religious subjects, and the arguments became tedious after a while.

"Why did you see Brigham Young?" Sternberg asked.

Cope shrugged. "There are no known fossil deposits in Utah now, but there are rumors of bones in the eastern regions near the Colorado border. I see no harm in making friendships for the future." And he added, "Marsh met him, last year."

The following day Mrs. Cope took the Union Pacific train back east, while the men traveled north by narrow gauge railway to Franklin, Idaho, "an alkali flats town," Johnson noted, "with nothing to recommend it save that rail and stage lines enable one to leave it as soon as possible."

But in Franklin, while buying stagecoach tickets, Cope was suddenly accosted by the sheriff, a large man with small eyes. "You are under arrest," he told Cope, taking him by the arm, "and charged with murder."

"Whom am I supposed to have murdered?" Cope asked, astonished.

"Your father," the sheriff said. "Back East."

"That's ridiculous—my father died last year of a heart attack." Despite being a Quaker, Cope was known for his flashing temper, and Johnson could see that he was doing his utmost to remain civil. "I loved my father with all my heart—he was kind and wise and support- ive of my irregular scholarly wanderings," he said with deep fury.

The sudden display of eloquence took everyone aback. The men all followed Cope and the sheriff to the jail, from a polite distance. It turned out a federal warrant for his arrest had been filed in the Idaho Ter- ritory. It also turned out that the federal marshal was in another district and would not return to Franklin until September. Cope, said the sheriff, would have to "cool his heels" in jail until then.

Cope protested that he was Professor Edward Drinker Cope, a United States paleontologist. The sher- iff showed him the telegram stating that "Prof. E. D. Cope, paleontologist" was the man wanted for murder.

"I know who is behind this," Cope said angrily. He was turning purple in the face.

"Now, Professor . . ." Sternberg said.

"I'm fine," Cope said stiffly. He turned to the sheriff. "I propose to pay the telegraph costs to verify that the charges against me are untrue."

The sheriff spat tobacco. "That's fair enough. You get your father to cable me back, and I'll apologize."

"I can't do that," Cope said.

"Why not?"

"I already told you, my father's dead."

"You think I'm a fool," the sheriff said, and grabbed Cope by the collar, to drag him into the jail cell. He was rewarded by a series of lightning-swift punches from Cope that knocked him to the ground; Cope proceeded to kick the sheriff repeatedly while the unfortunate man rolled in the dust and while Sternberg and Isaac cried, "Now, Professor!" and "That's enough, Professor!" and "Remember yourself, Professor!"

At length, Isaac managed to drag Cope away; Sternberg helped the sheriff to his feet and dusted him off. "I'm sorry, but the professor has a terrible temper."

"Temper? The man is a menace."

"Well, you see he knows that Professor Marsh sent you that telegram, along with a bribe to arrest him, and the injustice of your behavior makes him angry."

"I don't know what you're talking about," the sheriff sputtered, without conviction.

"You see," Sternberg said, "most places the professor goes, he encounters trouble from Marsh. Their rivalry has been going on for years now, and they are both able to spot it readily."

"I want all of you out of town," the sheriff shouted. "Do you hear me, out of town!"

"With pleasure," Sternberg said.

They left on the next stage.

From Franklin, they faced a six-hundred-mile journey on Concord stagecoach to Fort Benton, Montana Territory. Johnson, who had thus far experienced nothing more arduous than a railway carriage, was looking forward to the romance of a coach ride. Sternberg and the others knew better.

It was a horrible journey: ten miles an hour, day and night, with no stops except for meals, outrageously expensive at one dollar each, and awful. And at every coach stop, everyone would talk of the Indian troubles, and the prospect of scalping, so that if Johnson had had any desire for the coach stops' moldy army-surplus bacon, the rancid butter, and the week-old bread, he lost his appetite.

The landscape was uniformly dreary, the dust harshly alkaline; they had to walk up all the steep ascents, day or night; in the rattling, bouncing coach, sleep was impossible; and their chemical supplies leaked, so that at one point, "we were subjected to a gentle rain of hydrochloric acid, which drops etched a smoking pattern on the hats of the gentlemen, and elicited elaborate curses from all involved. The coach was stopped, and the driver accorded our left-over curses; the offending bottle stopped, and we were on our way once more."

Besides their group, the only other passenger was a Mrs. Peterson, a young woman married to an army captain stationed in Helena, Montana Territory. Mrs. Peterson seemed none too enthusiastic to be rejoining her husband; indeed, she cried frequently. Often she opened a letter, read it, wiped tears from her eyes, and tucked it away again. At the last coach stop before Helena, she burned the letter, dropping it to the ground to dissolve into ash. When the stage reached Helena, she was formally met by four army captains, their demeanor grave. They escorted her away; she walked erectly in their midst.

The others stared after her.

"He must be dead," Toad said. "That's what it's about. He's dead."

At the coach station, they were told that Captain Peterson had been killed by Indians. And there were rumors of a recent major cavalry defeat at Indian hands. Some said General Terry had been killed along the Powder River; others that General Crook had narrowly escaped death on the banks of the Yellowstone, and that he had suffered blood poisoning from the arrows removed from his side.

In Helena they were urged to turn back, but Cope never considered it. "Idle talk," he said, "foolish talk. We will go on." And they climbed back aboard the coach for the long trip to Fort Benton.

Located on the banks of the Missouri River, Fort Benton had been a trappers' refuge in the early days of the Montana Territory, back when John Jacob Astor was lobbying in Congress to prevent any legislation to protect the buffalo, and thus interfere with his lucrative trade in hides. Northern Montana was the source of other hides as well, including beaver and wolf. But now the fur trade was declining in importance, and the fastest-growing towns were located farther south, in the mining regions of Butte and Helena, where there was gold and copper. Fort Benton had seen better days, and looked it.

As their stagecoach arrived on July 4, 1876, they saw that the army stockade gates were closed, and there was a general air of tension. The soldiers were gloomy and distressed. The American flag flapped at half-mast. Cope went to see the commanding officer, Captain Charles Ransom.

"What's the trouble?" Cope asked. "Why is your flag lowered?"

"Seventh Cavalry, sir."

"What about it?" Cope asked.

"The whole of the Seventh Cavalry under General Custer was massacred at the Little Bighorn last week. More than three hundred army dead. And no survivors."

Fort Benton

George Armstrong Custer remained as controversial in death as he had been in life. Ol' Curly had always been the focus of strong feelings. He had graduated last in his class at West Point, accumulating ninety-seven demerits in his last half year, just three short of dismissal. Even as a cadet, he was making enemies who would dog him all his life.

But the insubordinate cadet proved a brilliant military leader, the Boy Wonder of Appomattox. Handsome, dashing, and reckless, he went on to earn a reputation as a great Indian fighter in the West, but his reputation was debated widely. A dedicated hunter, he traveled with greyhounds wherever he went, and it was said that he took better care of his dogs than he did his men. In 1867, he ordered his troops to shoot deserters from his company. Five men were wounded, and Custer refused them medical aid. One subsequently died.

Even for the army, this was too much. In July 1867, he was arrested, court-martialed, and suspended for a year. But he was a favorite of the generals, and he was back ten months later at Phil Sheridan's insistence, this time fighting the Indians along the Washita, in the Oklahoma Territory.

Custer led the 7th Cavalry against Black Kettle. His instructions were clear: to kill as many Indians as possible. General Sherman himself had said: "The more we can kill this year, the less will have to be killed the next year for the more I see of these Indians the more I am convinced they will all have to be killed or be maintained as a species of paupers."

It was a particularly vicious war. The Indians had been taking white women and children as hostages, whom they ransomed back to the settlers; whenever soldiers attacked an Indian village, the white hostages were summarily executed. This circumstance excused the kind of dashing bravado that was, in any case, Custer's trademark.

Forcing his troops on extended marches, forgoing food and rest, he ran down Black Kettle, killed the chief, and destroyed his village. Only then did he realize that Indians from surrounding villages were gathering for a massive counterattack, and that he had overextended himself and endangered all his troops. He managed to pull out, but left behind a company of fifteen men, presuming them to be already dead.

Later, the entire battle became embroiled in scandal. The Eastern press criticized Custer for his harsh treatment of Black Kettle's tribe, saying that Black Kettle was not a bad Indian but a scapegoat for military frustrations; this was almost certainly untrue. The army criticized Custer for his hasty attack and his equally hasty abandonment of the cut-off company; Custer was unable to provide a satisfactory explanation for his behavior in the crisis, but he felt, with justification, that he had only done what the army had expected him to do, to run down the Indians with his usual dash and bravado.

His personal style—his long curly hair, his greyhounds, his buckskin clothes, and his arrogant manner—remained notorious, as did the articles he wrote for the Eastern press. Custer had a peculiar affinity for his enemy, and often wrote admiringly of the Indians; this was no doubt the source of the persistent rumor he had fathered a child by a beautiful Indian girl after the Battle of the Washita.

And still the controversy continued. In 1874, it was Custer who led a party into the sacred Black Hills, discovered gold, and thus precipitated the Sioux War; in the spring of 1876, he had gone to Washington to testify against the corruption of Secretary of War Belknap, who received kickbacks for supplies from every army post in the country. His testimony had helped start impeachment proceedings against Belknap, but had not endeared him to the Grant administration, which ordered him to remain in Washington and, when he left without permission in March, demanded his arrest.

Now he was dead, in what was already being called the most shocking and humiliating military defeat in American history.

"Who did it?" Cope asked.

"Sitting Bull," Ransom said. "Custer charged Sitting Bull's camp without scouting it first. Sitting Bull had three thousand warriors. Custer had three hundred." Captain Ransom shook his head. "Mind you, Custer would have been killed sooner or later; he was vain and hard on his men; I'm surprised he wasn't 'accidentally' shot in the back on the way into battle, as often happens with his type. I was with him in the Washita, when he charged a village and then couldn't get himself out; luck and bluff saved the day, but luck runs out eventually. He almost certainly brought this one on himself. And the Sioux hated him, wanted to kill him. But it's going to be a bloody war now. This whole country's red-hot now."

"Well," Cope said, "we're going to search for fossil bones in the Judith badlands."

Ransom stared at him in astonishment. "I wouldn't," he said.

"There's trouble in the Judith River basin?"

"Not specifically, no, sir. Not that we know of."

"Well then?"

"Sir, most all the Indian tribes are on the warpath. Sitting Bull has three thousand warriors somewhere in the south—nobody knows where for sure—but we figure they'll head for asylum in Canada before winter, and that means they'll pass through the Judith basin."

"That's fine," Cope said. "We'll be safe for a few weeks during summer, for the reasons you just said. Sitting Bull isn't there."

"Sir," Ransom said, "the Judith River is the shared hunting grounds of the Sioux and the Crow. Now, the Crow are usually peaceable, but these days they'll kill you as soon as look at you, because they can blame your deaths on the Sioux."

"That's not likely," Cope said. "We're going."

"I have no orders to prevent you from going," Ransom said. "I'm sure nobody in Washington ever imagined that anyone would go. To go out there is suicide, sir. For myself, I wouldn't go out with less than five hundred trained cavalry at my side."

"I appreciate your concern," Cope said. "You have done your duty in informing me. But I left Philadelphia with the intention of going to the Judith, and I will not turn back within a hundred miles of my destination. Now, can you recommend a guide?"

"Certainly, sir," Ransom said.

But over the next twenty-four hours, the guides mysteriously became unavailable, as did horses, the provisions, and everything else that Cope had expected to obtain at Fort Benton. Yet he was undaunted. He simply offered more money, and more on top of that, until supplies began to become available after all.

It was here they had their first glimpse of the famous iron will of Professor Cope. Nothing stopped him. They demanded $180, an outrageous sum, for a broken-down wagon; he paid it. They wanted even more for his four "wheelers" and his four saddle ponies, "the meanest ponies that ever picketed together," in Sternberg's estimation. They would sell him no food except beans and rice and cheap Red Dog whiskey; he bought what he could. All together, Cope spent $900 for his motley outfit, but he never complained. He kept his gaze fixed on his destination—the fossils of the Judith basin.

Finally, on July 6, Ransom called him into the army stockade. It was the scene of bustling activity and preparation. Ransom told Cope that he had just received orders from the Department of War in Washington that "no civilians were permitted to enter the disputed Indian lands in the Montana, Wyoming, or Dakota Territories."

"I'm sorry to put a stop to your plans, sir," Ransom said politely, setting the telegram aside.

"You must do your duty, of course," Cope said, equally politely.

Cope rejoined his group. They had already heard the news.

"I guess we have to go back," Sternberg said.

"Not yet," Cope said cheerfully. "You know, I like Fort Benton. I think we should stay here a few days more."

"You like Fort Benton?"

"Yes. It's pleasant and agreeable. And full of preparations." And Cope smiled.

On July 8, the Fort Benton cavalry set off to fight the Sioux, the column riding out while the band played "The Girl I Left Behind Me." Later that day, a quite different group quietly slipped out. They were, wrote Johnson, a "particularly motley crew."

At the head of the column rode Edward Drinker Cope, United States paleontologist and millionaire. On his left rode Charlie Sternberg, occasionally bending to massage his stiff leg.

On Cope's right rode Little Wind, their Shoshoni scout and guide. Little Wind was proud in his bearing, and he had assured Cope that he knew the Judith River area like the face of his own father.

Behind these three came J.C. Isaac, who kept a sharp eye on Little Wind; with him were the students, Leander Davis, Harold Chapman, George Morton, and Johnson.

Bringing up the rear was the wagon pulled by its four stubborn horses, and driven by the teamster and cook "Sergeant" Russell T. Hill. He was a fat, weathered man whose girth had persuaded Cope that he could cook. Teamster Hill was distinguished not only by his size and proficiency at swearing so common among his trade, but also by his nicknames, which seemed to be endless. He was called "Cookie," "Chippie," "Squinty," and "Stinky." Hill was a man of few words, and those were most often repeated again and again.

So, for example, when the students would ask him why he was called Cookie or Stinky or another of his names, he would invariably reply, "I reckon you'll see soon enough."

And when confronted with an obstacle, however minor, Hill would always say, "Can't be done, can't be done."

Finally, tethered to the wagon was Bessie, the mule that carried all Johnson's photographic supplies. Bessie was Johnson's responsibility, and he grew to hate her as the expedition went on.

An hour after they started, they had left Fort Benton behind, and they were alone on the empty vastness of the Great Plains.

PART II

The Lost World

Night on the Plains

The first night they camped in a place called Clag-ett, on the banks of the Judith River. There was a trading post here, surrounded by a stockade, but it had been recently abandoned.

Hill cooked his first dinner, which they found heavy but otherwise acceptable. Hill used buffalo chips for fuel, thus explaining two of his nicknames: Chippie and Stinky. After dinner, Hill hung their food in a tree.

"What're you doing that for?" Johnson asked.

"That's to keep the food away from marauding grizzlies," Hill said. "Now go get ready to sleep."

Hill himself stamped the ground with his boots before laying out his bedding.

"What're you doing that for?" Johnson asked.

"That's to stop up the snake holes," Hill said, "so

the rattlers don't climb under the blankets with you at night."

"You're jobbing me," Johnson said.

"I ain't," Hill warned. "You ask anyone. Gets cold at night and they like the warm, so they crawl right in with you, coil up against your groin."

Johnson went to Sternberg, who was also laying out his bedding. "Aren't you going to stamp the ground?"

"No," Sternberg said. "This spot isn't lumpy, looks real comfortable."

"What about rattlesnakes crawling into the blankets?"

"That hardly ever happens," Sternberg said.

"It hardly ever happens?" Johnson's voice rose in alarm.

"I wouldn't worry over it," Sternberg said. "In the morning, just wake up slow, and see if you got any visitors. Snakes just run away, come morning."

Johnson shuddered.

They had seen no sign of human life all day long, but Isaac was convinced they were at risk from Indians. "With Mr. Indian," he grumbled, "the time you feel safest is the time you aren't." Isaac insisted they post guards throughout the night; the others grudgingly went along. Isaac himself would take the last watch, before dawn.

This was Johnson's first night out under the great domed sky of the prairie, and sleep was impossible. The very thought of a rattlesnake or a grizzly bear would have prevented any sleep, but there were too many other sounds besides—the whisper of the wind in the grass, the hooting of owls in the darkness, the distant howls of coyotes. He stared up at the thousands of stars in the cloudless sky, and listened.

He was awake for each changing of the guard, and saw Isaac take over from Sternberg at four o'clock in the morning. But eventually fatigue overcame him, and he was soundly asleep when a series of explosions jolted him awake. Isaac was shouting, "Halt! Halt, I say, halt!" as he fired his revolver.

They all jumped up. Isaac pointed east across the prairie. "There's something out there! Can you see it, there's something out there!"

They looked and saw nothing.

"I tell you, there's a man, a lone man!"

"Where?"

"There! Out there!"

They stared at the distant horizon of the plains, and saw nothing at all.

Cookie unleashed a stream of epithets. "He's Injun shy and he's crazy, too—he's going to see a red man behind every bush long as we're out here. We won't get a lick of sleep."

Cope quietly said that he would take over the watch, and sent the others back to bed.

It would be many weeks before they realized that Isaac had been right.

If Stinky's food and Isaac's guarding left something to be desired, so did Little Wind's scouting. The Shoshoni brave got them lost for much of the following day.

Two hours after they set out, they came across fresh horse manure on the plains.

"Indians," Isaac gasped.

Hill snorted in disgust. "Know what that is?" he said. "That's manure from our horses, that's what it is."

"That's impossible."

"You think so? See the wagon tracks over there?" He pointed to faint tracks, where the prairie grass had been pressed down. "You want to bet I put the wheels of this wagon in those tracks and they line up exactly? We're lost, I tell you."

Cope rode alongside Little Wind. "Are we lost?"

"No," Little Wind said.

"Well, what do you expect him to say?" Hill grumbled. "You ever heard an Indian admit he was lost?"

"I've never heard of an Indian being lost," Sternberg said.

"Well, we got one here, purchased at great expense," Hill said. "You mark my words, he's never been in this part of the country before, no matter what he says. And he's lost, no matter what he says."

For Johnson, the conversation filled him with strange dread. All day they had been riding under the great bowl of the sky, across uniformly flat country, a great vista without landmarks except for the occasional isolated tree or line of cottonwoods that marked a creek. It was truly a "sea of grass," and like the sea it was trackless and vast. He began to understand why everyone in the West talked so familiarly of certain landmarks—Pompey's Pillar, Twin Peaks, Yellow Cliffs. These few recognizable features were islands in the wide ocean of the prairie, and knowledge of their locations was essential for survival.

Johnson rode alongside Toad. "Can we really be lost?"

Toad shook his head. "Indians are born here. They can read the land in ways we can't begin to imagine. We're not lost."

"Well, we're going south," Hill grumbled, staring at the sun. "Why're we going south, when every man here knows that the Judith lands are east? Can someone tell me that?"

The next two hours were tense, until finally they came upon an old wagon track running east. Little Wind pointed. "This road for wagons to Judith lands."

"That's what the problem was," Toad said. "He's not used to traveling with a wagon, and he had to find the track for our wagon to use."

"The problem," Hill said, "is that he doesn't know the country."

"He knows this country," Sternberg said. "This is the Indian hunting lands we're in now."

They rode on in sober silence.

Incidents on the Plains

In the middle of the still hot afternoon, Johnson was riding alongside Cope, talking quite peaceably to him, when his hat suddenly flew away in the air, although there was no wind.

A moment later they heard the snapping report of a long rifle. Then another, and another.

Someone was shooting at them.

"Down!" Cope shouted. "Down!"

They dismounted and ducked for cover, crawling beneath the wagon. In the distance they could see a brown swirling dust cloud.

"Oh God," Isaac whispered. "Indians."

The distant cloud grew in size, resolving into many silhouetted horsemen. More bullets whizzed through the air; the fabric of the wagon ripped; bullets spanged off pots and pans. Bessie brayed in alarm.

"We're done for," Morton moaned.

"Any minute now we'll hear those arrows whistling," Isaac said, "and then, when they get closer, out come the tomahawks—"

"Shut up!" Cope said. He had never taken his eyes off the cloud. "They're not Indians."

"Damn if you're not a bigger fool than I thought you were! Who else'd be—"

Isaac fell silent. The cloud was now close enough that they could resolve the riders into individual figures. Blue-coated figures.

"Might still be red men," Isaac said. "Wearing Custer's jackets. For a surprise attack."

"Not much surprise if they are."

Little Wind squinted at the horizon. "Not Indians," he pronounced finally. "Saddle ponies."

"Damn!" Cookie shouted. "The army! My boys in blue!" He leapt up shouting, waving his hands. A fusillade of lead sent him diving back beneath the wagon.

The army horsemen rode around the wagon, whooping Indian-style, firing their pistols into the air. Finally, they stopped, and a young captain pulled up, his horse snorting. He aimed his revolver at the figures huddled beneath the wagon.

"Out, you slime. Out! By God, I've a mind to finish you right here, every last man of you."

Cope emerged, purple with fury. His fists were clenched at his sides. "I demand to know the meaning of this outrage."

"You'll know it in hell, you blackguard," the army captain said, and he shot twice at Cope, but his rearing horse threw off his aim.

"Wait, Cap'n," one of the soldiers said. By now Cope's party had all crawled from beneath the wagon and stood lined up along the wheels. "They don't look like gunrunners."

"Damn me if they're not," the captain said. They could see now that he was drunk; his words were slurred; his body rocked precariously in the saddle. "Nobody but gunrunners'd be out in this territory now. Supplying Mr. Indian with arms, when just last week six hundred of our own dear lads have fallen to the savages. It's slime like you make it—"

Cope drew himself up. "This is a scientific expedition," he said, "undertaken with the full knowledge and authorization of Captain Ransom at Fort Benton."

"Balls," said the captain, and discharged his gun into the air for punctuation.

"I am Professor Cope of Philadelphia, and I am a United States paleontologist and—"

"Kiss my calico-covered arse," the captain said.

Cope lost his temper and leapt forward, and Sternberg and Isaac hurried to intervene. "Now, Professor, control yourself, Professor!" Sternberg yelled as Cope struggled, shouting, "I want him, I want him!"

In the ensuing confusion, the army captain fired three more times, and wheeled on his horse. "Light 'em up, boys! Light 'em up!"

"But Captain—"

"I said light 'em up"—more gunshots—"and I mean light 'em up!"

There were still more gunshots, and Toad fell, shrieking, "I am hit, I am hit!" They rushed to help him; blood poured freely from his hand. One of the soldiers rode up with a torch. The dry canvas of the wagon burst into flames.

They turned to put out the fire, which roared fiercely. The cavalry wheeled around them, the captain shouting, "Teach 'em a lesson, boys! Teach 'em in hell!"

And then, still firing, they turned and rode off.

Cope's journal laconically notes:

Have experienced first open hostilities today at the hands of U.S. Cavalry. Fire put out with minimal damage although we are without protective covering for wagon and two of our tents are burned. One horse shot dead. One student received flesh wound in hand. No serious injuries, thank God.

That night it rained. Torrential cracking thunderstorms continued all the next day and all that night. Cold and shivering, they huddled beneath the wagon, trying to sleep with the intermittent glaring flash of lightning showing them each other's haggard faces.

The next day it rained again, and the trail was turned to mud, bogging down the wagons. They made only two miles of painful, soggy progress. But in the late afternoon, the sun burst through the clouds and the air became warmer. They felt better, especially when, climbing to the top of a gentle rise, they saw one of the great sights of the West.

A herd of buffalo, stretching as far as the eye could see, dark shaggy shapes clumping on the yellow-green grass of the plains. The animals seemed peaceful, except for occasional snorting and bellowing.

Cope estimated there were two million buffalo in the herd, perhaps more. "You are lucky to see it," he said. "In another year or two, herds like these will be only a memory."

Isaac was nervous. "Where there are buffalo, there

are Indians," he said, and he insisted they camp that night on high ground.

Johnson was fascinated by the indifference of the animals to the arrival of men. Even when Sternberg went out and shot an antelope for dinner, the herd hardly responded. But Johnson later remembered that Cookie had said to Cope, "Shall I unhitch the wagon tonight?" and Cope looked at the sky and said thoughtfully, "Better not tonight."

Meanwhile the antelope was butchered, and the flesh was found to be crawling with maggoty parasites. Cookie announced he had eaten worse, but they decided on a meal of biscuits and beans instead. Johnson recorded that "I am already thoroughly sick of beans, with six more weeks of them still before me."

But it was not all bad. They ate, sitting on a rocky outcrop beside the camp and watched the buffalo tinge with red as the sun set behind them. And then, in the light of the moon, the shaggy shapes, and the occasional distant snorting of the creatures, made "a vision of great majesty stretching away peacefully before us. Such were my thoughts as I turned in for a much-needed sleep."

Lightning cracked the sky at midnight, and the rain began again.

Grumbling and swearing, the students dragged their sleeping outfits under the wagon. Almost immediately, the rain stopped.

They rolled on the hard ground, trying to get back to sleep. "Hell," Morton said, sniffing. "What is that smell?"

"You're lyin' in horseshit," Toad said.

"Oh God, it's true."

They were laughing at Morton's predicament, with the steady rumble of thunder still in their ears. Then suddenly Cope ran around the wagon, rudely kicking them. "Up! Up! Are you mad? Get up!"

Johnson glanced up, and saw Sternberg and Isaac hastily loading the camp equipment, flinging it into the wagon; the wagon began to move over their heads as they scrambled out beneath. Cookie and Little Wind were shouting to each other.

Johnson ran to Cope. His hair was matted down by the rain; his eyes were wild. Overhead the moon raced among storm clouds.

"What is it?" Johnson shouted over the rumbling thunder. "Why are we moving?"

Cope shoved him roughly away. "The lee of the rocks! Get in the lee of the rocks!" Isaac had already gotten the wagon near the rocky outcrop, and Cookie was struggling with the horses, which snorted and reared, agitated. The students stared at each other, not understanding.

And then Johnson realized the rumble they were hearing was not thunder. It was the buffalo.

Terrorized by the lightning, the buffalo stampeded past the men in a wet, dense river of flesh that flowed around the rocks on both sides. They were all spattered by copious quantities of mud; for Johnson, it was a peculiar sensation, in that "the mud covered our clothing, our hair, our faces, and we grew heavier as we became transformed into mud-men, until finally we were all bowed over by the immense weight of it."

They eventually could see nothing, and could only listen to the thundering hooves, the snorting and grunting, as the dark shapes hurtled past them, ceaselessly. It seemed as if it went on forever.

In fact, the herd had stampeded past them, without interruption, for two hours.

Johnson awoke, his body stiff and aching. He was unable to open his eyes. He touched his face, felt the hard caked mud, and peeled it away.

"I was greeted by a sight of utter desolation," he later recalled, "as if a hurricane or a whirlwind had struck us. There was only choppy mud as far as the eye could see, and our pitiful human party picking their way through it. Whatever of our camp outfit had been protected by the rocks was safe; everything else was gone. Two tents trampled into the mud so deeply we could not locate them in the morning; heavy pots and cook pans dented and twisted by the passage of thousands of hooves; tattered fragments of a yellow shirt; a carbine shattered and bent."

They were greatly discouraged, particularly George Morton, who seemed to be in profound shock. Cookie argued to turn back, but as usual Cope was indomitable. "I am not here to excavate trifling possessions from mud," he said. "I am here to excavate prehistoric bones."

"Yes," Cookie said. "If you ever get there."

"We will." He ordered them to break camp and pull out.

Little Wind was particularly grim. He said something to Cope, and then galloped off to the north.

"Where's he going?" George Morton asked in alarm.

"He doesn't believe the buffalo stampeded because of lightning," Cope said. "He says they don't do that."

"I've known 'em to do it," Isaac said, "in Wyoming. Stupid and unpredictable, buffalo are."

"But what else could it be?" Morton said, still alarmed. "What does he think?"

"He thinks he heard gunshots just before the stampede began. He is going to look."

"He's going to contact his fellow red men," Isaac muttered, "and tell them where to find some nice white scalps."

"I think it's all ridiculous," Morton said petulantly. "I think we should give it up and stop these wild chases."

The shock of the stampede must have unnerved him, Johnson thought. He watched Morton poke through the mud, looking for his sketch pad.

Little Wind was gone an hour, and he came back riding hard.

"One camp," he said, pointing north. "Two men, two or three ponies. One fire. No tent. Many rifle shells." He opened his hand, and a cascade of copper jackets tumbled down in the sunlight.

"Well, I'll be!" Sternberg said.

"It's Marsh's men," Cope said grimly.

"Did you see them?" Morton asked.

Little Wind shook his head. "Left many hours."

"Which way did they go?"

Little Wind pointed east. The same direction they were going.

"Then we'll come across them again," Cope said. He clenched his fists. "I'd enjoy that."

Badlands

The Judith River, a tributary of the Missouri, flowed from the Little Belt Mountains and connected with large creeks in a confusing meander of waterways.

"There's damn good trout in those waters," said Cookie. "Not that I expect we will be fishing."

The Judith River basin itself consisted of badlands, rocky outcrops that formed, for the eye, into mysterious shapes, demons and dragons. A place of gargoyles, said Toad.

Toad's arm was now swollen and red; he complained of pain. Sternberg said privately he thought Toad would have to be sent back to Fort Benton, where the army surgeon could amputate his arm with the benefit of whiskey and a bone saw. But nobody mentioned it to Toad.

The scale of the rock formations in the Judith bad-lands was enormous; great cliffs—Cope called them "exposures"—reaching hundreds of feet into the air, in places towering more than a thousand feet above them. With pastel bands of pink and black rock, the land had a stark and desolate beauty. But it was a harsh land: there was little water nearby, and it was mostly brack-ish, alkaline, poisonous. "Hard to believe this was a great inland lake, surrounded by swamps," Cope said, staring at the soft sculpted rock. Cope always seemed to see more than the others did. Cope and also Stern-berg: the tough fossil hunter had the practiced eye of a plains explorer; he always seemed to know where to find game and water.

"We'll have water enough here," he predicted. "It won't be the water that troubles us. It'll be the dust."

There was indeed an alkaline bite in the air, but the others did not mind it so much. Their immediate prob-lem was to find a campsite near a suitable place for exca-vation, and this was no mean task. Moving the wagons over the terrain—there were no wagon trails here—was difficult and sometimes dangerous work.

They were also nervous about Indians, because they saw plenty of signs around them: pony tracks, aban-doned cook fires, the occasional antelope carcass. Some of the cook fires looked recent, but Sternberg professed complete indifference. Even the Sioux weren't crazy enough to stay in the badlands for long. "Only a crazy white man'd spend all summer here," he laughed. "And only a crazy, rich white man would spend his vacation here!" He slapped Johnson on the back.

For two days they pushed the wagons up hills and braced them down hills, until finally Cope announced that they were in a suitable bone region, and they could make camp at the next good site they found. Sternberg suggested the top of the nearby rise, and they pushed the wagons up a final time, coughing in the dust of the wheels. Toad, unable to help because of his swollen arm, said, "Do you smell fire?" but no one did.

As they came to the top of the rise, they had a view over the plains and a meandering stream, with cottonwoods growing alongside it. And stretching as far as they could see were white teepees, each with a thin column of smoke issuing from them.

"My God," Sternberg said. He quickly estimated the number.

"What do you make it?" Isaac said.

"I make it more'n a thousand teepees. My God," Sternberg said again.

I am persuaded," said Isaac, "that we are dead men."

"I reckon," said Cookie Hill. He spat on the ground.

Sternberg didn't think so. The question was what tribe of Indians they were. If they were Sioux, then Isaac was right; they were as good as dead. But the Sioux were supposed to still be farther south.

"Who cares where they're supposed to be?" Cookie said. "They're here, and so are we. It's that Little Weasel, he led us here—"

"That's enough. Let's go about our business," Cope said. "Make our camp, and act naturally."

"After you, Professor," Cookie said.

It was difficult to act naturally with a thousand teepees spread on the plains below, and the associated horses, fires, people. They had of course already been spotted; some of the Indians were pointing and gesturing.

By the time they had unloaded the cook wagon and started the fire for the night, a group of mounted horsemen splashed across the stream and rode up toward their camp.

"Here they come, boys," Cookie muttered.

Johnson counted twelve riders. His heart pounded as he heard their horses approach. They were superb horsemen, riding fast and easily, trailing a cloud of dust. They whooped and shouted savagely as they came closer.

"These were my first Indians," he later remembered,

"and I was consumed in equal parts with curiosity and terror. I confess that to see the swirling dust cloud, and hear their savage shrieks, increased the latter, and for the thousandth time on this journey I regretted the rashness of my wager."

The Indians were now close and rode in circles around the wagon, whooping enthusiastically. They knew the white men were frightened, and enjoyed it. Finally, they drew up, and their leader repeated several times, "Howah, howah." He said it in a grunting sort of way.

Johnson whispered to Sternberg, "What did he say?"

"He said, 'How.'"

"What does that mean?"

"It means, 'I agree, everything is fine, I feel friendly.'"

Johnson could now see the Indians clearly. Like many other first-time observers of Plains Indians, he was astonished at how handsome they were—"tall and muscularly endowed, their faces possessing pleasing regular features, their bearing naturally dignified and proud, their persons and buckskin garments surprisingly clean."

The Indians were not smiling, but they seemed friendly enough. They all said "Howah" in turn, and looked around at the camp. There was an awkward silence. Isaac, who knew some Indian language, ventured a few words of greeting.

Instantly their faces darkened. They wheeled on their horses and rode away, disappearing in an alkaline dust cloud.

Sternberg said, "You goddamn fool, what did you say?"

"I said, 'I bid you welcome and wish you success and happiness in the journey of your life.'"

"What'd you say it in?"

"Mandan."

"You goddamn fool, Mandan's Sioux talk. Those're Crows!"

Even Johnson had been long enough in the plains to know of the traditional enmity between the Sioux and the Crow tribes. The hatred between them was deep and implacable, especially since in recent years the Crows had allied themselves with the white soldiers in the fight against the Sioux.

"Well, Mandan's all I know," Isaac protested, "so I said it."

"You goddamn fool," Sternberg repeated. "If we didn't before, now we have a problem."

"I thought Crows never killed white people," Morton said, licking his lips.

DRAGON TEETH • 125

"That's what the Crows say," Sternberg said, "but they tend to exaggerate. Oh yes, lads, we have a problem."

"Well, we'll go down there and straighten it out," Cope said, in his usual forthright manner.

"After our last supper?" Cookie said.

"No," Cope said. "Now."

The Indian Village

Aboriginal peoples had hunted on the Western plains of America for more than ten thousand years. They had seen the glaciers recede and the land become warm; they had witnessed (and perhaps accelerated) the disappearance of the great mastodons, the hippo, and the feared saber-toothed tiger. They had hunted when the land was heavily forested, and they hunted now that it was a sea of grass. Through all the thousands of years, through all the changes of game and climate, Indians had continued to live as nomadic hunters on the vast spaces of the land.

The Plains Indians of the nineteenth century were colorful, dramatic, mystical, warlike people. They captured the imagination of all who saw them, and in many ways they stood, in the popular mind, for all American Indians. The antiquity of their rituals, the intricate organization of their way of life, was much admired by liberal thinkers.

But the truth was that the Plains Indian society that Westerners saw was hardly older than the white American nation that now threatened its existence. The Plains Indians were a nomadic hunting society organized around the horse, as were the Mongols of Asia. Yet there had been no horses in America until the Spaniards introduced them three hundred years earlier, changing Plains Indian society beyond recognition.

And even the traditional tribal structures, and tribal rivalries, were less ancient than often imagined. Most authorities believed the Crow Indians were once part of the Sioux nation, living in what is now Iowa; they had migrated west toward Montana, evolved a separate identity, and become the implacable antagonists of their former kin. As one expert wrote, "The Sioux and the Crow are virtually the same in dress, manner, habits, language, customs, values, bearing. This similarity might be thought to form the basis of friendship, yet it only heightens their antagonism."

It was these Crow Indians that they now rode down to visit.

———

First impressions of an Indian village were often contradictory. Henry Morton Stanley, the Welsh explorer and journalist who in 1871 famously found Dr. David Livingstone in Africa, entered Black Kettle's village with Custer and found it filthy: "so foul, indeed, as to defy description." Robes on the teepee floors were crawling with vermin; excremental odors assailed him.

Other first-time observers were unnerved to see Indians roasting a dog over a fire, or chewing bloody buffalo steaks. But Johnson's first impressions, riding that evening into the Crow village, seem more revealing about him than about the Crow:

"Anyone who imagines," he wrote,

that the nomadic Indian lives a free-spirited and open life will receive a rude shock on visiting his place of habitation. The Plains Indian village is, like the life of the warrior, regimented in the extreme. Teepees are regularly designed of elk hide, regularly set out, and regularly arranged according to fixed rules; there are rules for placement of the (back) rests inside the teepees, and rugs, and rawhide containers; there are rules for the designs that decorate the robes and clothes and teepees; rules for the making of fires and the manners of cooking; rules for the behavior of the Indian at every moment and at all times in his life; rules for war and rules for peace and rules for hunting and rules for behavior before hunting; and all these rules are followed with a rigid fixity and a serious determination which forcibly reminds the observer that one is among a warrior race.

They tethered their horses at the edge of the village and walked in, slowly. Curious stares greeted them from every side; laughing children fell silent, paused to watch the strangers pass; odors of cooking venison and the peculiar pungency of drying hides assaulted their nostrils. At length a young brave came up and made some elaborate movements with his hands.

"What's he doing?" whispered Johnson.

"Sign language," Toad said, cradling his swollen arm with the other.

"You understand it?"

"No," Toad said.

But Little Wind did, and he spoke to the brave in the Crow language. The Indian led them deeper into the village, to a large teepee where five older warriors sat around a fire in a semicircle.

"The chiefs," Toad whispered. At a gesture from one, the white men all sat in a semicircle facing them.

"Then began," wrote Johnson,

the most protracted negotiations I ever experienced in my life. The Indians love to talk and are in no rush. Their curiosity, the formal elaborateness of ceremonial speech, and the lack of urgency with regard to time peculiar to them, all conspired to a meeting of acquaintance that clearly would take all night. Everything was discussed: who we were (including our names, and the meaning of our names); where we had come from (the cities, the meanings of the names of cities, what routes we had taken, how we had chosen the route, and what experiences we had had on our journey); why we were here (the reason for our interest in the bones, and how we planned to excavate them, and what we planned to do with them); what we were wearing as clothing and why, the meaning of rings and trinkets and belt buckles, and so on *ad infinitum et ad nauseam.*

If the powwow seemed interminable, it must have in part been because of the tension the whites felt.

Sternberg noted that "they didn't care overly for our answers." It soon emerged that they knew about Cope, had been told that he was unfriendly to Indians, and had killed his own father. The Crow had been advised to kill him in turn.

Cope was furious, but kept his temper. Smiling pleasantly, he said to the others, "Do you see the villainy, the black scoundrel's techniques, finally exposed to all eyes? Do I harass Marsh? Do I attempt at every juncture to impede his progress? Am I jealous of him? I ask you. I ask you."

The chiefs could tell that Cope was upset, and Little Wind hastened to assure them of an error.

The Indians insisted there was no error: Cope had been described well and true.

Who has said these things about him? Little Wind asked.

Red Cloud Agency.

Red Cloud Agency is a Sioux agency.

This is so.

The Sioux are your enemy.

This is so.

How can you believe the words of an enemy?

The discussion dragged on, hour after hour. At length, to control his temper or perhaps his nerves, Cope began to sketch. He drew the chief, and the likeness aroused great interest. The chief wanted the sketch, and Cope gave it to him. The chief wanted Cope's pen. Cope refused.

"Professor," Sternberg said, "I think you'd better give him your pen."

"I will do nothing of the sort."

"Professor . . ."

"Very well." Cope handed over the pen.

Shortly before dawn, the discussion turned from Cope to Toad. Some kind of new chief was called for, a very pale, very thin man with a wild look in his eyes. His name was White Deer. White Deer looked at Toad, and muttered something, and left.

The Indians then announced they wanted Toad to remain in the camp, and for the others to leave.

Cope refused.

"It's all right," Toad said. "I will serve as a kind of hostage."

"They may kill you."

"But if they kill me," Toad pointed out, "they'll almost certainly kill all of you soon after."

In the end, Toad remained, and the others left.

From their camp, they looked down on the Indian encampment as dawn broke. The braves had begun whooping and riding in circles; a large fire was being built.

"Poor Toad," Isaac said. "They'll torture him for sure."

Cope watched through his glass, but the smoke obscured everything. Now a chanting began; it kept up until nine in the morning, when it abruptly stopped.

A party of braves rode up to the camp, bringing Toad with them on a spare horse. They came upon Cope washing his false teeth in a tin bowl. The Indians were entranced and, before Toad dismounted, insisted that Cope pop his lifelike teeth in and then take them out again.

Cope did this several times, contrasting a dazzling smile with a gaping, toothless hole, and the Indians departed much entertained.

Dazed, Toad watched them go.

"That one chief, White Deer, did magic on my hand," he said, "to cure it."

"Did it hurt?"

"No, they just waved feathers over it and chanted. But I had to eat some awful stuff."

"What stuff?"

"I don't know, but it was awful. I'm very tired now." He curled up beneath the wagon, and slept for the next twelve hours.

———————

Toad's arm was improved the following morning. In three days he was cured. Each morning, the Indians would ride up to see Cope. And they would watch Funny Tooth wash his teeth. The Indians would often hang around the camp, but they never took anything. And they were very interested in what the whites were doing: finding bones.

Bone Country

With these preliminary problems resolved, Cope was impatient to begin the work. The students found him standing in the dawn chill, glancing up at the cliffs near the camp, which were being struck with light for the first time that day. Abruptly, he leapt up and said, "Come along, come along. Quickly now, this is the best time to look."

"Look for what?" the students asked, surprised.

"You'll know soon enough." He led them to the cliff face exposure nearest the camp and pointed. "See anything?"

They looked. They saw bare, eroded rock, predominantly gray in color with pink and dark gray striations highlighted in the weak morning sunlight. That was all they saw.

"No bones?" Cope asked.

Encouraged by this hint, they looked hard, squinting in the light. Toad pointed. "How about up there?"

Cope shook his head. "Just embedded boulders."

Morton pointed. "Near the rise there?"

Cope shook his head. "Too high, don't look up there."

Johnson tried his luck. "Over there?"

Cope smiled. "Dead sagebrush. Well, it seems you can see everything but the bones. Now: look in the middle of the cliff, for a cliff this high will have its Cretaceous zone near the middle—a lower cliff, it might be nearer the top—but this one, it will be in the middle—just below that pink striation band there. Now run your eye along the band until you see a kind of roughness, see there? That oval patch there? Those are bones."

They looked, and then they saw: the bones caught the sunlight ever so differently from the rock, rounded edges more muted than jagged stone, their color a shade different. Once pointed out, it became easy: they saw another patch there—and more there—and there again—and still more. "We realized," wrote Johnson,

that the entire cliff face was fairly stuffed to bursting with bones, which previously were invisible to us, yet now were as plain as the nose on your face. But as Professor Cope says, we had to learn to recognize the nose on your face, too. He likes to say, "Nothing is obvious."

They were discovering dinosaurs.

In 1876, scientific acceptance of dinosaurs was still fairly recent; at the turn of the century, men did not suspect the existence of these great reptiles at all, although the evidence was there to see.

Back in July 1806, William Clark, of the Lewis and Clark Expedition, explored the south bank of the Yellowstone River, in what would later become Montana Territory, and found a fossil "semented [sic] within the face of the rock." He described it as a bone three inches in circumference and three feet in length, and considered it the rib of a fish, although it was probably a dinosaur bone.

More dinosaur bones were found in Connecticut in 1818; they were believed to be the remains of human beings; dinosaur footprints, discovered in the same region, were described as the tracks of "Noah's raven."

The true meaning of these fossils was first recognized in England. In 1824, an eccentric English clergyman named Buckland described "the *Megalosaurus* or Great Fossil Lizard of Stonesfield." Buckland imagined the fossil creature to be more than forty feet long, "and with a bulk equal to that of an elephant seven feet high." But this remarkable lizard was considered an isolated specimen.

The following year, Gideon Mantell, an English physician, described "*Iguanodon*, a newly-discovered Fossil Reptile." Mantell's description was based largely on some teeth found in an English quarry. Originally the teeth were sent to Baron Cuvier, the greatest anatomist of his day; he pronounced them the incisors of a rhinoceros. Dissatisfied, Mantell remained convinced that "I had discovered the teeth of an unknown herbivorous reptile," and eventually demonstrated that the teeth most resembled those of an iguana, an American lizard.

Baron Cuvier admitted his error, and wondered: "Do we not have here a new animal, an herbivorous reptile . . . of another time?" Other fossil reptiles were unearthed in rapid succession: *Hylaeosaurus* in 1832; *Macrodontophion* in 1834; *Thecodontosaurus* and *Paleosaurus* in 1836; *Plateosaurus* in 1837. With each new discovery came the growing suspicion that the bones represented a whole group of reptiles that had since vanished from the earth.

Finally, in 1841, another physician and anatomist, Richard Owen, proposed the entire group be called *Dinosauria*, or "terrible lizards." The notion became so widely accepted that in 1854, full-size reconstructions of dinosaurs were built in the Crystal Palace in Sydenham, and attained wide popularity with the public. (Owen, knighted by Queen Victoria for his accomplishments, later became a bitter opponent of Darwin and the doctrine of evolution.)

By 1870, the focus of dinosaur hunting shifted from Europe to North America. It had been recognized since the 1850s that there were large numbers of fossils in the American West, but recovery of these giant bones was impractical until the completion of the transcontinental railroad in 1869.

The following year, Cope and Marsh began their furious competition to acquire fossils from this new region. They undertook their labors with all the ruthlessness of a Carnegie or a Rockefeller. In part this aggressiveness—new to scientific endeavors—reflected the prevailing values of their age. And in part it was a recognition of the fact that dinosaurs were no longer mysterious. Cope and Marsh knew exactly what they were about: they were discovering the full range of a great order of vanished reptiles. They were making scientific history.

And they knew that fame and honor would accrue to the man who discovered and described the largest number.

The two men were consumed by the search. "Hunting for bones," wrote Johnson, "has a peculiar fascination, not unlike hunting for gold. One never knows what one will find, and the possibilities, the potential discoveries lying in wait, fuels the quest."

And they did indeed make discoveries. While they dug the hillside, Cope was kept busy on the ground below, sketching, making notes, and classifying. He insisted that the students be meticulous in recording which bones were found in proximity to which others. Shovel and pickax were used to loosen the stone, but they gave way to the smaller tools, which appeared simple enough: hammer, chisel, pick, and brush. Despite the students' earnestness, there was first a great deal of technique to be learned; they had to learn to choose among the three weights of wide-head hammer, four widths of rock chisel (imported from Germany, explained Cope, for the quality of the cold steel), two sizes of steel points to pick at the stone, and a variety of stiff brushes for whisking away dirt and dust and gravel.

"We've come too far not to do this the correct way," Cope said. "The fossils don't always give themselves up easily, too."

One did not just bang a fossilized bone out of the rock, he explained to them. One studied the position of the fossil, tapped the stone with a chisel when necessary, hammered vigorously only rarely. To find the subtle demarcation between bone and stone, it was necessary to see color difference.

"Sometimes it helps just to spit on it," Cope said. "The moisture heightens the contrast."

"I'm going to die of thirst pretty quickly," muttered George Morton.

"And don't just look at what you are doing," Cope instructed. "Listen, too. Listen to the sound of the chisel hitting the stone. The higher the note, the harder the stone."

He also demonstrated the right position to extract the fossils, depending upon the slope of the rock. They worked on their bellies, on their knees, squatting, and sometimes while standing. When the rock face was especially sharp, they hammered in a spike and secured themselves with ropes. They were to understand how the angle of the sun revealed not just the face of the stone but also its fissures and unexpected depths.

Johnson found himself recalling how challenging it had been for him to learn to take photographs; extracting fossils from the grasp of stone without damaging them was far more difficult.

Cope showed them how to position their tools next to the hand that would use those tools and to work as efficiently as possible, for in a day each student would switch from hammer and chisel to pick to brush and back again in all combinations hundreds of times. Left-handers kept their chisels to their right, brushes to their left.

"The work is more tiring than you expect," he told them.

And, indeed, it was.

"My fingers hurt, my wrists hurt, my shoulders hurt, and also my knees and feet," said George Morton after the first few days.

"Better you than me," Cookie said.

As the bones came down to the camp, Cope laid them on a dark wool blanket for contrast, staring at them until he saw how they related to each other. In late July, he announced a new duck-billed *Hadrosaurus*; a week later, a flying reptile. And then in August they found a *Titanosaurus*, and finally the teeth of a *Champsosaurus*. "We are finding wonderful dinosaurs!" exulted Cope. "Wonderful, marvelous dinosaurs!"

The work was exhausting, backbreaking, sometimes dangerous. For one thing, the scale of the landscape was, as in the rest of the West, deceptive. What appeared to be a small cliff exposure turned out, on climbing, to be five or six hundred feet high. Scrambling up these sheer crumbling faces, working halfway up the hill, maintaining balance on the incline, was fatiguing in the extreme. It was a strange world: often, working on these huge rocky faces, they were so far apart they could hardly see each other, but because the land was so quiet and the curving cliffs acted like giant funnels, they could hold clear conversations no louder than a whisper, even within the constant sound of the reverberating pings and soft clicks of hammers striking chisel and chisel striking stone.

At other times, the broader silence and desolation became oppressive. Especially after the Crow moved on, they were uncomfortably aware of the silence.

And Sternberg had been right: in the end, the worst thing about the badlands was the dust. Harshly alkaline, it billowed up with every stab of pick and shovel; it burned the eyes, stung the nose, caked the mouth, caused coughing spasms; it burned in open cuts; it covered clothes and chafed at elbows and armpits and backs of knees; it gritted in sleeping bags; it dusted food, sour and bitter, and flavored coffee; stirred by the wind, it became a constant force, a signature of this harsh and forbidding place.

Their hands, which they needed in order to do everything, especially dig fossils, were soon scraped and calloused, the dust burning in any cracks. Cope insisted they thoroughly wash their hands at the end of the day and dispensed a small dollop of yellowish emollient to rub into their palms and fingers.

"Smells bad," Johnson said. "What is it?"

"Clarified bear fat."

But the dust was everywhere. Nothing they tried worked. Bandanas and facecloths did not help, since they could not protect the eyes. Cookie built a tent to try to keep the dust off the food he was preparing, but it burned down on the second day. They complained to each other for a while, and then after the second week, they no longer mentioned it. It was like a conspiracy of silence. They would no longer talk about the dust.

Once dug out, the fragile bones had to be lowered down with ropes in a difficult, painstaking process. One slip, and the fossils would break free of the ropes and tumble down the hillside, crashing to the ground, smashed beyond value.

At such times, Cope turned waspish, reminding them that the fossils had "lain for millions of years in perfect peace and remarkable preservation, waiting for you to drop them like idiots! Idiots!"

These hot speeches led them to anxiously await some slip by Cope himself, but it never happened. Sternberg finally said that "except for his temper, the professor is perfect, and it seems best to recognize it."

But the rock was fragile, and breaks in the fossils did occur, even with the most careful handling. Most frustrating of all was a break days or weeks after the fossil was lowered to the ground.

It was Sternberg who first proposed a solution.

When they set out from Fort Benton, they had brought with them several hundred pounds of rice. As the days went on, it became clear that they would never eat all the rice ("at least not the way Stinky cooks it," Isaac grumbled). Rather than leave it behind, Sternberg boiled the rice to a gelatinous paste, which he poured over the fossils. This novel preservative technique left the fossils looking like snowy blocks—or, as he put it, "gigantic cookies."

But whatever they called it, the paste provided a protective covering. They had no further breaks.

Around the Fire

Each evening, when the sunlight was fading and the light was soft, making the sculptured terrain look less stark, Cope reviewed with them the finds of the day, and spoke of the lost world in which these giant animals roamed.

"Cope could speak like an orator when he chose to," noted Sternberg, "and of an evening, the dead gray rocks became dense green jungle, the trickling streams vast vegetation-choked lakes, the clear sky turned close with hot rainclouds, and indeed the entire barren landscape before our eyes was transformed into an ancient swamp. It was mysterious, when he spoke that way. We felt goose-bumps and a chill on the spine."

In part, that chill came from the lingering tinge of heresy. Unlike Marsh, Cope was not an open Darwinian, but he appeared to believe in evolution, and certainly in great antiquity. Morton was going to be a preacher, like his father. He asked Cope, "as a man of science," how old the world was.

Cope said he had no idea, in the mild way he had when he was concealing something. It was the opposite side of his snapping temper, this almost lazy indifference, this tranquil, calm voice. This mildness overcame Cope whenever the discussion moved into areas that might be considered religious. A devout Quaker (despite his pugilistic temperament), he found it difficult to tread on the religious feelings of others.

Was the world, Morton asked, six thousand years old, as Bishop Ussher had said?

A great many serious and informed people still believed this date, despite Darwin and the fuss that the new scientists who called themselves "geologists" were making. After all, the trouble with what the scientists said was that they were always saying something different. This year one idea, next year something else. Scientific opinion was ever changing, like the fashions of women's dress, while the firm and fixed date 4004 BC invited the attention of those seeking greater verity.

No, Cope said, he did not think the world was so recent.

How old, then? asked Morton. Six thousand years? Ten thousand years?

No, Cope said, still tranquil.

Then how much older?

A thousand thousand times as old, said Cope, his voice still dreamy.

"Surely you're joking!" Morton exclaimed. "Four billion years? That is patently absurd."

"I know of no one who was there at the time," Cope said mildly.

"But what about the age of the sun?" Morton said, with a smug look.

In 1871, Lord Kelvin, the most eminent physicist of his day, posed a serious objection to Darwin's theory. It had not been answered by Darwin, or anyone else, in subsequent years.

Whatever else one might think of evolutionary theory, it obviously implied a substantial period of time—at least several hundred thousand years—to carry out its effects on earth. At the time of Darwin's publication, the oldest estimates of the age of the earth were around ten thousand years. Darwin himself believed the earth would have to be at least three hundred thousand years old to allow enough time for evolution. The earthly evidence, from the new study of geology, was confusing and contradictory, but it seemed at least conceivable that the earth might be several hundred thousand years old.

Lord Kelvin took a different approach to the question. He asked how long the sun had been burning. At this time, the mass of the sun was well established; it was obviously burning with the same processes of combustion as were found on earth; therefore one could estimate the time it would take to consume the mass of the sun in a great fire. Kelvin's answer was that the sun would burn up entirely within twenty thousand years.

The fact that Lord Kelvin was a devoutly religious man and therefore opposed to evolution could not be thought to have biased his thinking. He had investigated the problem from the impersonal vantage point of mathematics and physics. And he had concluded, irrefutably, that there was simply not enough time for evolutionary processes to take place.

Corroborating evidence derived from the warmth of the earth. From mine shafts and other drilling, it was known that the earth's temperature increased one degree for every thousand feet of depth. This implied that the core of the earth was still quite hot. But if the earth had really formed hundreds of thousands of years ago, it would have long since become cool. That was a clear implication of the second law of thermodynamics, and there was no disputing it.

There was only one escape from these physical dilemmas, and Cope echoed Darwin in suggesting it. "Perhaps," he said, "we do not know everything about the energy sources of the sun and the earth."

"You mean there may be a new form of energy, as yet unknown to science?" Morton asked. "The physicists say that it is impossible, that the rules governing the universe are fully understood by them."

"Perhaps the physicists are wrong," Cope said.

"Certainly someone is wrong."

"That is true," Cope said evenly.

If he was open-minded when listening to Morton's beliefs, he was equally so with Little Wind, the Snake scout.

Early in the bone digging, Little Wind became agitated and objected to their excavations. He said they would all be killed.

"Who will kill us?" Sternberg inquired.

"The Great Spirit, with lightning."

"Why?" Sternberg asked.

"Because we disturb the burial ground."

Little Wind explained that these were the bones of giant snakes that had inhabited the earth in ages past, before the Great Spirit had hunted them down and killed them all with bolts of lightning so that man could live on the plains.

The Great Spirit would not want the serpent bones disturbed, and would not look kindly on their adventures.

Sternberg, who did not like Little Wind anyway, duly reported it to Cope.

"He may be right," Cope said.

"It's nothing but savage superstition," Sternberg snorted.

"Superstition? Which part do you mean?"

"All of it," Sternberg said. "The very idea."

Cope said, "The Indians think these fossils are the bones of serpents, which is to say reptiles. We think they were reptiles, too. They think these creatures were gigantic. So do we. They think these gigantic reptiles lived in the distant past. So do we. They think the Great Spirit killed them. We say we don't know why they disappeared—but since we offer no explanation of our own, how can we be sure theirs is superstition?"

Sternberg walked away, shaking his head.

Bad Water

Cope chose his campsites for convenience to fossils, and no other reason. One difficulty with their
first site was lack of water. Nearby Bear Creek was so
badly polluted they did not draw water from there after
the first night, when they all experienced dysentery and
cramps. And the water elsewhere in the badlands was,
in Sternberg's words, "like a dense solution of Epsom
salts."

So they drew all their water from springs. Little Wind
knew several, the nearest a two-mile ride from camp.
Since Johnson was fussiest about the water, which he
used for his photographic processes, it became his job to
ride to and from the spring each day, and fetch the water.

Someone always accompanied him on these excursions. They had seen no trouble with the Crows, and

the Sioux were still presumed to be far south, but these were Indian hunting grounds, and they never knew when they might meet small parties of hostile Indians. Solitary riders were always at risk.

Nevertheless, for Johnson it was the most exhilarating part of the day. To ride out under the great dome of blue sky, with the plains stretching in all directions around him, was an experience that approached the mystical.

Usually, Little Wind rode with him. Little Wind liked to get out of camp, too, but for different reasons. As the days passed and more bones were unearthed, he became increasingly fearful of the retribution of the Great Spirit, or, as he sometimes called it, the Everywhere Spirit—the spirit that existed in all things in the world, and was found everywhere.

They would usually arrive at the spring, located in flat prairie, around three in the afternoon, as the sun was cooling and the light turning yellow. They filled their water bags and slung them onto the horses, and paused to drink directly from the stream, and then rode back.

One day as they reached the spring, Little Wind gestured for Johnson to stay some distance away while he dismounted and inspected the ground around the spring closely.

"What is it?" Johnson said.

Little Wind was moving quickly all around the spring, his nose inches from the ground. Occasionally he picked up a clod of prairie sod, smelled it, and dropped it again.

This behavior always filled Johnson with a mixture of amazement and irritation—amazement that an Indian could read the land as he read a book, and irritation because he could not learn to do it himself, and he suspected that Little Wind, knowing this, added a theatrical touch to his procedures.

"What is it?" Johnson asked again, annoyed.

"Horses," Little Wind said. "Two horses, two men. This morning."

"Indians?" The word came out more nervously than he had intended.

Little Wind shook his head. "Horses have shoes. Men have boots."

They had seen no white men for nearly a month, except their own party. There was little reason for white men to be here.

Johnson frowned. "Trappers?"

"What trappers?" Little Wind gestured to the flat expanse of the plains in all directions. "Nothing to trap."

"Buffalo hunters?" There was still a trade in buffalo hides, which were fashioned into robes for sale in the cities.

Little Wind shook his head. "Buffalo men don't hunt on Sioux land."

That was true, Johnson thought. To invade the Sioux lands looking for gold was one thing, but buffalo hunters would never take the risk.

"Then who are they?"

"Same men."

"What same men?"

"Same men at Dog Creek."

Johnson dismounted. "The same men whose camp you found, back at Dog Creek? How do you know that?"

Little Wind pointed in the mud. "This one boot crack heel. Same heel. Same man."

"I'll be damned," Johnson said. "We're being followed."

"Yes."

"Well," he said, "let's get the water and tell Cope. Maybe he'll want to do something."

"No use water here." Little Wind pointed to the horses, which were standing quietly by the spring.

"I don't get it," Johnson said.

"Horses no drink," Little Wind said.

The horses always drank as soon as they reached the spring. That was the first thing they did, let the horses drink before they filled their water bags.

But Little Wind was right: today the horses were not drinking.

"I'll be," Johnson said.

"Water not so good," Little Wind said. He bent close to the water and sniffed. Suddenly he plunged his arm up to his shoulder into the spring, and pulled out great clumps of a pale green grass. He reached in again, pulled out more. With each clump he removed, the spring flowed more freely.

He named the weed for Johnson, and explained that it would cause sickness if men drank it. Little Wind was speaking quickly, and Johnson did not understand it all, except that apparently it caused fevers and vomiting and men acted crazy, if they didn't die.

"Bad thing," he said. "Tomorrow water is good."

He stared off across the plains.

"We go find those white men?" Johnson said.

"I go," Little Wind said.

"Me, too," Johnson said.

They rode at a gallop for nearly an hour in the yellowing afternoon light, and soon they were far from camp.

It would be difficult, Johnson realized, to make it back by nightfall.

Periodically, Little Wind would pause, dismount, check the ground, and mount up again.

"How much farther?"

"Soon."

They rode on.

The sun dropped behind the peaks of the Rockies, and still they rode. Johnson began to worry. He had never been out on the plains at night before, and Cope had repeatedly warned him always to return to camp before dark.

"How much farther?"

"Soon."

They rode for perhaps fifteen minutes more and stopped again. Little Wind seemed to be stopping more often. Johnson thought it was because it was too dark to see the ground clearly.

"How much farther?"

"You want go back?"

"Me? No, I was just asking how much farther."

Little Wind smiled. "Get dark, you afraid."

"Don't be ridiculous. I was just asking. Is it much farther, do you think?"

"No," Little Wind said. He pointed. "There."

Beyond a far ridge, they saw a thin line of gray smoke climbing straight into the sky. A campfire.

"Leave horses," Little Wind said, dismounting. He pulled up a bunch of grass, let the blades fall in the wind. They drifted south. Little Wind nodded, and explained that they must approach the camp downwind or the other men's horses would smell them.

They crept forward, over the next ridge, lay on their stomachs, and looked down into the valley below.

In the deepening twilight, two men, a tent, a glowing fire. Six horses picketed behind the tent. One of the men was stocky, the other tall. They were cooking an antelope they had killed. Johnson could not see their faces well.

But he found the sight of this solitary camp, surrounded in all directions by miles of open plains, oddly disturbing. Why were they here?

"These men want bones," Little Wind said, echoing his own thoughts.

And then the tall man leaned close to the fire as he adjusted the leg on the spit, and Johnson saw a face he knew. It was the tough man he had spoken to in the Omaha train station. The man Marsh had spoken to near the cornfields. Navy Joe Benedict.

And then they heard a murmuring voice. The tent flap opened, and a balding, heavyset man emerged. He was rubbing something in his hands—spectacles he was cleaning. The man spoke again, and even from a distance Johnson recognized the slight halt, the formality of the speech.

It was Marsh.

Cope clapped his hands in delight. "So! The learned professor of Copeology has followed us here! What better proof of what I have been saying? The man is not a scientist—he is a dog in the manger. He does not pursue his own discoveries—he seeks to spy on mine. I have neither time nor inclination to spy on him. But Daddy Marsh can come all the way from Yale College to the Territory of Montana just to keep track of me!" He shook his head. "The asylum will yet receive him."

"You seem amused, Professor," Johnson said.

"Of course I am amused! Not only is my theory of the man's dementia amply confirmed—but so long as he is tracking me, he cannot be finding any new bones of his own!"

"I doubt that follows," Sternberg said soberly. "Marsh has nothing if not money, and his students are not with him. He is probably paying his bone hunters to dig for him simultaneously in three or four territories, even as we speak."

Sternberg had done some work for Marsh several years before, in Kansas. He was undoubtedly right, and Cope stopped smiling.

"Speaking of finds," Cookie said, "how did he find us?"

"Little Wind said that these are the same men that were following us back at Dog Creek."

Isaac leapt up. "See? I told you we were being followed!"

"Sit down, J.C.," Cope said. He was frowning now, his good humor vanished.

"What are they doing here, anyway?" Cookie said. "They're not on the square. They're gonna kill us and take the bones."

"They're not going to kill us," Cope said.

"Well then, take the bones, for sure."

"They wouldn't dare. Even Marsh wouldn't dare."

But in the darkness of the plains, he sounded unconvinced. There was a silence. They listened to the moan of the night wind.

"They poisoned the water," Johnson said.

"Yes," Cope said. "They did."

"I wouldn't call that neighborly," Cookie said.

"True . . ."

"You've made some important discoveries, Professor. Discoveries any scientist'd give his left arm to claim as his own."

"True."

There was another long silence.

"We surely are a long way from home, out here," Isaac said. "If something happened to us, who'd be the wiser? They'd just blame the Indians if we never showed back in Fort Benton."

"They blame Indians." Little Wind nodded.

"Quite true."

"Better do something about them," Isaac said.

"You're right," Cope said finally. He stared at the campfire. "We will do something. We will invite them to dinner tomorrow night."

Dinner with Cope and Marsh

The search for fossils was abandoned the next day in feverish preparation for Marsh. The camp was cleaned, clothes and bodies washed. Sternberg shot a deer for dinner and Cookie roasted it.

Cope was busy with preparations of his own. He picked through the piles of fossils they had found, selecting a piece here, a piece there, setting them aside.

Johnson asked if he could help, but Cope shook his head. "This is a job for an expert."

"You are selecting finds to show Marsh?"

"In a way. I am making a new creature: *Dinosaurus marshiensis vulgaris.*"

By the end of the day he had assembled from fragments a passable skull, with two horned projections that stuck out laterally from the jaw like curving tusks.

Isaac said it looked like a wild boar, or a warthog.

"Exactly," Cope said, excited. "A prehistoric por-cine giant. A piglike dinosaur! A pig for a pig!"

"It's nice," Sternberg allowed, "but it won't stand close scrutiny from Marsh."

"It won't have to."

Cope ordered them to lift the skull, which was held together with paste, and under his instructions they moved it first farther from the fire, then closer, then far-ther again. Next to one side, and to another. Cope stood by the fire, squinted, and then ordered it moved again.

"He's like a woman decorating his house, and we're movin' the furniture," Cookie said, panting.

It was late afternoon when Cope pronounced himself satisfied with the skull's position. They all went off to clean up, and Little Wind was dispatched to invite the other camp to join them for dinner. He returned a few minutes later to say that three riders were approaching the camp.

Cope smiled grimly. "I should have known he'd in-vite himself."

There was a theatrical aspect to both men," ob-served Sternberg, who had worked for both, "although it manifested differently. Professor Marsh was heavy and solemn, a man of judicious pauses. He spoke slowly and had a way of making the listener hang on his next words. Professor Cope was the opposite—his words came in a tumbling rush, his movements were quick and nervous, and he captivated attention as a hummingbird does, so brilliantly quick you did not want to miss anything. At this meeting—the only face-to-face encounter I ever witnessed—it was clear no love was lost between them, though they were at pains to hide this fact in frosty Eastern formality."

"To what do we owe this honor, Professor Marsh?" Cope asked when the three men had ridden into camp and dismounted.

"A social visit, Professor Cope," Marsh said. "We happened to be in the neighborhood."

"Quite extraordinary, Professor Marsh, considering how large a neighborhood it is."

"Similar interests, Professor Cope, lead down similar paths."

"I am astonished you even knew we were here."

"We didn't know," Marsh said. "But we saw your cook fire and came to investigate."

"Your attention honors us," Cope said. "You must stay to dinner, of course."

"We have no wish to intrude," Marsh said, his eyes darting around the camp.

"And likewise, I am sure we have no wish to detain you on your journey—"

"Since you insist, we will be delighted to stay to dinner, Professor Cope. We accept with gratitude."

Cookie produced some decent bourbon; as they drank, Marsh continued to look around the camp. His gaze fell on several fossils, and at length, the unusual tusked skull set off to one side. His eyes widened.

"I see you are looking around—" Cope began.

"No, no—"

"Ours must strike you as a very small expedition, compared to the grand scale of your own endeavors."

"Your outfit appears efficient and compact."

"We have been fortunate to make one or two significant finds."

"I'm certain you have," Marsh said. He spilled his bourbon nervously, and wiped his chin with the heel of his hand.

"As one colleague to another, perhaps you'd enjoy a tour of our little camp, Professor Marsh."

Marsh's excitement was palpable, but all he said was, "Oh, I don't want to pry."

"I can't tempt you?"

"I wouldn't want to be accused of anything improper," Marsh said, smiling.

"On second thought," Cope said, "you are correct as always. Let's forgo a tour, and simply have dinner."

In that instant, Marsh shot him a look of such murderous hatred that it chilled Johnson to see it.

"More whiskey?" Cope asked.

"Yes, I will have more," Marsh said, and he extended his glass.

Dinner was a comedy of diplomacy. Marsh reminded Cope of the details of their past friendship, which had begun, of course, in Berlin, of all places, when both men were much younger and the Civil War raged. Cope hastened to add his own warm, confirming anecdotes; they fell all over each other in eagerness to declare their fervent admiration for one another.

"Professor Cope has probably told you how I got him his first job," Marsh said.

They demurred politely: they had not heard.

"Well, not quite his first job," Marsh said. "Professor Cope had quit his position as zoology professor at Haverford—quit rather suddenly, as I recall—and in 1868 he was looking to go west. True, Professor Cope?"

"True, Professor Marsh."

"So I took him down to Washington to meet Ferdinand Hayden, who was planning the Geological Survey expedition. He and Hayden liked each other, and Professor Cope signed on as expedition paleontologist."

"Very true."

"Though you never actually accompanied the expedition, I believe," Marsh said.

"No," Cope said. "My baby daughter was ill, and my own health not excellent, so I worked from Philadelphia, cataloging the bones the expedition sent back."

"You have the most extraordinary ability to draw deductions from bones without benefit of having seen them in the actual site or having dug them out yourself."

Marsh managed to turn this compliment into an insult.

"You are no less talented in just that way, Professor Marsh," Cope said quickly. "I often wish I had, like you, the ample funds from multiple patrons needed to pay for the large network of bone hunters and fossil scouts you employ. It must be difficult for you to keep up with the quantities of bones sent you in New Haven, and to write all the papers yourself."

"A problem you face as well," Marsh said. "I am amazed you are no more than a year behind in your own reporting. You must often be obliged to work with great haste."

"With great speed, certainly," Cope said.

"You always had a facile ability," Marsh said, and he then reminisced about some weeks they had spent as young men in Haddonfield, New Jersey, searching for fossils together. "Those were great times," he said, beaming.

"Of course we were younger then, and didn't know what we know now."

"But even then," Marsh said, "I remember that if we found a fossil, I was obliged to ponder it for days to deduce its meaning, whereas Professor Cope would simply glance at it, snap his fingers, and give it a name. An impressive display of erudition—despite the occasional error."

"I recall no errors," Cope said, "though in the years since then, you have been kind enough to hunt down all my errors and point them out to me."

"Science is an exacting mistress, demanding truth above all."

"For myself, I've always felt that truth is a by-product of a man's character. An honest man will reveal the truth with every breath he takes, while a dishonest man will distort in the same way. More whiskey?"

"I believe I'll have water," Marsh said. Navy Joe Benedict, sitting by his side, nudged him. "On second thought, whiskey sounds good."

"You don't want water?"

"The water in the badlands doesn't always agree with me."

"That's why we draw ours from a spring. Anyway, you were saying, Professor Marsh, about honesty?"

"No, I believe honesty was your subject, Professor Cope."

Johnson later recorded:

Our fascination at seeing these legendary giants of paleontological science meet head-to-head eventually faded as the evening grew older. It was of interest to note how long they had known each other, and how similar were their backgrounds. Both men had lost their mothers in infancy and had been raised by strict fathers. Both men had evinced a fascination with fossils from early childhood—a fascination that their fathers had opposed. Both men were difficult, lonely personalities—Marsh because he had grown up on a rural farm, Cope because he had been a childhood prodigy who made anatomical notes at the age of six. Both men had followed parallel careers, such that they met in Europe, where they were both abroad studying the fossils of the Continent. At that time, they had been good friends, and now were implacable enemies.

As the hours passed, interest in their banter faded. We were tired from the exertions of the day, and ready for sleep. On Marsh's side, his roughneck companions looked equally fatigued. And still Cope and Marsh talked on into the night, sniping, bickering, trading insults as pleasantries.

Finally, Toad fell asleep, beside the fire. His loud snores were inescapable proof that these two had lost their audience, and having lost the audience to witness their jibes, they seemed to lose interest in each other.

The evening had dragged to a seemingly undramatic conclusion—no hollering, no gunfire—and too much had been drunk on all sides. Marsh and Cope shook hands, but I noticed that the handshake was extended; one man was holding the other's hand tightly, not releasing it, as the two men stared hatefully into each other's eyes, the light from the fire flickering over both their faces. I could not tell which man was the aggressor in this instant, but I could plainly see each man silently swearing his undying enmity toward the other. Then the handshake broke off almost violently and Marsh and his men rode off into the night.

"Sleep with Your Guns Tonight, Boys"

No sooner were they gone over the nearest ridge than Cope was wide awake, alert and energized.

"Break out your guns!" he said. "Sleep with your guns tonight, boys."

"Why, what do you mean?"

"We'll have visitors tonight, mark my words." Cope bunched his fists in his pugilistic way. "That vertebrate vulgarity will be back, crawling in on his belly like a snake for a closer look at my pig skull."

"You don't mean to shoot at them?" Isaac said, horrified.

"I do," Cope said. "They have opposed us and impeded us, they have got the army after us, they have poisoned our water and insulted our persons, and now they are going to steal our finds. Yes, I mean to shoot at them."

This seemed to them extreme, but Cope was angry and would not be talked out of it.

An hour passed. Most of the camp fell asleep. Johnson was lying next to Cope, and his twisting and turning kept him awake.

Thus he was awake when the first dark figure crept over the ridge.

Cope gave a soft sigh.

A second figure, then a third. The third was heavy-set, lumbering.

Cope sighed again, and swung his rifle around.

The figures crept toward the camp, and made for the fossil head.

Cope raised his rifle to shoot. He was a crack shot, and for a horrified moment Johnson thought he really intended to kill his rival.

"Now, Professor—"

"Johnson," he said quietly, "I have him in my sights. It is within my power to kill a trespassing sneak and thief. Remember this night."

And Cope raised his rifle higher into the air, and fired twice at the sky, and shouted, "Indians! Indians!"

The cry brought the camp to its feet. Soon rifles were

discharged from all sides; the night air was clouded with gun smoke, and acrid with the smell of powder.

Across the camp, they heard the intruders scrambling up the ridge. There was an occasional shout of "Damn you! Damn your eyes!"

Finally, a deep, distinctive voice cried, "Just your way, Cope! It's a damnable fake! Just your way! A fake!"

And the three men were gone.

The firing stopped.

"I believe we have seen the last of Othy Marsh," Cope said. Smiling, he rolled over to sleep.

Moving Camp

I n early August, they were visited by a party of soldiers passing through the badlands on their way to
the Missouri River. Steamboats came as far upriver as
Cow Island, where the army maintained a small camp.
The soldiers were on their way to reinforce the garrison
there.

They were young Irish and German boys, no older
than the students, and they seemed amazed to find
white men alive in the region. "I surely would pull out
of here," one said.

They brought news of the war, and it was not good:
Custer's defeat was still unavenged; General Crook had
fought an inconclusive battle at the Powder River in
Wyoming but had seen no Indians since; General Terry
had not engaged any large parties of Sioux at all. The

war, which the Eastern newspapers had confidently predicted would be over in a matter of weeks, appeared now to be dragging on indefinitely. Some generals were predicting that it would not be resolved for at least a year, and perhaps not even by the end of the decade.

"Trouble with Indians," one soldier explained, "is when they want to find you they find you—and when they don't want you to find them, you'd never know they were there." He paused. "It is their country, after all, but I didn't say it."

Another soldier looked at their stacked crates. "You mining here?"

"No," Johnson said. "These're bones. We're digging fossil bones."

"Sure you are," the soldier said, grinning broadly. He offered Johnson a drink from his canteen, which was filled with bourbon. Johnson gasped; the soldier laughed. "Makes the miles shorter, I can tell you," he explained.

The soldiers grazed their horses for an hour with Cope's party and then went on.

"I surely wouldn't dawdle here much longer," their Captain Lawson said. "Best we know, Sitting Bull, Crazy Horse, and his Sioux'll make for Canada before winter, which means they'll be here any day now. They find you here, they'll kill you for sure."

And with that final advice, he rode off.

(Much later, Johnson heard that when Sitting Bull went north, he killed all the white men he came across, among them the troops stationed at Cow Island, including Captain Lawson.)

"I think we ought to be going," Isaac said, scratching his chin.

"Not yet," Cope said.

"We've found plenty of bones."

"That's so," Cookie said. "Plenty so far. More'n enough."

"Not yet," Cope said, in an icy tone that ended all discussion. As Sternberg noted in his account of the expedition, "We had long since learned there was no purpose served in arguing with him when his mind was made up. Cope's indomitable will could not be conquered."

But Cope did decide to break camp and move to another location. For the last three weeks, they had been located at the foot of thousand-foot-high shale cliffs. He had been scouting the area, and he felt there was a more promising fossil location three miles distant.

"Where?" Sternberg said.

Cope pointed. "Up on the plains."

"You mean on the flat tablelands?"

"That's right."

Isaac protested: "But, Professor, it'll take three days to move out of the badlands, find a new route, and come back in up there."

"No, it won't."

"We can't scale these cliffs."

"Yes, we can."

"A man can't walk up, a horse can't ride up, and certainly this wagon can't be pulled up those cliffs, Professor."

"Yes, it can. I will show you."

Cope insisted they pack up at once, and moved two miles to the east, where he proudly pointed to a sloping bank of shale.

It was much gentler than the surrounding cliffs, but still far too steep to negotiate. While there were some level ridges, the shale was loose and crumbling, affording treacherous footing.

Cookie, the teamster, looked at the proposed route and spat tobacco. "Can't be done, can't be done."

"It can," Cope said, "and it will."

It took them fourteen hours to climb a thousand feet—backbreaking work, and continuously dangerous. Using shovels and picks, they dug a trail up the side. Then they unloaded the wagon and put everything they could on the horses and got the horses up; now only the wagon remained.

Cookie drove it halfway up the incline from the floor below, but when he arrived at a level ridge so narrow that one wheel was hanging over empty space, he refused to go any farther.

This enraged Cope, who said he would drive the wagon himself: "Not only are you a revolting cook, but you are a wretched teamster!" The others quickly interceded, and Isaac climbed on to drive the wagon.

They had to unhitch the lead horses, and pull the wagon with the remaining two ponies.

Sternberg later described it in *The Life of a Fossil Hunter*:

Isaac had driven about thirty feet when the inevitable happened. I saw the wagon slowly begin to tip, pulling the ponies over sideways, and then the whole outfit, wagon and horses, began to roll down the slope. Whenever the wheels stuck up in the air, the ponies drew in their feet to their bellies, and at the next turn, stretched out their legs for another roll.

My heart was in my mouth for fear that Isaac would be killed in one of the turns, or that the wagon would roll over [the] precipice below, but after three complete turns, they landed, the horses on their feet, the wagon on its wheels, on a level ledge of sandstone, and stood there as if nothing had happened.

Eventually they unhitched all the horses and pulled the wagon up on ropes, but they succeeded, and late in the day they made camp, on the prairie.

Cope snapped at Cookie, "This dinner better be your best."

"Just wait and see," Cookie said. And he served them the usual fare of hardtack, bacon, and beans.

Despite the grumbling, their new camp was a decided improvement. The breeze made it cooler, for they were on the open plains, wrote Johnson, with "a magnificent view of mountains in every direction—to the west the towering craggy Rockies, with white snow gleaming on their peaks; to the south, east, and north, the Judith River, Medicine Bow, Bearpaw, and Sweet Grass Mountains, completely encircling us. Especially in the early morning, when the air was clear and we would see herds of deer and elk and antelope and the mountains beyond, it was a sight of such glory as surely cannot be matched elsewhere in all creation."

But the herds of deer and antelope were migrating northward, and the snow was creeping down the slopes of the Rockies as the days passed. One morning they awoke to find a thin carpet of snow had fallen during the night, and although it burned off by midday, they could not ignore the inevitable fact. The seasons were changing, fall was coming, and with the fall, the Sioux.

"It's time to leave, Professor."

"Not yet," Cope said. "Not just yet."

The Teeth

One afternoon, Johnson came across some knobby
protuberances of rock, each roughly the size of a
fist. He was working in a promising deposit midway up
the side of a shale slope, and these knobs got in his way;
he pulled several out of the exposed surface, and they
tumbled down the hillside, narrowly missing Cope,
who was at the base of the cliffs, sketching a newly discovered *Allosaurus* leg bone. Cope heard them coming
and took a practiced step to the side.

"Hey there!" he shouted up the slope.

"Sorry, Professor," Johnson called sheepishly. One
or two rocks continued to fall; Cope moved aside again
the other way and dusted himself off.

"Be careful!"

"Yes, sir. Sorry!" Johnson repeated. Gingerly, he returned to his work, digging with his pick around still other rocks, trying to pry them free and—

"Stop!"

Johnson looked down. Cope was scrambling up the hillside toward him like a madman, one of the fallen rocks in each hand.

"Stop! Stop, I say!"

"I'm being careful," Johnson protested. "Really I—"

"Wait!" Cope slid several yards down the slope. "Do nothing! Touch nothing!" Still shouting, he slid backwards, disappearing in a dust cloud.

Johnson waited. After a moment, he saw Professor Cope scrambling out of the dust, coming up the hill with frenzied energy.

Johnson thought he must be very angry. It was foolish and nearly impossible to climb straight up the hill; they had all learned that long ago. The surface was too sheer and too friable; a climber had to zigzag his way up, and even that was so difficult they usually preferred a detour of as much as a mile to find an easy route to the top, and from there to descend to where they wanted to go.

Yet here was Cope scrambling straight up as if his life depended upon doing so. "Wait!"

"I'm waiting, Professor."

"Don't do anything!"

"I'm not doing anything, Professor."

At length Cope arrived beside him, covered in dirt, gasping for breath. But he did not hesitate. He wiped his face with his sleeve and peered at the excavation.

"Where is your camera?" he demanded. "Why don't you have your camera? I want a picture in situ."

"Of these rocks?" Johnson asked, astonished.

"Rocks? You think these are rocks? They are nothing of the sort."

"Then what are they?"

"They are teeth!" Cope exclaimed.

Cope touched one, and traced with his finger the gentle hills and indentations of the cusp pattern. He placed the two he held next to each other, then found a third at Johnson's feet and set it in a row with the other two; it was clear from their similarity in size and form that they went together.

"Teeth," he repeated. "Dinosaur teeth."

"But they are enormous! This dinosaur must be of fantastic size."

For a moment the two men silently contemplated just how large such a dinosaur must have been—the jaw needed to hold rows of such large teeth, the thick skull needed to match such a massive jaw, the enormous neck the width of a stout oak to lift and move such a skull and jaw, the gigantic backbone commensurate to the neck, with each vertebra as big around as a wagon wheel, with four staggeringly huge and thick legs to support such a beast. Each tooth implied an enormity of every bone and every joint. An animal that large might even need a long tail to counterweight its neck, in fact.

Cope stared across the rocky expanse and beyond, into his own imagination and knowledge. For a moment his usual ferocious confidence gave way to quiet wonder. "The full creature must be at least twice the dimensions of any previously known," he said, almost to himself.

They had already made several discoveries of large dinosaurs, including three examples of the genus *Monoclonius*, a horned dinosaur that resembled a gigantic rhinoceros. *Monoclonius sphenocerus*, one of the specimens, was estimated by Cope to stand seven feet tall at the hip joint, and to be twenty-five feet long, including the tail.

Yet this new dinosaur was far larger than that. Cope measured the teeth with his steel calipers, scratched some calculations on his sketch pad, and shook his head. "It doesn't seem possible," he said, and measured again. And then he stood looking across the expanses of rock, as if expecting to see the giant dinosaur appear before him, shaking the ground with each step. "If we are making discoveries such as this one," he said to Johnson, "it means that we have barely scratched what is possible to learn. You and I are the first men in recorded history to glimpse these teeth. They will change everything we think we know about these animals, and much as I hesitate to say such a thing, man becomes smaller when we realize what remarkable beasts went before us."

Johnson saw then that all that was done in Cope's mission—all that even he, Johnson, did now—would have meaning to scientists in the future.

"Now, your camera," Cope reminded him. "We must record this moment and place."

Johnson went off to collect his equipment, from the flat plains above. When he returned, careful not to fall, Cope was still shaking his head. "Of course you can't be sure from teeth alone," he said. "Allometric factors may be misleading."

"How big do you make it?" Johnson asked. He glanced at the sketch pad, now covered with calculations, some scratched out and done again.

"Seventy-five, possibly one hundred feet long, with a head perhaps thirty feet above the ground."

And right there he gave it the name, *Brontosaurus*, "thundering lizard," because it must have thundered when it walked. "But perhaps," he said, "I should call it *Apatosaurus*, or 'unreal lizard.' Because it is hard to believe such a thing ever existed . . ."

Johnson took several plates, up close and from farther away, with Cope in all of them. They hurried back to camp, told the others of their discovery, and then in the fading twilight paced out the dimensions of *Brontosaurus*—a creature as long as three horse-drawn wagons, and as tall as a four-story building. It made the imagination run wild. It was altogether astonishing, and Cope announced that "this discovery alone justifies our entire time in the West," and that they had made "a momentous discovery, in these teeth. These are," Cope said, "the teeth of dragons."

The trouble the teeth would soon cause them, they could not have imagined.

Around the Campfire

A ny discovery led Cope to wax philosophical around the campfire at night. Each man had examined the teeth, felt their ridges and knobs, weighed their heft in one hand. The discovery of the gigantic *Brontosaurus* provoked an unusual degree of speculation.

"There are so many things in nature we would never imagine," Cope said. "At the time of this *Brontosaurus*, the glacial ice had receded and our entire planet was tropical. There were fig trees in Greenland, palm trees in Alaska. The vast plains of America were then vast lakes, and where we are sitting now was at the bottom of a lake. The animals we find were preserved because they died and sank to the bottom of the lake, where muddy sediment silted over them, and that sediment in turn compressed into rock. But who would have conceived such things until the evidence for them was found?"

No one spoke. They stared at the crackling fire.

"I am thirty-six years old, but at the time I was born," Cope said, "dinosaurs were unknown. All the generations of mankind had been born and died, lived and inhabited the earth, and none ever suspected that long, long before them, life on our planet was dominated by a race of gigantic reptilian creatures who held sway for millions upon millions of years."

George Morton coughed. "If this is so, then what about man?"

There was an uncomfortable silence. Most discussions of evolution sidestepped the question of man. Darwin himself had not dealt with man for more than a decade after his book was published.

"You know of the German finds in the Neander Valley?" Cope asked. "No? Well, back in '56 they discovered a complete skull in Germany—heavy-boned, with brutish brow ridges. The strata is disputed, but it seems to be very old. I myself saw the find in Europe in '63."

"I heard the Neander skull was an ape, or a degenerate," Sternberg said.

"That is unlikely," Cope said. "Professor Venn in Düsseldorf has devised a new method of measuring the brain size of skulls. It's quite simple: he fills the brain case with mustard seeds, then pours the seeds out into a measuring vessel. His researches show that the Neander skull held a larger brain than we possess today."

"You are saying this Neander skull is human?" Morton said.

"I don't know," Cope said. "But I do not see how one can believe that dinosaurs evolved, and reptiles evolved, and mammals such as the horse evolved, but that man sprang fully developed without antecedents."

"Aren't you a Quaker, Professor Cope?"

Cope's ideas were still unacceptable to most faiths, including the Religious Society of Friends, which was the Quakers' formal name.

"I may not be," Cope said. "Religion explains what man cannot explain. But when I see something before my eyes, and my religion hastens to assure me that I am mistaken, that I do not see it at all . . . No, I may no longer be a Quaker, after all."

Leaving the Badlands

The morning of August 26 was distinctly chilly as they set out on the one-day journey to Cow Island, located at one of the few natural fords along a two-hundred-mile stretch of the Missouri River, where the Missouri Breaks formed a barrier on each side. The island also served as a steamboat landing, and it was here Cope planned to meet the steamboat that came up from St. Louis. They were all eager to leave, and frankly worried about Indians, but they had too many fossils to take with them in the wagon. Nothing would do but to make two trips. Cope marked the most precious box, the one with the *Brontosaurus* teeth, with a subtle X on one side.

"I'm going to leave this one here," Cope said, "for the second trip."

Johnson said he didn't understand. Why not take it on the first trip?

"The chances we get raided on our first leg are probably better than the chances the second load will get discovered here," he said. "Plus we should be able to pick up some extra hands at Cow Island to protect us on the second trip."

Their initial journey was uneventful; they reached Cow Island in the early evening and dined with the army troops stationed there. Marsh and his men had gone down the Missouri on the previous steamer, after warning the troops of "Cope's cutthroats and vagabonds," who might appear later.

Captain Lawson laughed. "I think Mr. Marsh bears no love for your party," he said.

Cope affirmed that was the case.

The steamboat was due in two days, but the schedule was uncertain, especially so late in the year. It was imperative that they make their final trip to the plains camp the following day. Cope would remain in Cow Island, repacking the fossils for the steamboat journey, while Little Wind and Cookie drove the wagon back in the morning under Sternberg's supervision.

But early the next morning, Sternberg awoke with severe chills and fever, a recurrence of his malaria. Isaac was too jumpy about Indians to go back, Cookie and

Little Wind too unreliable to go unsupervised. There was the question as to who would lead the expedition.

Johnson said, "I'll lead it."

It was the moment he had been waiting for. Summer on the plains had toughened him, but he had always been under the supervision of older and more experienced men. He longed for a chance to prove himself on his own, and this short trip seemed the perfect opportunity for independence, and a fitting conclusion to the summer's adventures.

Toad felt the same way. He immediately said, "I'll go, too."

"You two shouldn't make the trip alone," Cope said. "I haven't been able to find any extra hands. The soldiers are unavailable to us."

"We won't be alone. We'll have Cookie and Little Wind."

Cope frowned. He drummed his fingers nervously on his sketchbook.

"Please, Professor. It's important that you repack the fossils. We will be fine. And the day is passing as we stand here discussing it."

"All right," Cope said finally. "This is against my better judgment, but all right."

Delighted, Johnson and Toad left at seven that morning, with Cookie and Little Wind driving the wagon.

———

Cope organized the wooden boxes of fossils, repacking those not sufficiently safe to suffer the depredations of the steamboat's stevedores. Isaac looked after Sternberg, who was delirious most of the time; he boiled him a tea made of the bark of willow branches, which he said helped with fevers. Morton assisted Cope.

Six or seven other passengers waited at Cow Island for the steamboat. Among them was a Mormon farmer named Travis and his young son. They had come to Montana to bring the gospel to the settlers, but had had little success, and were disgruntled.

"What you got in those crates there?" Travis asked.

Cope looked up. "Fossil bones."

"What for?"

"I study them," Cope said.

Travis laughed. "Why study bones when you can study living animals?"

"These are the bones of extinct animals."

"That can't be."

"Why not?" Cope asked.

"Are you a God-fearing man?"

"Yes, I am."

"Do you believe God is perfect?"

"Yes, I do."

Travis laughed again. "Well then, you must agree there can be no extinct animals, because the good Lord in His perfection would never allow a line of His creatures to become extinct."

"Why not?" Cope asked.

"I just told you." Travis looked annoyed.

"You just told me your belief about how God goes about His business. But what if God attains His perfection by degrees, casting aside His past creations in order to create new ones?"

"Men may do that, because men are imperfect. God does not, because He is perfect. There was only one Creation. Do you think God made mistakes in His Creation?"

"He made man. Didn't you just say man is imperfect?"

Travis glowered. "You're one of those professors," he said. "One of those educated fools who has departed from righteousness to blasphemy."

Cope was in no mood for theological dispute. "Better an educated fool than an uneducated fool," he snapped.

"You are doing the work of the Devil," Travis said, and he kicked one of the fossil crates.

"Do that again," Cope said, "and I'll beat your brains out."

Travis kicked another crate.

In a letter to his wife, Cope wrote:

I am dreadfully ashamed of what occurred next, and can offer no excuse save the effort I had expended in collecting these fossils, their priceless value, and my own fatigue after a summer in the heat and bugs and searing alkali of the Bad Lands. To be confronted by this stupid bigot was too much for me, and my patience abandoned me.

Morton described what happened directly:

Without preamble or warning, Cope fell upon this man Travis and pounded him into insensibility. It could not have taken more than a minute at most, for Professor Cope was of a pugilistic disposition. Between blows, he would say "How dare you touch my fossils! How dare you!" and at other times he would say scornfully "In the name of religion!" The fight ended when the soldiers pulled Cope off the poor Mormon gentleman, who had said nothing other than what a great many people in the world thought to be utter and indisputable truth.

This was certainly still so in 1876. Much earlier in the century, Thomas Jefferson had carefully concealed his own view that fossils represented extinct creatures. In Jefferson's day, public espousal of belief in extinction was considered heresy. Attitudes had since changed in many places, but not everywhere. It was still controversial to espouse evolution in certain parts of the United States.

Soon after the fight ended, the steamboat, the *Lizzie B.*, rounded the bend and whistled her imminent arrival. All eyes were on the boat, except for those of one soldier who glanced back across the plains and shouted, "Look there! Horses!"

And from across the plains, two riderless horses approached.

"My heart sank," Cope wrote in his journal, "to imagine what this might mean."

They quickly mounted up and rode out to meet them. As they came closer they saw Cookie, bent over, clutching the saddle, near death. A half dozen Indian arrows pierced his body; blood streamed freely from his wounds. The other horse belonged to Johnson: there was blood on the saddle, and arrows were stuck in the leather.

The army soldiers got Cookie off the horse and laid him on the ground. His lips were swollen and crusted dry; they gave him sips from the canteen until he could speak.

"What happened?" Cope said.

"Indians," Cookie said. "Damn Indians. Nothing we could—"

And he coughed blood, fitfully, writhing with the effort, and died.

"We must return at once and search for survivors," Cope said. "And our bones."

Captain Lawson shook his head. He yanked one arrow from the saddle. "These're Sioux arrows," he said.

"So?"

The captain nodded toward the plains. "There won't be anything to go back for, Professor. I'm sorry, but if you find your friends at all—which I doubt—they'll be scalped and mutilated and left to rot on the plains."

"There must be something we can do."

"Bury this 'un and say a prayer for the others is about all," Captain Lawson said.

The next morning, they mournfully loaded their fossils onto the steamboat and headed back down the Missouri. The nearest telegraph station was in Bismarck, Dakota Territory, which was nearly five hundred miles to the east, on the Missouri. When the *Lizzie B.*

stopped there, Cope sent the following cable to Johnson's family in Philadelphia:

I PROFOUNDLY REGRET TO INFORM YOU OF THE DEATH OF

YOUR SON WILLIAM AND THREE OTHER MEN YESTERDAY,

AUGUST 27, IN THE BAD LANDS OF THE JUDITH BASIN, MON-

TANA TERRITORY, AT THE HANDS OF HOSTILE SIOUX INDI-

ANS. MY SINCERE CONDOLENCES.

EDWARD DRINKER COPE, U.S. PALEONTOLOGIST.

PART III

Dragon Teeth

On the Plains

From the journal of William Johnson:

Our enthusiasm was absolute, as we set out on the morning of August 27 to collect the remainder of the fossils. There were four in our party: Little Wind, the Crow scout, Toad and myself, riding a little behind, surveying the ground ahead with watchful eyes, and finally Cookie, the teamster, whipping and cursing his animals as he drove the wagon across the prairie. Our journey would take us twelve miles to the Bad Lands, and twelve miles back again. We rode quickly in order to get there and back to Cow Island by dark.

It was a clear, chill, beautiful morning. Feathery cirrus clouds streaked the blue dome of the sky. The Rocky Mountains directly before us gleamed with white snow, which now reached down from the peaks to the deep crevices. The plains grass whispered in a gentle wind. Herds of pale antelope leapt across the distant horizon.

Toad and I imagined ourselves as pioneers, leading our little expedition into the wilderness, into excitement and dangers to be met bravely. For two Eastern college students of eighteen years, it was hugely exciting. We sat straight in our saddles; we scanned the horizon with narrowed eyes; we kept our hands on our pistol butts and our minds on the business at hand.

As the morning continued, we saw a tremendous amount of game—not only antelope, but elk and bison as well. It was far more game than we had seen in our previous weeks on the plain, and we commented on it to each other.

We had traveled no more than half the distance to the camp—perhaps six miles or so, out into the plains—when Cookie called for a halt. I refused. "No halts until we reach camp," I said.

"You little bastards will halt if I say so," Cookie said.

I turned and saw that Cookie was leveling a shotgun at our midsections. That gave him a deal of authority. We halted.

"What is the meaning of this?" I demanded, in a loud voice.

"Shut up, you little blanking blanking so-and-so," Cookie said, climbing off the wagon. "Now get off your horses, boys."

I looked at Little Wind, but he avoided our eyes.

"Come on, off of your horses!" Cookie snarled, so we dismounted.

"What do you mean by this outrage?" Toad said, blinking his eyes rapidly.

"End of the line, boys," Cookie said, shaking his head. "This is where I get off."

"Where you get off?"

"I can't help it if you're too stupid to see the noses on your faces. You seeing all the game today?"

"What about it?"

"Didn't you ever wonder why you're seeing so much game? It's being driven north, that's why. Look there." He pointed to the south.

We looked. Streaky lines of smoke rose into the sky in the distance.

"That's the Sioux camp, you damn fools. That's Sitting Bull." Cookie was taking our horses, mounting up.

I looked again. The fires—if that is what they were—were very far away. "But that must be at least a day away from here," I protested. "We can make our camp, load up, and be back to Cow Island before they reach us."

"You boys go right ahead," Cookie said. He was mounted on Toad's horse, and leading my own.

I looked at Little Wind, but he would not meet my eyes. He shook his head. "Bad day now. Many Sioux warriors in Sitting Bull camp. Kill all Crows. Kill all white men."

"You heard the man," Cookie said. "Me, I value my scalp. See you, boys. Come on, Little Wind." And he started to ride off to the north. A moment later, Little Wind wheeled his horse around and rode off with him.

Toad and I stood by the wagon and watched them leave.

"They planned this," Toad said. He shook his fist at them as they disappeared toward the horizon. "Bastards! Bastards!"

As for me, my good spirits evaporated. I suddenly realized our predicament—we were two boys alone on the vast and empty plains of the West. "What do we do now?"

Toad was still angry. "Cope paid them in advance, otherwise they would never dare to do this."

"I know," I said, "but what are we going to do now?"

Toad squinted at the lines of smoke to the south. "Do you really think those camps are a day away?"

"How would I know?" I cried. "I just said that so they wouldn't leave."

"Because the thing about Indians is," Toad said, "that when they have a large camp, like Sitting Bull's, they keep hunting and raiding parties out in front of the main camp."

"How far out in front?" I asked.

"Sometimes one, two days."

We both stared at the fires again. "I make it six fires, maybe seven," Toad said. "So that can't be the main camp. The main camp'd have hundreds of fires."

I made up my own mind. I was not going to

return to Cow Island without the fossils. I could not face the Professor. "We have to get the fossils," I said.

"Right," Toad said.

We climbed aboard the wagon and headed west. I had never driven a wagon before, but I made a tolerable job of it. Beside me, Toad whistled nervously. "Let's sing a song," he suggested.

"Let's not," I said. And so we drove in silence, with our hearts in our mouths.

They got lost.

Their own trail from the day before should have been easy enough to follow, but large stretches of the plains were as flat and featureless as any ocean, and they lost their way several times.

They expected to reach the plains camp before noon, but instead finally found the camp in late afternoon. They loaded the wagon with the remaining ten wooden crates of fossils, which weighed about a thousand pounds in all, plus some final supplies and Johnson's photographic equipment. He was pleased they had come back, for among the fossils they now packed was of course the box with the X, containing the precious *Brontosaurus* teeth. "Couldn't go home without these," he said.

But by the time they were ready to head back, it was after four o'clock, and growing dark.

They were pretty sure they could never find their way to Cow Island in darkness. That meant they would have to spend the night on the plains—and in another day, the advancing Sioux might come upon them. They were debating just what to do when they heard the savage, bloodcurdling cries of Indians.

"Oh my God," Toad said.

A dust cloud, stirred up by many riders, appeared on the eastern horizon. It was coming toward them.

They scrambled aboard the wagon. Toad broke out the rifles and loaded them.

"How much ammunition have we got?" Johnson asked.

"Not enough," Toad said. His hands were shaking, dropping shells.

The whooping grew louder. They could see a single rider, hunched low in the saddle, pursued by a dozen others. But they heard no gunshots.

"Maybe they don't have any guns," Toad said hopefully. At that moment, the first arrow whistled past them. "Let's get out of here!"

"Which way?" Johnson said.

"Any way! Away from them!"

Johnson whipped up the team, and the horses responded with unaccustomed enthusiasm. The wagon rumbled forward at frightening speed, bouncing and tossing over the prairie, the cargo creaking and sliding around in the bed. In the growing darkness, they headed west, away from the Missouri River, away from Cow Island, away from Cope, away from safety.

The Indians closed in on them. The solitary rider drew abreast of their wagon, and they saw it was Little Wind. He was soaked in sweat; his horse lathered. Little Wind came very close to the wagon and gracefully leapt aboard. He smacked his pony, and set it racing to the north.

Several Indians chased it, but the main party continued in pursuit of the wagon.

"Damn Sioux! Damn, damn Sioux!" Little Wind shouted, grabbing a rifle. More arrows streaked through the air. Little Wind and Toad fired at the pursuing Indians. Glancing over his shoulder, Johnson estimated there were a dozen warriors, perhaps more.

The riders came closer, and easily surrounded the wagon on three sides. Toad and Little Wind fired at them, and both hit one at virtually the same time, blasting him backwards off his horse. Another veered closer until Toad took careful aim and fired; the Sioux warrior clutched his eye, slumped forward, arms limp, then toppled sideways off his horse.

One Indian managed to climb aboard the wagon, as Little Wind had done. He was swinging his tomahawk over Johnson when Little Wind shot him in the mouth. In the same instant that the blade cut across Johnson's upper lip, the warrior's face burst red and he fell back, off the wagon, and was lost in the dust.

Johnson grabbed his bleeding face, but there was no time for horror; Little Wind turned to him. "Where you drive? Go south!"

"South is the badlands!" It was already quite dark; it would be suicide to enter the abrupt cliffs and gullies of the badlands at night.

"Go south!"

"We'll die if we go south!"

"We die anyway! Go south!"

And then Johnson realized what he was being told. Their only hope, a slim hope, was to head where the Indians would not follow. He whipped the team, and the wagon plunged southward, toward the badlands.

A mile of open prairie stretched ahead of them, and the Indians again surrounded them on all sides, whooping and shouting. An arrow seared Johnson's leg, pinning his trouser leg to the wooden wagon seat, but he felt no pain and drove on. It was darker and darker; their guns glowed brightly with each discharge. The Indians, recognizing their plan, pursued them with greater intensity.

Soon Johnson could make out the eroded dark line of the badlands at the edge of the prairie. The flat plains just seemed to drop away into black nothingness. They were approaching at frightful speed.

"Hold on, boys!" he shouted, and without reining his horses, the wagon plunged over the lip, into darkness.

Badlands

Silence, under a waning moon.

Water trickled over his face, onto his lips. He opened his eyes and saw Little Wind leaning close. Johnson raised his head.

The wagon sat upright. The horses snorted softly. They were at the base of dark cliffs, looming high.

Johnson felt a pinching in his leg. He tried to move.

"Stay," Little Wind said. His voice was tight.

"Is something wro—"

"Stay," he repeated. He put down his canteen and held out another. "Drink."

Johnson sipped, sputtered, coughed. The whiskey burned his throat, and some splashed on the slash above his lip, making that burn, too.

"Drink more," Little Wind said. He was cutting the cloth of Johnson's trouser leg with a knife. Johnson started to look.

"No look," Little Wind said, but it was too late.

The arrow had pierced the flesh of his right leg, passing under the skin, pinning him to the seat. The flesh around the wound was puffed and purple and ugly.

Johnson felt a wave of dizziness and nausea. Little Wind grabbed him. "Wait. Drink."

Johnson took a big drink. The dizziness returned.

"I fix," Little Wind said, bent over Johnson's leg. "No look."

Johnson stared at the sky, at the moon. Thin clouds drifted past. He felt the whiskey.

"What about Toad?"

"Stay now. No look."

"Is Toad all right?"

"No worry now."

"Where is he? Let me talk to him!"

"You feel hurting now," Little Wind said, his body tensing. There was a whacking sound, and Johnson felt a pain so sharp he screamed, his voice echoing off the dark cliffs. Immediately he felt a searing, burning pain that was worse; he could not scream; he gasped for breath.

Little Wind held the arrow up, bloody in the moon-light.

"Finish now. I finish."

Johnson started to get up, but Little Wind pushed him back. He gave him the arrow. "You keep." Johnson felt warm blood pouring from the open wound; Little Wind bandaged it with a strip of cloth cut from his bandana.

"Good. Good now."

Johnson pushed up, felt pain as he stood, but it was bearable; he was all right. "Where's Toad?"

Little Wind shook his head.

Toad was stretched out in the back of the wagon. One arrow had pierced sideways all the way through his neck; two others were lodged in his chest. Toad's eyes stared to the left; his mouth gaped open, as if he were still surprised to be dead.

Johnson had never seen a dead man before, and felt odd as he closed Toad's eyes and turned away. He was not sad so much as he felt that he was not here in this desolate Western place, that he was not alone with some Indian scout, that he was not in mortal danger. His mind simply refused to accept it. He sought something to do, and said, "Well, we better bury him."

"No!" Little Wind seemed horrified.

"Why not?"

"Sioux find him."

"Not if we bury him, Little Wind."

"Sioux find place, they dig him, take scalp, take fingers. Women come, take more." He pointed to his crotch.

Johnson shivered. "Where are the Sioux now?"

Little Wind pointed to the plains above the cliffs.

"They leave, or they stay?"

"They stay. They come in morning. Maybe bring more warriors."

Weariness overcame Johnson, and his leg throbbed. "We'll leave as soon as it's light."

"No. Leave now."

Johnson looked up. The clouds were heavier, and there was a faint blue ring circling the moon.

"It'll be pitch-dark in a few minutes. There won't even be starlight."

"Must leave," insisted Little Wind.

"It's a miracle we've survived this far, but we can't go on through the badlands in darkness."

"Leave now," Little Wind said.

"But we'll die."

"We die anyway. Leave now."

They moved through utter blackness.

Johnson drove the wagon, with Little Wind walking

a few paces ahead. Little Wind carried a long stick and a handful of rocks. When he could not see the terrain ahead, he threw rocks.

Sometimes, it took a long time for the rocks to land, and when the sound came back, it was distant and hollow and echoing. Then Little Wind would edge forward, tapping the ground with the stick like a blind man until he found the edge of the precipice. He would then point the wagon in a different direction.

Their progress was exhausting, and painfully slow. Johnson could not believe they were making more than a few hundred yards in an hour's time; it seemed pointless. At dawn, the Indians would charge down the ravines, pick up their trail, and find them in a matter of minutes.

"What is the point?" he would demand when the throbbing in his leg became especially bad.

"Look at sky," Little Wind would say.

"I see the sky. It's black. The sky is black."

Little Wind said nothing.

"What about the damned sky?" he demanded.

But Little Wind explained no further.

Shortly before dawn, it began to snow.

They had reached Bear Creek, at the edge of the badlands, and they paused to water the team.

"Snow good," Little Wind said. "Unkpapa warriors see snow, know they follow us easy. They wait, stay warm by fire one, two hours in morning."

"And meanwhile, we go like hell."

Little Wind nodded. "Go like hell."

From Bear Creek they headed west across open prairie, as fast as they could with the horses. The wagon jolted over the prairie; the pain in his leg was severe.

"Where are we going, Fort Benton?"

Little Wind shook his head. "All white men go to Fort Benton."

"You mean the Sioux expect us to go there?"

He nodded.

"Then where are we going?"

"Sacred Mountains."

"What sacred mountains?" Johnson asked, alarmed.

"Thunder Mountains of Great Spirit."

"Why are we going there?"

Little Wind did not answer.

"How far away are these sacred mountains? What will we do when we get there?"

"Four days. You wait," Little Wind said. "You find many white men."

"But why are you going there?"

Johnson noticed now that Little Wind's buckskin shirt was seeping red, staining with blood.

"Little Wind, are you hurt?"

In a high falsetto voice, Little Wind began to chant a song. He did not speak again.

They turned south, across the plains.

Little Wind died silently on the third night. Johnson awoke at dawn to find him lying stiffly by the smoldering campfire, his face covered with snow, his skin cold to the touch.

Using his rifle for support, Johnson dragged Little Wind's body to the wagon, painfully hoisted it up into the bed, next to Toad's, and drove on. He was feverish, hungry, and often delirious. He was sure he was lost, but he did not care. He began to remind himself to keep sitting up, even as his mind separated itself from his ordeal, creating distracting and confusing visions. At one point he believed that the wagon was approaching Rittenhouse Square in Philadelphia, and that he was searching unsuccessfully for his family's mansion.

Early in the fourth day, he found a clear wagon track, freshly used. The track wound eastward, toward a range of low purple hills.

He went into the hills. As he continued on, he found places where timber had been cut and initials had been carved in trees—evidence of white men. It was very cold and the snow was falling heavily when he climbed a final ridge and saw a town in the gulley below—a single muddy street of square, utilitarian wooden buildings. He whipped up the horses and rode down to it.

And that was how, on August 31, 1876, William Johnson, nearly fainting from hunger, thirst, exhaustion, and blood loss, rode with a wagonload of bones, and the dead bodies of a white man and a Snake scout, into the town of Deadwood Gulch.

Deadwood

Deadwood presented a bleak aspect: a single street of unpainted wooden buildings surrounded by bare hills—the trees had been cut down to provide lumber for the town. Everything was covered in a thin crust of dirty snow. But despite the dreary appearance, the town had the charged excitement of a boomtown. The main street of Deadwood consisted of the usual mining-town variety—a tin shop, a carpenter shop, three dry goods stores, four stables, six grocery stores, a Chinatown with four Chinese laundries, and seventy-five saloons. And in the center of it all, boasting a wooden second-story balcony, stood the Grand Central Hotel.

Johnson staggered up the front steps, and the next thing he knew he was lying on a padded bench inside the hotel, attended to by the proprietor, an older man with thick glasses and thinning greased hair.

"Young fellow," he joked, "I seen men in worse shape, but a percentage of them was dead."

"Food?" Johnson croaked.

"We got plenty of food here. I'm going to help you into the dining room and we'll get some vittles into you. You got any money?"

An hour later, he was feeling distinctly better and looked up from his plate. "That was good. What was it?"

The woman clearing the table said, "That's buffalo tongue."

The proprietor, who was named Sam Perkins, looked in. Considering the rough surroundings, he was extremely polite. "I'm thinking you need a room, young man."

Johnson nodded.

"Four dollars, payable in advance. And a bath can be obtained down the street at the Deadwood public baths."

"Much obliged," Johnson said.

"That pretty slash on your face is going to heal by itself, leave a scar, but that leg needs attention."

"I am in agreement," said Johnson wearily.

Perkins asked where Johnson had come from. He said he had come from the badlands of Montana near Fort Benton. Perkins looked at him in disbelief, but said only that it was a long way to come.

Johnson stood up and asked if there was someplace he could store the crates on his wagon. Perkins said he had a room in the back, available to hotel guests, and that only he had the key to the lock on its door. "What do you have to store?"

"Bones," Johnson said, realizing the warm food had given him some strength.

"You mean, animal bones?"

"That's right."

"You making soup?"

Johnson didn't appreciate the joke. "These are valuable to me."

Perkins said he didn't think that anyone in Deadwood would be interested in stealing his bones.

Johnson said he had gone through hell and back for these bones, and he had two dead bodies in his wagon to prove it, and he wasn't taking any chances. Could he please store his bones in the storeroom?

"How much space you need? It ain't a barn."

"I got ten wood boxes of bones and then some other supplies."

"Well, let's see them."

Perkins followed Johnson back out onto the street, looked in the wagon, and nodded. While Johnson started moving crates, Perkins inspected the snow-covered bodies. He brushed the snow away.

"This one's an Indian."

"That's right."

Perkins squinted at Johnson. "How long you had these two with you?"

"One's been dead almost a week. The Indian died yesterday."

Perkins scratched his chin. He asked, "You thinking of burying your friend?"

"Now I've got him away from the Sioux, I guess I will."

"There's a graveyard at the north end of town. What about the Indian?"

"I'll bury him, too."

"Not in the graveyard."

"He's a Snake."

"Good for him," Perkins said. "We don't have no problem with Snakes that is alive, but you can't bury any Indian in the graveyard."

"Why not?"

"Town won't stand for it."

Johnson glanced at the unpainted wood buildings. The town didn't seem to have been there long enough to have formed a civic opinion on any subject, but he simply asked why not.

"He's a heathen."

"He's a Snake, and I didn't bury him for the same reason I didn't bury the white man. If the Sioux found the grave, they'd dig him up and mutilate him. This Indian led me to safety. I owe him a decent burial."

"That's fine, you do what you want with him," Perkins said, "long as you don't bury him in the graveyard. You don't want to cause trouble. Not in Deadwood."

Johnson was too tired to argue. He carried the crates of fossils inside, stacking them to take up as little space as possible, and made sure Perkins locked the room after he exited. Then he asked the proprietor to arrange for his bath, and went off to bury the bodies.

It took a long time to dig the hole for Toad in the graveyard at the end of town. He had to use a pick before shoveling out the rocky earth. He dragged Toad out of the wagon and into the grave, which didn't look comfortable, even for a dead man. "I'm sorry, Toad," he said aloud. "I'll tell your family when I get the chance."

When the first shovel of earth landed on Toad's face, Johnson stopped. *I'm not who I used to be*, he thought. Then he finished filling in the grave.

He took Little Wind's body outside the town, along a side road, and dug a grave beneath a spreading fir tree on the slope of a hill. The ground was easier to dig in this location, which made him think the town should have located the graveyard there instead. The hill faced north, and from the site you could not see any sign of habitation or white men.

Then he sat down and cried until he was too cold to stay out anymore. He returned to town, had his bath, carefully cleaning and bandaging his wounded leg. Then he pulled on his dirty, blood-crusted clothes again.

In his hotel room, there was a small mirror above the washbasin, and he inspected the slash above his lip for the first time. The edges of the wound had started to heal but hadn't closed up. There would be quite a scar.

The bed was a thin straw mattress over a simple lumber frame.

He slept for thirty hours, straight through.

From Johnson's journal:

When I went down to eat in the hotel dining room, two days later, I discovered that I had become the most famous person in Deadwood. Over antelope steaks, the five other hotel guests—all rough miners—plied me with bourbon and questions about my recent activities. Like the proprietor, Mr. Perkins, they were exceedingly polite in their manner, and everyone kept their hands on the table when they ate. But I noticed, polite or not, that they did not believe my story.

It took some time to learn why. Apparently anyone who claimed to have crossed from Montana into Dakota was on the face of it a liar, since anyone who tried it would be certain to die at the hands of the Sioux. But the fact was I had encountered no Indians at all since the attack on the wagon; Sitting Bull's Sioux must have been to the north of us when we had made our crossing.

But in Deadwood, the story was not believed, and this drew attention on my "bones," which I had stored. One interested guest was a hard customer called Broken Nose Jack McCall, whose moniker was likely the result of a barroom altercation. Broken Nose also had one eye that looked steadfastly to the left, with a pale blue cast to it, like a bird of prey. Whether because of this eye, or some other reason, he was very mean, but not so mean as his companion, Black Dick Curry, who had a snake tattoo on his left wrist and the unlikely nickname "the Miner's Friend." When I asked Perkins why he was called the Miner's Friend, the proprietor said it was a kind of joke.

"What do you mean, a joke?" I asked.

"We can't get proof of it, but most folks reckon Dick Curry and his brothers, Clem and Bill, are the highwaymen who rob the stagecoaches and gold shipments going from Deadwood down to Laramie and Cheyenne," Perkins explained.

"We're near Cheyenne?" I asked, suddenly excited. For the hundredth time I cursed my lack of geographical knowledge.

"Near to there as anywhere," the proprietor said.

"I want to go there," I said.

"Nobody keeping you here, is there?"

In high excitement, thinking of Lucienne, he returned to his room to pack. But after he unlocked the door, he discovered the room had been searched, and his personal articles scattered around. His wallet was missing; all his money was gone.

He went downstairs to Perkins, at the desk.

"I've been robbed."

"How can that be?" Perkins said, and accompanied him upstairs. Perkins viewed the room with equanimity. "Just one of the boys, burdened with curiosity, checking out your story. They didn't take anything, did they?"

"Yes, they took my wallet."

"How can that be?" Perkins said.

"It was here, in my room."

"You left your wallet in your room?"

"I was only going downstairs to dinner."

"Mr. Johnson," Perkins said gravely, "you're in Deadwood. You can't leave your money unattended for a breath."

"Well, I did."

"That is a problem," Perkins said.

"You better call the town marshal and report the robbery."

"Mr. Johnson, there's no marshal in Deadwood."

"No marshal?"

"Mr. Johnson, there was no town here this time last year. We surely haven't gotten around to hiring a marshal. Besides, I don't think the boys'd stand for one. They'd kill him first thing. Just two weeks back, Bill Hickok was killed here."

"Wild Bill Hickok?"

"That's him." Perkins explained that Hickok was playing cards in Nuttal and Mann's Saloon when Jack McCall came in and shot him through the back of the head. The bullet passed through Hickok's head and lodged in the wrist of another player. Hickok was dead before his hands touched his guns.

"The Jack McCall I had dinner with?"

"That's him. Most folks figure Jack was hired to shoot Wild Bill by folks who were afraid he'd be hired as town marshal. Now I reckon nobody's eager for the job."

"Then who keeps the law here?"

"There is no law here," Perkins said. "This is Deadwood." He was speaking slowly, as if to a stupid child. "Judge Harlan presides over the inquests, when he's sober enough, but other'n that, there's no law at all, and people like it that way. Hell, every saloon in Deadwood is technically against the law; this is Indian territory, and you can't sell spirits in Indian territory."

"All right," Johnson said. "Where is the telegraph office? I'll wire my father for funds, pay you, and be gone."

Perkins shook his head.

"No telegraph office?"

"Not in Deadwood, Mr. Johnson. Not yet, anyway."

"What do I do about my stolen money?"

"That is a problem," Perkins agreed. "You been here three days now, you owe six dollars plus your dinner tonight, that's a dollar more. And you stabled your horses with Colonel Ramsay?"

"Yes, down the street."

"Well, he's going to want two dollars a day, so that makes six or eight dollars more you owe him. I reckon you can sell him your wagon and team to square it."

"If I sell my wagon and team, how can I leave with my bones?"

"That is a problem," Perkins said. "It surely is."

"I know it is a problem!" Johnson began to shout.

"Now, Mr. Johnson, keep a cool head," Perkins said soothingly. "You still intending to go to Laramie and Cheyenne?"

"That's right."

"Then that wagon is no good to you, anyhow."

"Why not?"

"Mr. Johnson, why don't you come downstairs and allow me to pour you a drink? I suspect there's one or two facts that ought to make your acquaintance."

The facts were these:

There were two roads to Deadwood, north and south.

Johnson had driven into Deadwood unmolested only because he had arrived from the north. Nobody was ever expected from the north; the route was bad and there were hostile Indians in the north, and consequently the road was unattended by brigands and highwaymen.

On the other hand, the road to Laramie and Cheyenne ran south. And that road was thick with thieves. They sometimes preyed on emigrants coming up to seek their fortune, but they especially preyed on anything moving south out of Deadwood.

In addition, there were marauding bands of Indians, assisted by white bandits, such as the notorious "Persimmons Bill," who was said to have led the savages responsible for the massacre of the entire Metz party in Red Canyon earlier that year.

The stagecoach line had started up that spring with a single armed guard, or messenger, riding shotgun up with the driver. Pretty soon they laid on two messengers, then three. Lately there were never less than four. And when the Gold Stage went south once a week, it traveled in a convoy with a dozen heavily armed guards.

Even then, they didn't always make it through. Sometimes, they were driven back to Deadwood, and sometimes they were killed and the gold stolen.

"You mean the guards were killed?"

"Guards and passengers both," Perkins said. "These highwaymen just naturally kill anyone they come across. It's their way of doing business."

"That's appalling!"

"Yep. It's bad, too."

"How am I going to leave?"

"Well, this is what I've been trying to explain," Perkins said patiently. "It's a good deal easier to come to Deadwood than to leave."

"What can I do?"

"Well, come spring, things should cool down a bit. They say Wells Fargo will start a coach line, and they have experience cleaning up desperadoes. You'll be safe then."

"In the spring? But this is September."

"I believe so," Perkins said.

"You're trying to tell me I'm stuck here in Deadwood until spring?"

"I believe so," Perkins said, pouring him another drink.

Life in Deadwood

There was a good deal of gunfire during the late hours, and Johnson spent a restless night. He awoke with an aching head; Perkins gave him strong black coffee, and he went out to see what he could do to raise funds.

The snow had melted during the night; the street was now ankle deep with stinking mud, the wooden buildings streaked with damp. Deadwood looked especially dreary, and the prospect of remaining there for six or seven months depressed him. Nor were his spirits improved when he saw a dead man lying on his back in the muddy street. Flies buzzed around the body; three or four loungers stood over it, smoking cigars and discussing its former owner, but no one made any attempt to move the corpse, and the passing teams of horses just wheeled past it.

Johnson stopped. "What happened?"

"That's Willy Jackson. He was in a fracas last night."

"A fracas?"

"I believe he engaged in disputing with Black Dick Curry, and they settled it outside in the street."

Another man said, "Willy always did drink overmuch."

"You mean Dick shot him?"

"Ain't the first time. Dick likes to kill. Does it when he can."

"You just going to leave him there?"

"I don't know who'll move him," one said.

"Well, he's got no relatives to fret over him. He had a brother, but he died of dysentery about two months back. They had a small claim couple of miles east of here."

"Whatever happened to that claim?" one man asked, flicking his cigar.

"I don't believe it amounted to nothing."

"Never did have luck."

"No, Willy never did."

Johnson said, "So the body will just stay here?"

One man jerked a thumb to the store behind them. The sign read KIM SING WASHING AND IRONING. "Well, he's in front of Sing's place, I reckon Sing'll move him before he gets too ripe and ruins business."

"Sing's son'll move him."

"Too heavy for the son, I imagine. He's only about eleven."

"Naw, that little 'un is strong."

"Not that strong."

"He moved old Jake when the carriage ran him down."

"That's so, he did move Jake."

They were still discussing it when Johnson walked on.

At Colonel Ramsay's stables, he offered his wagon and team for sale. Cope had purchased them in Fort Benton for the inflated price of $180; Johnson thought he could get forty or perhaps fifty dollars.

Colonel Ramsay offered ten.

After a long complaint, Johnson agreed to it. Ramsay then explained Johnson owed six already, and plunked down the difference—four silver dollars—on the countertop.

"This is an outrage," Johnson said.

Silently, Ramsay picked one of the four dollars off the counter.

"What's that for?"

"That's for insulting me," Ramsay said. "Care to do it again?"

Colonel Ramsay was a hard-bitten man well over six feet tall. He wore a long-barreled Colt six-shooter on each hip.

Johnson took the remaining three dollars, and turned to leave.

"You got a mouth, you little bastard," Ramsay said. "I was you, I'd learn to keep it shut."

"I appreciate the advice," Johnson said quietly. He was beginning to understand why everyone in Deadwood was so polite, so almost preternaturally calm.

He next went to the Black Hills Overland and Mail Express, at the north end of the street. The agent there informed him that the fare to Cheyenne was eight dollars by regular coach, and thirty dollars by the express coach.

"Why does the express cost so much more?"

"Your express coach is pulled by a team of six. Standard coach is pulled by a team of two, and it's slower."

"That's the only difference?"

"Well, of late the slow coach hasn't been making it through regular."

"Oh."

Johnson then explained that he had some freight to transport as well. The agent nodded. "Most folks do. If it's gold, it's one and a half percent of appraised value."

"It's not gold."

"Well then, it goes at freight rate, five cents a pound. How much you got?"

"About a thousand pounds."

"A thousand pounds! What on earth you got weighs a thousand pounds?"

"Bones," Johnson said.

"That's highly unusual," the agent said. "I don't know as we could accommodate you." He scratched figures on a sheet of paper. "These, ah, bones can ride up top?"

"I guess they can, if they're safe up there."

At five cents per pound, Johnson figured, the cost would be fifty dollars.

"Be eighty dollars, plus five dollars loading fee."

More than he expected. "Oh, fifty for the freight and thirty for the express. Eight-five in all?"

The clerk nodded. "You want to book passage?"

"Not right now."

"You know where to find us if you do," he said, and turned away.

As Johnson was leaving, he paused at the door. "About the express coach," he said.

"Yes?"

"How often does it get through?"

"Well, it gets through mostly," the agent said. "It's your best bet, no question of that."

"But how often?"

The agent shrugged. "I'd say three out of five get through. A few of them get ventilated on the way, but mostly they're fine."

"Thank you," Johnson said.

"Don't mention it," the agent said. "You sure you don't got gold nuggets in them boxes?"

The agent wasn't the only one who had heard about the boxes of bones. All of Deadwood had, and there was plenty of speculation. It was known, for example, that Johnson had arrived in Deadwood with a dead Indian. Since Indians knew better than any white man where the gold was in their sacred Black Hills, many people figured the Indian had shown Johnson the gold, and then Johnson had killed him and his own partner and made off with the ore, now disguised as crates of "bones."

Others were equally sure the crates didn't contain gold, since Johnson hadn't taken it across the street to the assayer, which was the only sensible thing to do with gold. But the crates might still be plenty valuable, containing jewels or even cash money.

But in that case, why didn't he take them to the Deadwood bank? Here, the only possible explanation was that the crates contained some recognizable stolen treasure that would be identified at once by the bankers. What that treasure might be was hard to say, but everybody talked about it a great deal.

"I think you might want to move those bones," said Sam Perkins. "People are talking. I can't guarantee they won't get stolen from the storeroom."

"Can I carry them up to my own room?"

"Nobody will help you, if that's what you're asking."

"I wasn't asking that."

"Suit yourself. You want to sleep in the same room with a lot of animal bones, nobody will say nothing."

So that is what he did. Ten boxes, up the stairs, stacked carefully against the wall, more or less blocking all the light from his one window.

"Course everybody knows you moved them upstairs," said Perkins, tagging along. "That makes them look even more valuable."

"I thought of that."

"The posts in that wall are good, but anybody could bust open that door."

"I could build a thick timber slide lock on the inside, same as a stable door."

Perkins nodded. "That keeps those boxes safe when you are in the room, but what about when you ain't?"

"Cut two holes around the post, one in the wall and one in the door, use a chain with a padlock."

"You got a good padlock?"

"Nope."

"I do, but you got to buy it from me. Ten dollars. Came off a Sioux City and Pacific boxcar door that caught fire. Heavier than it looks."

"I would be much obliged."

"You would be further obliged, financially speaking."

"Yes."

"So I expect you'll have to get a job," Perkins said. "You need to raise over a hundred dollars, plus what you owe me. That's a good deal of money to come by honestly."

Johnson didn't need to be told that.

"Any work you can do, useful work?"

"I dug all summer."

"Everybody here can dig. That's the only reason folks come to the Black Hills—to mine. No, I mean can you cook or shoe horses or do carpentry, anything like that. A skill."

"No. I am a student." Johnson looked at the crates of fossils. He rested his hand on one, touched it. He could leave the fossils here. He could take the stage from Deadwood to Fort Laramie, and from there cable home for money. He could tell Cope—assuming Cope was still alive—that the fossils had been lost. A story formed in his mind: they had been ambushed, the wagon had overturned, fallen over a cliff, all the fossils were lost or smashed. It was a pity, but it couldn't be helped.

Anyway, he thought, these fossils weren't so important, for the entire American West was full of fossils. Wherever you dug into a cliff, you found old bones of one sort or another. There were certainly far more fossils than gold in this wilderness. These few wouldn't be missed. At the rate Cope and Marsh were collecting bones, in a year or two these would hardly even be remembered.

Another idea came to him: leave the fossils here in Deadwood, go to Laramie, wire for money, and with proper funds return to Deadwood, collect the fossils, and leave again.

But he knew that if he ever got out of Deadwood alive, he'd never come back. Not for anything. He must either take them now, or turn tail and run without them.

"Dragon teeth," he said softly, touching the crate, remembering the moment of their discovery.

"What's that?" said Perkins.

"Nothing," Johnson said. Try as he might, he could not diminish the importance of the fossils in his mind. It was not merely that he had dug them with his own hands, his own sweat. It was not merely that men had died, that his friends and companions had died, in the course of finding them. It was because of what Cope had said.

These fossils were the remains of the largest creatures that ever walked on the face of the earth—creatures unsuspected by science, unknown to mankind, until their little party had dug them up in the middle of the Montana badlands.

"With all my heart," he wrote in his journal,

> I wish to leave these accursed rocks right here in this accursed town right here in this accursed wilderness. With all my heart, I wish to leave them and go home to Philadelphia and never think again in my life of Cope or Marsh or rock strata or dinosaur genera or any other of this exhausting and tedious business. And to my horror, I find I cannot. I must take them back with me, or stay with them as a mother hen stays with her eggs. Damn all principles.

While Johnson was examining the fossils, Perkins pointed to a jumble of material under a tarp. "This yours, too? What's all this?"

"That's photographic equipment," Johnson said absently.

"Know how to use it?"

"Sure."

"Well then, your troubles are over!"

"How's that?"

"We had a man who made photographic pictures. He took his camera out on the road south out of town last spring. Just him and a horse, to take photos of the land. Why, I do not know. Ain't nothing there. The next stagecoach found him on his back, with the turkey vultures on him. That camera was in a thousand pieces."

"What happened to all his plates and chemicals?"

"We still got them, but nobody knows what to do with them."

The Black Hills Art Gallery

H ow quickly can one's disadvantages be turned to profit!" Johnson wrote in his journal.

   With the opening of my studio, the Black Hills Art Gallery, my every character flaw is perceived in a new light. Before, my Eastern habits were seen as lacking masculinity; now they are proof of artistry. Before, my disinterest in mining was viewed with suspicion; now, with relief. Before, I had nothing that anyone wanted; now, I can provide what everyone will pay dearly to possess—a portrait.

   Johnson rented a location in the south bend of Deadwood, because the light was stronger there for more of the day; the Black Hills Art Gallery was located behind Kim Sing's laundry, and business was brisk.

Johnson charged two dollars for a portrait and later, as demand increased, raised his prices to three. He could never get used to the demand: "In this rude and bleak setting, hard men want nothing more than to sit as like death, and walk away with their likeness."

The life of a miner was backbreaking and exhausting; all these men had come a long and dangerous way to seek their fortune in the rugged wilderness, and it was clear that few would succeed. Photographs provided a tangible reality to men who were far from home, fearful and tired; they were posed proofs of success, souvenirs to send to sweethearts and loved ones, or simply ways of remembering, of grasping a moment in a swiftly changing and uncertain world.

His business was not limited to portraits. When the weather was bright, he made excursions to placer mines outside town, to photograph men working at their claims; for this he charged ten dollars.

Meanwhile, most of the businesses in town hired him to portray their establishments. There were moments of minor triumph: on September 4, he tersely records:

Photograph of Colonel Ramsay Stablery. Charged $25 because of "large plate required." He hated to pay! F11, at 22 sec., dull day.

And he was apparently pleased to become a full citizen of the town. As the days passed, "Foggy" Johnson (a contraction of "photographer"?) became a familiar figure in Deadwood, known to everyone.

He also acquired the frustrations of commercial photographers everywhere. On September 9:

Broken Nose Jack McCall, a notorious gunman, returned to complain of his portrait made yesterday. He showed it to his inamorata, Sarah, who said it did not flatter him, so he was back to demand a more sympathetic version. Mr. McCall has a face like a hatchet, a sneer that would kill a cow from fright, a pox-scarred complexion, and a wall-eye. I told him politely that I had done the best I could, considering.

He discharged his pistols in the Art Gallery, until I offered to try again at no charge.

He sat once more, and he wanted a different pose, with his chin resting on his hand. But the effect of his pose was to portray him as a pensive, effeminate scholar. It was wholly unsuited to his station in life, but he would hear no disagreement about the pose. Upon my retiring to the darkroom, Broken Nose waited outside, allowing me to hear the clicking of his pistol chambers as he reloaded his revolver, in anticipation

of my latest effort. Such is the nature of art crit-
ics in Deadwood, and under such circumstances,
my work surpassed my own expectations, although I lost a deal of sweat before Broken Nose
and Sarah pronounced themselves satisfied.

Apparently Johnson knew the rudiments of retouch-
ing photographs; by the judicious use of pencils, it was
possible to soften signs of scarring and to make other
adjustments.

Not everyone wanted his picture taken.

On September 12, Johnson was hired to photograph
the interior of the Deadwood Melodeon Saloon, a
drinking and gambling establishment at the south end
of the main street. Interiors were dark, and he often
had to wait several days for strong light to carry out
a commission. But a few days later the weather was
sunny, and he arrived at two o'clock in the afternoon
with his equipment and set up to make an exposure.

The Melodeon Saloon was a dingy place, with a long
bar on the back wall and three or four rough tables for
playing cards. Johnson went around throwing back the
curtains on the windows, flooding it with light. The
patrons groaned and cursed. The proprietor, Leander
Samuels, cried out, "Now, gents, be easy!"

Johnson ducked under the cloth of his camera to

compose the shot, and a voice said, "What the hell you doing, Foggy?"

"Taking a picture," Johnson said.

"Like hell."

Johnson looked up. Black Dick, the Miner's Friend, had risen from one of the card tables. His hand rested on his gun.

"Now, Dick," said Mr. Samuels, "it's just a picture."

"It's disturbing my peace."

"Now, Dick—" Mr. Samuels began.

"I've said my say," Dick threatened. "I'm playing cards now and I don't want no picture."

"Perhaps you'd like to step outside while the picture is made," Johnson said.

"Perhaps you'd like to step outside with me," Dick said.

"No thank you, sir," Johnson said.

"Then you just take yourself and your contraption out, and don't come back."

"Now, Dick, I hired Foggy. I want a picture for the wall behind the bar, I think it'd look fine."

"That's all right," Dick said. "He can come back any time he likes, long as I'm not here. No one takes my likeness." He poked a finger at Johnson, showing off the snake tattoo on his wrist, which he was vain about. "Now you remember that. And you git out."

Johnson got out.

That was the first sure indication that Black Dick was a wanted man somewhere or other. Nobody in Deadwood was surprised to hear it, and the mystery it added to Dick only increased his reputation.

But it was also the beginning of trouble between Johnson and the three Curry brothers—Dick, Clem, and Bill—that would later cause him so much misery.

But while his business prospered, he didn't have much time to amass his profits. On September 13 he wrote:

> I am generally informed that the mountain roads close with snow by Thanksgiving latest, and perhaps by November first. I must be ready to make my departure before the end of October, or remain until the following spring. Each day I record my accounts and my costs. For the life of me, I do not see how I can possibly make enough money in time to leave.

His journal for the next few days was filled with despairing comments, but two days after that, Johnson's fortunes again underwent a dazzling change.

"My prayers are answered!" he wrote. "The army has come to town!"

The Army Arrives

On September 14, 1876, two thousand miners lined the streets of Deadwood, firing pistols into the air and shouting their welcome as General George Crook and his column of the 2nd Cavalry rode through the town. "It would be hard to imagine a more popular sight to the locals," wrote Johnson, "for everyone here fears Indians, and General Crook has waged a successful war against them since spring."

The arriving army presented a notably rugged appearance after their months on the plains. When General Crook signed into the Grand Central Hotel, Perkins, in his polite way, suggested that the general might wish to visit the Deadwood baths, and perhaps also to obtain a set of new clothing from a dry goods store. General Crook took the hint, and was cleaned up when he stepped onto the Grand Central balcony and made a brief speech to the throng of miners below.

Johnson viewed the festivities, which ran long into the night, with an entirely different perspective. "Here at last," he wrote, "is my ticket to civilization!"

Johnson asked Crook's quartermaster, Lieutenant Clark, about joining the cavalry for the march south. Clark said that would be fine, but he would have to square it with the general himself. Wondering how to meet the man, Johnson thought perhaps he should offer to take his picture.

"General hates pictures," Clark advised him. "Don't do it. Go up directly and just ask him."

"Very well," Johnson said.

"One other thing," Clark said. "Don't shake hands. General hates to shake hands."

"Very well," Johnson said.

Major General George Crook was every inch a military man: short-cropped hair; piercing eyes; a full, flowing beard; and ramrod-erect posture as he sat in his chair in the dining room. Johnson waited until the man had finished his coffee and some of his admirers had departed for the gambling halls before he approached and explained his situation.

Crook listened patiently to Johnson's tale, but before

long he was shaking his head, murmuring that he could not take civilians on a military expedition with all the hazards involved—he was sorry, but it was impossible. Then Johnson mentioned the fossil bones he wished to take home.

"Fossil bones?"

"Yes, General."

Crook said, "You have been digging fossil bones?"

"Yes, General."

"And you are from Yale?"

"Yes, General."

His whole manner changed. "Then you must be associated with Professor Marsh of Yale," he said.

After the briefest hesitation, Johnson said that he was indeed associated with Professor Marsh.

"Marvelous man. Charming, intelligent man," Crook said. "I met him in Wyoming in '72, we went hunting together. Outstanding man. Remarkable man."

"None quite like him," Johnson agreed.

"You're with his party?"

"I was. I became separated from it."

"Damned bad luck," Crook said. "Well, anything I can do for Marsh, I will. You are welcome to join my column, and we will see your fossil bones safely to Cheyenne."

"Thank you, General!"

"Have your bones loaded on a suitable wagon. Quartermaster Clark will assist you in any way you need. We march at dawn, day after tomorrow. Happy to have you with us."

"Thank you, General!"

Last Day in Deadwood

On September 15, his last full day in Deadwood, Johnson undertook two final photo assignments.

In the morning, he rode out to Negro Gulch to photograph the colored miners who had made a fabulous strike there. Six miners had been taking out nearly two thousand dollars a day for weeks; their ore was shipped home, and they had already sold their claim. Now they were posing, putting on their old work clothes and standing by the flume for the photograph, then dressing again in their new duds and burning the old clothes.

They were in high spirits, and wanted the picture to take to St. Louis. For his part, Johnson was pleased to see miners so well disciplined that they were taking their findings home with them. Most left their earnings in the saloons or on the green felt of the gaming tables, but these men were different. "They are ever so cheerful," Johnson wrote, no doubt cheerful himself, "and I wish them the best of luck in their journey home."

In the afternoon, he photographed the facade of the Grand Central Hotel for its owner, Sam Perkins. "You photographed everyone else," Perkins said, "and since you're leaving town, it's the least you can do."

Johnson was obliged to set up his camera across the street. Had he set up closer, the passing horses and carriages would have kicked mud in the lens. The intervening street traffic would appear to obstruct the view of the hotel, but Johnson knew that moving objects—horses and wagons—would not leave more than a ghostly streak in a time exposure; for all intents and purposes, the hotel would appear to stand on an empty street.

Indeed, it was a problem when photographers tried to represent the busy street activity of towns, because the movement of horses and pedestrians and wagons was too quick for the film to record.

Johnson made his usual exposure—F11 and 22 seconds—and then, since the light was especially strong and he had a spare plate that was wet and waiting, he decided to try to capture the street life of Deadwood in a final quick shot. He exposed the last plate at F3.5 and 2 seconds.

Johnson developed both plates in his darkroom at the Black Hills Art Gallery and, while they were drying, purchased a suitable wagon to transport his bones with the cavalry. Then he went to the hotel to load the fossils, and have his final dinner in Deadwood.

He arrived just in time to see a body carried out into the street.

Norman H. "Texas Tom" Walsh had been found strangled in his room on the second floor of the Grand Central Hotel. Texas Tom was a short, feisty man who was rumored to be a member of the Curry gang of stage robbers. Suspicion of murder naturally fell on Black Dick Curry, also staying in the hotel at the time, but no one was brave enough to make an accusation.

For his part, Black Dick claimed to have spent all afternoon in the Melodeon Saloon, and to be innocent of any knowledge of what might have happened to Texas Tom.

And there the matter might have ended, had not Sam Perkins decided to stop by Johnson's table and ask, during dinner, about the hotel portrait.

"Did you make it today?" Perkins asked.

"I did."

"And how did it turn out?"

"Very nicely," Johnson said. "I will have a print for you tomorrow."

"What time'd you take it?" Perkins asked.

"Must have been about three o'clock in the afternoon."

"Aren't there shadows then? I'd hate the place to look all depressing, with shadows."

"There were some shadows," Johnson said, but he explained that shadows made a picture look better, giving it more depth and character.

It was then that Johnson noticed that Black Dick was listening to their conversation with interest.

"Where'd you take the picture from?" Perkins asked.

"Across the street."

"Where, over by Donohue's store?"

"No, farther south, by Kim Sing's."

"What're you fellers yammering on about?" Black Dick asked.

"Foggy took a portrait picture of the hotel today."

"Did he." The voice went cold. "When was that?"

Johnson instantly felt danger in the situation, but Perkins was oblivious to it. "What'd you just say, Foggy, 'bout three o'clock?"

"Something about there," Johnson said.

Dick cocked his head; he fixed Johnson with a watchful eye. "Foggy, I warned you once about photographin' when I was around."

"But you weren't around, Dick," Perkins said. "Remember, you told Judge Harlan that you were at the saloon all afternoon."

"I know what I told Judge Harlan," Dick growled. He turned slowly to Johnson. "Where'd you take the picture from, Foggy?"

"Across the street."

"Turn out good?"

"No, as a matter of fact it didn't turn out at all. I'm going to have to take it again tomorrow." He kicked Perkins under the table as he said it.

"I thought your pictures always turned out."

"Not always."

"Where's the picture you did today?"

"I scrubbed the glass plate. It wasn't any good."

Dick nodded. "All right, then." And he turned back to his meal.

"You thinkin' what I'm thinkin'?" Perkins asked later.

"Yep," Johnson said.

"Texas Tom had a room right at the front of the hotel, facing out on the street. Middle of the afternoon, sunlight would shine right in. Did you look real close at your picture?"

"No," Johnson said. "I didn't."

At that moment, Judge Harlan came in, puffing. They quickly told him the conversation with Black Dick. "I can't see as there's any case against Dick at all," he said. "I've just come from the Melodeon. Everybody swears Dick Curry was playing faro there all afternoon, just like he says."

"Well, he must have paid them off!"

"There's twenty or more seen him. I doubt he paid 'em all," Judge Harlan said. "No, Dick was there all right."

"Then who killed Texas Tom?"

"I'll worry over it at the inquest, in the morning," Judge Harlan said.

Johnson intended to pack after dinner, but curiosity— and Perkins's urging—led him to the Black Hills Art Gallery instead. "Where are they?" Perkins asked when they had locked the door behind them.

They inspected the two exposed plates.

The first exposure was as Johnson had remembered— a deserted hotel, with no people visible at all.

The second plate showed horses in the streets and people walking through the mud.

"Can you see the window?" Perkins asked.

"Not really," Johnson said, squinting, holding the plate to a kerosene lantern. "I can't see."

"I think there's something there," Perkins said. "You have a glass?"

Johnson held a magnifying glass to the plate.

Clearly visible in the second-floor window were two figures. One was being strangled by a second man, who stood behind him.

"I'll be damned," Perkins said. "You took a picture of the murder!"

"Can't see much, though," Johnson said.

"Make it bigger," Perkins said.

"I have to pack," Johnson said. "I'm leaving with the cavalry at dawn."

"Cavalry's drunk in the saloons all over town," Perkins said, "and they'll never leave at dawn. Make it bigger."

Johnson had no enlarging equipment, but he managed to rig an impromptu outfit and exposed a print. They both peered into the developing tray as the image slowly appeared.

In the window, Texas Tom struggled, his back arched with effort, his face contorted. Two hands gripped his neck, but the killer's body was blocked by the curtain to the left, and the killer's head was in deep shadow.

"Better," Perkins said. "But we still can't see who it is."

They made another print, and then another still

larger. The work became slower as the evening progressed. The rigged system was sensitive to vibration at great magnification, and Perkins was so excited he could not stand still during the long exposure.

Shortly before midnight, they got a clear one. At great magnification, the picture was speckled and grainy. But one detail came through. There was a tattoo on the left wrist of the strangling arm: it showed a curled snake.

"We got to tell Judge Harlan," Perkins insisted.

"I got to pack," Johnson said, "and I got to get some sleep before I leave tomorrow."

"But this is murder!"

"This is Deadwood," Johnson said. "Happens all the time."

"You're just going to leave?"

"I am."

"Then give me the plate, and I'll go tell Judge Harlan."

"Suit yourself," Johnson said, and gave him the plate.

Back in the Grand Central Hotel lobby, he passed Black Dick Curry himself. Dick was drunk.

"Howdy, Foggy," Dick said.

"Howdy, Dick," Johnson said, and he went up to his room. It was, he observed in his journal, a fine ironic last touch to his last day in notorious Deadwood.

He had been packing for half an hour when Perkins showed up in his room with Judge Harlan.

"You take this picture?" Judge Harlan said.

"I did, Judge."

"You doctor this picture in any way, pencil touch-ups or whatever?"

"No, Judge."

"That's fine," Judge Harlan said. "We got him dead to rights."

"I'm glad for you," Johnson said.

"Inquest will settle it in the morning," Judge Harlan said. "Be there at ten o'clock, Foggy."

Johnson said he was leaving town with General Crook's cavalry.

"I'm afraid you can't," Judge Harlan said. "In fact, you're at some risk right here tonight. We're gonna have to take you into protective custody."

"What're you talking about?" Johnson asked.

"I'm talking about jail," Judge Harlan said.

The Next Day in Deadwood

J ail was an abandoned mine shaft at the edge of town. It was fitted with iron bars and a solid lock. After spending a night in the freezing cold, Johnson was able to look through the bars and watch the cavalry under the command of General George Crook ride south out of Deadwood.

He shouted to them—shouted until he was hoarse—but no one paid any attention. No one came to let him out of jail until nearly noon, when Judge Harlan showed up, groaning and shaking his head.

"What's the trouble?" Johnson said.

"Bit much to drink last night," the judge said. He held the door wide. "You're free to go."

"What about the inquest?"

"Inquest's been cancelled."

"What?"

Judge Harlan nodded. "Black Dick Curry hightailed it out of town. Seems he got word of what was coming, and chose the better part of valor, as Shakespeare would say. An inquest's beside the point, with Dick gone. You're free to go."

"But the cavalry's a half day ahead of me now," Johnson said. "I can never catch up with them."

"True," the judge said. "I'm real sorry for the inconvenience, son. I guess you'll be staying with us in Deadwood a while longer, after all."

The story of Johnson's incriminating photograph, and how he had come to miss leaving with the cavalry, went through the town. It had serious consequences.

The first was to worsen relations between Johnson and Black Dick Curry, the Miner's Friend. All the Curry brothers now were openly hostile to him, especially as Judge Harlan seemed uninterested in setting another inquest into the death of Texas Tom. When they were in town, which was whenever there was no stage leaving Deadwood for a day or so, they stayed at the Grand Central Hotel. And when they ate, which was seldom, they took their meals there.

Johnson irritated Dick, who announced that Johnson behaved superior to everybody else, with what he called "his Phil-a-del-phia ways. 'Pass the butter, would you please?' Faugh! Can't bear his fairy-airy ways."

As the days passed, Dick took to bullying Johnson, to the amusement of his brothers. Johnson bore it quietly; there was nothing he could do since Dick was only too ready to take an argument out into the street and settle it with pistols. He was a steady shot, even when drunk, and killed a man every few days.

No one in town who knew Dick would go up against him, and certainly Johnson did not intend to. But it got so bad that he would leave the dining room before finishing his meal if Dick entered.

And then there was the business of Miss Emily.

Emily

Women in Deadwood were few, and no better than they needed to be. Most of them lived in a house called the Cricket, down at the end of the south bend, where they plied their trade under the cold watchful eye of Mrs. Marshall, who smoked opium and owned the house. Others were independent, like Calamity Jane, who in recent weeks had made a great show of mourning the death of Bill Hickok, much to the disgust of Hickok's friends. Calamity Jane was so masculine she often wore a soldier's uniform and traveled undetected with the boys in blue, giving them service in the field; she had gone with Custer's 7th Cavalry on more than one occasion. But she was so male that she often boasted that "give me a dildo in the dark, and no woman can tell me from a true man." As one observer noted, this left Jane's appeal somewhat obscure.

A few Deadwood miners had brought their wives and families, but they did not often show in town. Colonel Ramsay had a fat squaw wife named Sen-a-lise; Mr. Samuels had a wife, too, but she was consumptive and always stayed indoors. So for the most part, the feminine element was provided by the Cricket women, and the girls who worked in the saloons. In the words of one Deadwood visitor, they were "pleasant women of a certain age, but in appearance as hard and mean as the rest of the landscape of that wretched mining town. The ones that ran tables in the saloons smoked and swore with the best of the men, and were so full of tricks that seasoned gamblers avoided them, and preferred men as dealers."

Into this hard-bitten world, Miss Emily Charlotte Williams appeared as a floating vision of loveliness.

She arrived one noon on a miner's buckboard, dressed entirely in white, her blond hair tied back fetchingly. She was young—though perhaps a few years older than Johnson; she was immaculate; she was delicate and fresh and sweet, and possessed some notable curvatures. When she took a room at the Grand Central Hotel, she became the most interesting new arrival since young Foggy had showed up with a wagonload of mysterious crates and two dead men covered in snow.

News of Miss Emily, her lovely appearance and her tender story, raced around the town. Perkins's dining room, never before full, was packed that night as everyone came to get a look at the creature.

She was an orphan, the daughter of a preacher, the Reverend Williams, who had been killed in the nearby town of Gayville while building a church. At first it was said that he had been shot by a devilish desperado, but it later turned out he had fallen from the roof under construction and broken his neck.

In her grief, it was also said, Miss Emily had collected her few belongings, and set out to find her brother Tom Williams, whom she knew to be prospecting somewhere in the Black Hills. She had already been to Montana City and Crook City, and had not succeeded in finding him. Now she was in Deadwood, where she planned to stay three or four days, perhaps more.

The men in the Grand Central Hotel that night had bathed, and were wearing the cleanest clothes they owned; Johnson recorded in his journal that "it was amusing, to see these hard men preen and puff up their chests while they tried to eat their soup without slurping."

But there was a good deal of tension in the room as well, which was increased when Black Dick went over to Miss Emily's table (the object of all eyes was dining alone) and introduced himself. He offered to escort her around the town that evening; with admirable poise she thanked him but said she would be retiring early. He offered to assist her in finding her brother; she thanked him but said that she had already had many offers of assistance.

Dick was being watched by all the others, and knew it. He sweated; his face turned red and he glowered.

"Seems I can't be of help to you, then, is that it?"

"I appreciate your courteous offer, I surely do," she said softly.

Dick appeared somewhat mollified as he stomped back to his table and huddled, commiserating, with his brothers.

And there the matter might have rested, had not Miss Emily turned to Johnson, and said in her sweetest voice, "Oh, are you the young photographer I have heard so much about?"

Johnson said he was.

"I should appreciate seeing your gallery of pictures," she said. "Perhaps my brother is among them."

"I will be happy to show them to you in the morning,"

Johnson answered, and she responded with a graceful smile.

Black Dick looked fit to kill—Johnson, in particular.

"There is no greater pleasure than to win what everyone desires," Johnson noted in his pages; he went to bed a happy man. He had become accustomed to sleeping in the room next to the stacked crates, accustomed not only to the fine powder that fell from them and dusted the floor, but also to the tomb-like darkness of the room itself and a strange sense of intimacy to be sleeping with the bones of the great creatures themselves. And of course the immense teeth, the teeth of actual dragons that once walked the earth. He found their presence oddly comforting.

And tomorrow would bring his appointment with Emily.

But his happiness was short-lived. Emily was disappointed by his pictures, not finding her dear brother among them.

"Perhaps you could look again," he suggested. She had gone through them very quickly.

"No, no, I know he is not to be found in these." She prowled his shop restlessly, looking around. "Have you shown me all you have?"

"All I have taken in Deadwood, yes."

She pointed to a corner shelf. "You haven't shown me those."

"Those are from my time in the badlands. Your brother is not among those plates, I assure you."

"But I am interested to see. Bring them here, and come sit beside me, and tell me about the badlands."

She was so charming he could not possibly refuse her. He brought down the plates and showed her his pictures, which seemed now to belong to another lifetime.

"Who is this man with the tiny pick?"

"That's Professor Cope, with his geological hammer."

"And that beside him?"

"That's a skull of a saber-tooth tiger."

"And this man?"

"That's Cookie. Our teamster and cook."

"And this? Is he standing with an Indian?"

"That's Charlie Sternberg and Little Wind. He was a Snake scout. He died."

"Oh dear. And this is the badlands? It looks like the desert."

"Yes, you can see how eroded it is."

"How long did you spend there?"

"Six weeks."

"And why would you go to such a place?"

"Well, where there is erosion, the bones stick out and are easier to uncover."

"You went there for bones?"

"Yes, of course."

"How very odd," she said. "Did bones pay you a lot?"

"No, I paid my own way."

"You paid your own way?" She pointed to the desolate picture. "To go there?"

"It's a long story," he said. "You see, I made a bet at Yale and then I had to go."

But he could tell she was not listening anymore. She thumbed through the glass plates, holding each to the light, glancing quickly, going on to the next.

"What do you hope to find?" he asked, watching her.

"It is all so strange to me," she said. "I was merely curious about you. Here, put them back."

As he replaced them on the shelf, she said, "And did you find bones?"

"Oh yes, lots of them."

"Where are they now?"

"Half were taken down the Missouri River by steamer. I have the other half."

"You have them? Where?"

"In the hotel."

"Can I see these bones?"

Something about her manner made him suspicious. "Why would you want to do that?"

"I am just curious to see them, now that you have mentioned them."

"Everyone in the town is curious to see them."

"Of course, if it is too much trouble—"

"Oh no," Johnson said. "It's no trouble."

In his room, he opened one crate for her to see. Some gritty dirt fell to the floor.

"That's just old rocks!" she said, peering at the pieces of black shale.

"No, no, this is a fossil. Look here," he said, and he traced the shape of a dinosaur leg. It was a perfect specimen.

"But I thought you had found old bones, not rock."

"Fossil bones are rock."

"There's no need to snip."

"I'm sorry, Emily. But you see, these things have no value at all in Deadwood. They are bones which have lain in the earth for millions of years and which belonged to creatures long gone. This bone is from the leg of an animal with a horn on its nose, like a rhinoceros, but much larger."

"Really?"

"Yes."

"That seems wonderful, Bill," she said, having decided to call him by that name. Her gentle enthusiasm touched him. She was the first sympathetic person he had come across in a long time.

"I know," he said, "but no one believes me. The more I explain them, the more they disbelieve. And eventually they will break in and smash them all, if I don't get out of Deadwood first."

And despite himself, tears rolled down one cheek, and he turned away, so that she would not see him cry.

"Why, Bill, what's the matter?" she said, sitting down close to him on the bed.

"It's nothing," he said, wiping his face and turning back. "It is just that—I never asked for this job, I just came west and now I am stuck with these bones and they are my responsibility, and I want to keep them safe so the professor can study them, and people never believe me."

"I believe you," she said.

"Then you are the only one in Deadwood who does."

"Shall I tell you a secret of my own?" she said. "I am not really an orphan."

He paused, waiting.

"I am from Whitewood, where I have lived since the summer."

He still said nothing.

She bit her lip. "Dick put me up to it."

"Put you up to what?" he asked, wondering how she knew Dick.

"He thought you would confide in a lady, and tell me what the crates really contained."

"So you said you would ask me?" he said, feeling hurt.

She looked down, as if ashamed. "I was curious myself, too."

"They really contain bones."

"I see that, now."

"I don't want them—I don't want anything to do with them—but they are my responsibility."

"I believe you." She frowned. "Now I must convince Dick. He is a hard man, you know."

"I know."

"But I will talk to him," she said. "I will see you at dinner."

That night in the Grand Central dining room there were two new visitors. At first glance, they seemed to be twins, so similar was their appearance: they were both tall, lean, wiry men in their twenties, with identical broad mustaches, and identical clean white shirts.

They were quiet, self-contained men who emanated a forceful calmness.

"Know who those two are?" Perkins whispered to Johnson, over coffee.

"No."

"That's Wyatt Earp and his brother Morgan Earp. Wyatt's taller."

At the mention of their names, the two men looked over at Johnson's table and nodded politely.

"This here's Foggy Johnson, he's a photographer from Yale College," Perkins said.

"Howdy," the Earp brothers said, and went back to their dinner.

Johnson didn't recognize the names, but Perkins's manner suggested that they were important and famous men. Johnson whispered, "Who are they?"

"They're from Kansas," Perkins said. "Abilene and Dodge City?"

Johnson shook his head.

"They're famous gunfighters," Perkins whispered. "Both of 'em."

Johnson still had no notion of their importance, but any new visitor to Deadwood was fair game for a photograph, and after dinner he suggested it. In his journal, Johnson recorded his first conversation with the famous Earp brothers. It was not exactly a dramatic high point.

"How would you gents like a photograph?" Johnson asked.

"A photograph? Could be," Wyatt Earp said. Seen close, he was boyish and slender. He had a steady manner, a steady gaze, an almost sleepy calmness. "What'll it cost?"

"Four bucks," Johnson said.

The Earp brothers exchanged a silent glance.

"No thanks," Wyatt Earp said.

Emily's News

I t's no good," she whispered to him outside on the porch of the hotel before dinner. "The Curry boys are rattled by the Earp brothers arriving. It makes them jumpy. So they're coming for your bones tonight. They boasted about it."

"They're not going to get them," Johnson said.

"I believe they're in the habit of getting whatever they want."

"Not this time."

"What're you going to do?"

"I'll stand guard over them," Johnson said, reaching for his gun.

"I wouldn't."

"What do you think I should do?"

"Best thing is step aside, let them have 'em."

"I can't do that, Emily."

"They're hard men."

"I know that. But I must guard the bones."

"They're just bones."

"No, they're not."

He saw her eyes light up. "They're valuable, then?"

"They're priceless. I told you."

"Tell me really. What are they, really?"

"Emily, they really are bones. Like I told you."

She looked disgusted. "If it was me, I wouldn't risk my life for a bunch of old bones."

"It's not you, and these bones are important. They are historical bones and important to science."

"The Curry boys don't care a hoot for science, and they'd be happy to kill you in the bargain."

"I know it. But I got to keep the bones."

"Then you better get help, Bill."

He found the famous gunfighter Wyatt Earp in the Melodeon Saloon, playing blackjack. Johnson drew him aside.

"Mr. Earp, could I hire your services for the night?"

"I imagine so," Earp said. "In what capacity?"

"As a guard," Johnson said, and explained about his fossil bones, the room, and the Curry brothers.

"That's fine," Earp said when he had heard it all. "I will want five dollars."

Johnson agreed.

"In advance."

Johnson paid him, right there in the saloon. "But I can count on you?"

"You surely can," Wyatt Earp said. "I will meet you in your room at ten o'clock tonight. Bring ammunition and plenty of whiskey, and don't worry any further. You have Wyatt Earp on your side now. Your problems are over."

He had dinner with Emily, in the hotel dining room.

"I wish you would give this up," she said.

They were exactly his sentiments. But he said, "I can't, Emily."

She kissed him lightly on the cheek.

"Then good luck, Bill. I hope I see you tomorrow."

"Rest assured," he said, and smiled bravely for her.

She went up to her room. He went to his room and locked himself in.

It was nine o'clock in the evening.

Ten o'clock passed, and ten thirty. He shook his pocket watch, wondering if it was running right. Finally, he unlocked the room, and went down into the hotel lobby.

A pimply boy was behind the desk as night clerk. "Howdy, Mr. Johnson."

"Howdy, Edwin. You seen Mr. Earp?"

"Not tonight, I haven't. But I know of his whereabouts."

"What do you know?"

"He's at the Melodeon, playing blackjack."

"He was at the Melodeon this afternoon."

"Well, he's still there."

Johnson looked at the wall clock. It, too, said ten thirty. "He was supposed to meet me here."

"Probably forgot," Edwin said.

"We had an arrangement."

"Probably drinking," Edwin said.

"Can you go over there and get him for me?"

"I wish I could. But I have to stay here. Don't worry, Mr. Earp is a responsible sort. If he says he'll come, I'm sure he'll be along shortly."

Johnson nodded and locked himself back in his room.

And waited. *If they come in the door,* he thought, *I better be ready.* He put a loaded pistol into each of his boots at the foot of the bed.

The hours dragged by. At midnight, he went out again in his wool socks to ask about Earp, but Edwin was asleep and Earp's key was on the wall behind him, which meant he had not yet returned from the saloon.

Johnson went back to his room and waited.

All around him, the hotel was silent.

He stared at the hands of his watch. He listened to it tick, and he waited.

At two, there was a scratching on the wall. He jumped up, raising his gun.

He heard the scratching again.

"Who's there!"

There was no reply. More scratching.

"Get away!" he said, his voice quavering.

He heard a low squeaking, and the scratching moved quickly off. He recognized the sound now.

"Rats."

He slumped back down, tense and exhausted. He was sweating. His hands were shaking. This was not his line of business. He didn't have the nerve for it. Where was Wyatt Earp, anyway?

"I can't figure what you're so hot about," Earp said, the next day.

"We had a deal," Johnson said. "That's what I'm so hot about." He had not slept at all the night before; he was angry and tired.

"Yes, we did," Earp said. "To protect your fossils from the Curry boys."

"And I paid you in advance."

"Yes, you did."

"And where were you?"

"Doing what I was hired to do," Earp said. "I played blackjack all night. With the Curry boys."

Johnson sighed. He was too tired to argue.

"Well, what do you expect me to do," Earp said. "Leave 'em to come and sit in the dark with you?"

"It's just that I didn't know."

"You look peaked," Earp said sympathetically. "You go get sleep."

Johnson nodded, started back to the hotel.

"You want to hire me again tonight?" Earp called to him.

"Yes," Johnson said.

"That'll be five dollars," Earp said.

"I'm not paying you five dollars to play blackjack," Johnson said.

Earp shrugged. "Suit yourself, boy."

That night he put the loaded pistols and extra bullets in his boots again. He must have fallen asleep after midnight, because he awoke to the sound of wood splintering. The broken door opened, and a figure slid into the room. The door closed again. It was pitch-dark because of the crates blocking the window.

"Foggy," a voice whispered.

"Wyatt?" Johnson whispered.

The sharp clock of a gun being cocked. A footstep. Silence. Breathing in the dark. Johnson realized he made an easy target and eased out of the bed and beneath it. He took one of the pistols out of its boot and flung the boot against the wall.

At the sound of the boot hitting the wall, there was a tongue of flame as the man fired at the noise. Someone yelled immediately elsewhere in the hotel.

"You get out, whoever you are!" Johnson said, the room filled with smoke now. "I have a loaded gun, you get on out."

Silence. Another footstep. Breathing.

"That you, Foggy boy?"

The door opened again and another man came in.

"He's in his bed," came a voice.

"Foggy, we are going to light a lamp now. Just sit still and we will get this all straightened out."

Instead, the men opened fire into his bed, splintering the frame. Johnson grabbed his second pistol and lifted both guns, emptying each without skill.

He heard wood splintering, groaning, something falling, then maybe the door being opened.

He paused to reload, fumbling in the darkness. He heard breathing—he was sure of it. That made him nervous. He could imagine the killer squatting there, listening to Johnson's panicked exhalations, listening to the clink of the bullets going into the chambers, focusing on the sound, locating Johnson . . .

He finished reloading. Still nothing.

"Oh, Carmella," came a sad and tired voice. "I know I've been—" The man's breathing became labored. "If'n I can just get my breath good . . ." He coughed and there was a kick against the floor. Then a crackling, choking noise. Then nothing.

In his journal, Johnson wrote,

> I apprehended then that I had killed a man, but the room was too dark to see who it was. I waited there on the floor with my guns ready in case the other shootist came back, and I resolved to fire first and ask questions afterward. But then I heard Mr. Perkins, the proprietor, calling from the hallway. I answered back. I told him I wasn't going to shoot, and then he appeared in the doorway with a lamp, throwing light across the room and down to the floor,

where a big man lay dead, his blood a wet rug beneath him.

There were three neat bullet wounds in the man's broad back.

Perkins rolled the body over. In the guttering light of the lamp, he looked into the sightless eyes of Clem Curry. "Dead as a doornail," he muttered.

The hallway filled with voices, and then heads poked their way through the doorway to gawk.

"Stand back, folks, stand back."

Judge Harlan pushed roughly through the onlookers into the room. Harlan was in ill humor, probably, Johnson thought, because he had been called out of bed. It turned out to be nothing of the sort. "I left a hell of a poker game," the judge said, "to deal with this here murder."

He stared at the body.

"That's Clem Curry, isn't it?"

Johnson said it was.

"No loss to the community, as far as I'm concerned," the judge said. "What was he doing here?"

"Robbing me," Johnson said.

"Figures," Judge Harlan said. He took a drink from a hip flask, passed it to Johnson. "Who shot him?"

Johnson said he had.

"Well," the judge said, "as far as it matters to me, that's fine. The only trouble is, you shot him in the back."

Johnson explained that it was dark, and he could not see.

"I am sure of it," the judge said. "But the problem is, you shot him three times in the back."

Johnson said he hadn't intended to kill anyone at all.

"I am sure of it. You have no problem with me, but you may have some difficulty when Black Dick hears of it, tomorrow or the next day, depending if he's in town."

This had already occurred to Johnson, and he did not like to think about it too long.

"You planning to leave Deadwood?" the judge said.

"Not just yet," Johnson said.

Judge Harlan took another pull from the flask. "I would," he said. "Myself, I'd be gone before daybreak."

"**Well, damn** me," Sam Perkins said, fingering the bullet holes in the wall after the crowd had left. "You surely had some hot work here, Mr. Johnson."

"They didn't get the bones."

"That's so, but they got every one of my guests out of bed in the middle of the night, Mr. Johnson."

"I'm sorry about that."

"Scared Edwin the night clerk so bad he wet his trousers. I'm not fooling."

"I'm sorry."

"I can't run a hotel this way, Mr. Johnson. The Grand Central has its reputation. I want these bones out of here today," Perkins said.

"Mr. Perkins—"

"Today," Perkins said, "and that's final. And I'll charge you to repair the bullet holes. That'll be on your bill."

"Where am I going to move them to?"

"Ain't my problem."

"Mr. Perkins, these bones are valuable to science."

"We're a long way from science. Just get 'em out of here."

Moving the Bones

With the crates loaded in his wagon the next morning, he went first to the Deadwood bank, but they had no space to store anything but gold dust.

Then he tried Sutter's Dry Goods. Mr. Sutter had a strong room in the back where he stored his firearms for sale. Mr. Sutter refused outright. But Johnson took the opportunity to buy more bullets for his guns.

The National Hotel was not as particular as the Grand Central, and was known to be accommodating. But the man at the desk said he had no storage facilities.

Fielder's Saloon and Gaming House was open around the clock, and the scene of so many altercations that Fielder kept an armed guard to maintain order. He had a back room that was large enough.

Fielder said no.

"It's just bones, Mr. Fielder."

"Maybe so, maybe not. Whatever it is, the Curry boys are after 'em. I want no part of it."

Colonel Ramsay was feisty, and had plenty of room in his stables. He just shook his head when Johnson asked him.

"Is everybody afraid of the Curry brothers?"

"Everybody with sense," Ramsay said.

The afternoon was drawing to an end, the light starting to fail, and the temperature in town was dropping quickly. Johnson went back to his photo studio, the Black Hills Art Gallery, but he had no customers. It seemed he had become extremely unpopular overnight. He was looking around the studio, trying to see whether he could store the bones there, when his landlord, Kim Sing, came in from the laundry with his young son, the one who had dragged away the dead body out of the street.

Sing nodded and smiled, but as usual said nothing. The son said, "You need place to store some things?"

The boy's English was pretty good. "Yes, I do. What's your name?"

"Kang."

"I like your boots there, Kang."

The boy smiled. Chinese boys never wore leather boots. His father said something to him. "You store your things in Chinese Town."

"I can?"

"Yes. You can."

"It would have to be a safe place."

"Yes. Ling Chow has tool shed, very strong and just new, it has lock and no windows except small windows at the top."

"Where is it?"

"Behind Ling Chow restaurant."

In the middle of Chinatown. It would be perfect. Johnson felt a rush of gratitude. "That's very kind of you, I appreciate your offer very much. No one else in this town will even—"

"Ten dollar a night."

"What?"

"Ten dollar a night. Okay?"

"I can't afford ten dollars a night!"

Unblinking: "You can."

"That's outrageous."

"That's the price. Okay?"

Johnson thought it over. "Okay," he said. "Okay."

At this time, I still had more than a thousand pounds of fossils," Johnson later recalled.

Ten boxes weighing about a hundred pounds each. I hired Kim Sing's boy, Kang, to help me with the wagon. I paid him two dollars for the afternoon, and he earned it. He kept saying, "What is this?" and I kept telling him it was old bones. But my story didn't get more persuasive. I also didn't know there were so many Chinamen in Deadwood. It seemed to me their smooth impassive faces were everywhere, watching me, commenting to each other, standing four deep around the tool shed, peering from windows in the surrounding buildings.

Finally when all the crates were stacked neatly in the tool shed, Kang looked at them and said, "Why you care so much?"

I said I didn't know anymore. Then I went to the Grand Central for dinner, and returned to the tool shed at nightfall, to keep my evening watch over the dinosaur bones.

He did not have long to wait. Around ten, shadowy figures appeared around the high transom windows. Johnson cocked his gun. There were several figures outside; he heard whispered voices.

The window creaked open. A hand reached down.

Johnson saw a dark head appear in the narrow glass. He aimed his gun.

"Get away, you bastards!"

A sharp giggle startled him. They were kids, Chinese kids. He lowered his gun.

"Get away. Go on, get away."

The giggling continued. Scraping footsteps, and he was alone again. He sighed. It was a good thing he hadn't shot hastily, he thought.

There was more scraping.

"Didn't you hear me? Get out of here!"

Probably they didn't speak English, he thought. But most of the young ones had passable English. And the older ones spoke a lot more English than they were willing to admit they did.

Another head at the window, shadowy.

"Get away, you kids!"

"Mr. Johnson." It was Kang.

"Yes?"

"I have the bad news for you."

"What?"

"I think everybody know you here. People in laundry say talking you move boxes to this place."

Johnson froze. Of course they knew. He'd merely exchanged one room in town for another. "Kang, you know my wagon?"

"Yes, yes."

"It's at the stable. Can you get it and bring it here?"

"Yes."

It seemed he returned only a few minutes later.

"Tell your friends to load the boxes as fast as possible."

Kang did that, and soon the wagon was loaded. Johnson gave them a dollar and told them to run away. "Kang, stay with me."

Chinese Town was larger than it looked, with new streets being built constantly. Kang showed him how to guide the wagon through the narrow lanes. At one point they stopped as four horsemen went by in a hurry in the street ahead.

"Look for you, I think," said Kang.

They eased out onto a side road, and in a few minutes they came to the tall pine where Johnson had buried Little Wind. The ground was still soft, and he and Kang gently exhumed Little Wind, holding their breaths as they pulled him out of the hole. The stench was wretched. The ten boxes took up the space of about two more graves, and Johnson widened the hole he had made for Little Wind and stacked the boxes as evenly as he could. Then he laid Little Wind on top of the boxes, as if he were sleeping atop them.

If I had my camera and it was daytime, I would take a photograph of that, Johnson told himself.

He piled the dirt back over Little Wind, spreading it around so the excess would not be so apparent, then brushed pine needles over the spot.

"This is our secret," he told Kang.

"Yes, but it can be a better secret."

"Yes, of course." Johnson pulled a five-dollar gold piece from his pocket. "You do not tell anyone."

"No, no."

But he did not trust the boy not to talk. "When I leave, Kang, I will pay you another five dollars if you have kept the secret."

"Another five dollar?"

"Yes, the day I leave Deadwood."

A Shootout

Black Dick showed up in a rage at the Grand Hotel at breakfast time the same morning. He kicked open the door. "Where is the little bastard?"

His gaze fell on Johnson.

"I'm not a shooting man," Johnson said, as calmly as he could.

"No coward is."

"You may hold whatever opinion you like."

"You shot Clem in the back. You are a yellow-bellied snake."

"He was robbing my property."

Dick spat. "You shot him in the back, you son of a poxy whore."

Johnson shook his head. "I won't be provoked."

"Then hear this," Dick said. "You meet me outside now, or I'll go to that shed in Chinese Town and plug every one of your precious crates with dynamite and blow 'em to smithereens. Might blow up some of those Chinamen who helped you, too."

"You wouldn't dare."

"I can't see who might stop me. You care to watch me blow your precious bones?"

Johnson felt a strange deep fury fill him. All his frustrations, all the difficulties of his weeks in Deadwood, overwhelmed him. He was glad he had moved the crates. He began to breathe deeply, slowly. His face felt oddly tight.

"No," Johnson said. He stood. "I'll see you outside, Dick."

"That's fine," Dick said. "I'll be waiting on you."

And Dick left, slamming the door behind him.

Johnson sat in the hotel dining room. The other breakfasters looked at him. Nobody spoke. Sunlight came in through the windows. He heard a bird chirping.

He heard the rattle of wagons in the street outside, the people shouting to each other to clear out, that there was going to be some gunplay. He heard Mrs. Wilson's piano lessons in the next building, a child playing scales.

Johnson felt completely unreal.

Minutes later, Wyatt Earp hurried into the dining room. "What's this foolishness about you and Dick Curry?"

"It's true."

Earp stared at him a moment, then said, "Take my advice and back out."

"I'm not backing out," Johnson said.

"Can you shoot?"

"Not real good."

"That's unfortunate."

"But I'm going up against him anyway."

"You want some advice, or you want to die your own way?"

"I will be grateful for any advice," Johnson said. He noticed that his lip was quivering, his hand shaking.

"Sit down," Earp said. "I been through lots of these, and it's always the same. You get a pistoleer like Dick, he is pretty full of himself, and he has shot a man or two. He's fast. But mostly his victims have been drunk or scared or both."

"I surely am scared."

"That's fine. Just remember, most of these gunmen are cowards and bullies, they have a trick that works for them. You must avoid his tricks."

"Such as what? What tricks?"

"Some of 'em try and rush you, some of 'em try and distract you—they smoke a cigar, toss it away, expecting your eyes naturally to follow it. Some of 'em try and talk to you. Some of 'em yawn, try to get you to yawn. Tricks."

"What should I do?" Johnson's heart was hammering so loudly he could hardly hear his own voice.

"When you go out there, you take your time. And never take your eyes off him—he may try and shoot you while you're stepping into the street. Never take your eyes off him. Then take your position, put your feet wide, get your balance. Don't let him engage you in talk. Concentrate on him. Never take your eyes off him, no matter what he does. Watch his eyes. You'll see in his eyes when he's going to make his play, even before his hand moves."

"How will I see it?"

"You'll see it, don't worry. Let him fire first, you draw deliberate, you aim deliberate, and you squeeze off one shot right to the middle of his stomach. Don't do anything fancy like aim for the head. Make it count. Shoot him in the stomach and kill him."

"Oh God." The reality of it was settling in on him.

"You sure you won't back out?"

"No!"

"Fine," Earp said. "I believe you'll come out. Dick's cocky, he thinks you're a mark. You can't ask for better than a cocky man to go up against."

"I'm glad to hear of it."

"You'll come out," Earp said again. "Is your gun loaded?"

"No."

"Better load it, boy."

Johnson stepped out of the hotel into the morning light. The main street of Deadwood was deserted. There was silence, except for Mrs. Wilson's piano lesson, monotonous scales.

Black Dick was at the north end of the street, waiting. He puffed on a cigar. His broad hat put his face in deep shadow. Johnson had trouble seeing his eyes. He hesitated.

"Come on out, Foggy," Dick called.

Johnson stepped away from the hotel, into the street. He felt his feet squish in the mud. He did not look down.

Keep your eyes on him. Never take your eyes off him.

Johnson moved to the middle of the street, stopped.

Get your balance, get your feet wide.

Clearly, he heard Mrs. Wilson's voice say, "No, no, Charlotte. Tempo."

Concentrate. Concentrate on him.

They were thirty feet apart, on the main street of Deadwood in the morning sunshine.

Dick laughed. "Come closer, Foggy."

"This'll do," Johnson said.

"I can't hardly see you, Foggy."

Don't let him talk to you. Watch him.

"I see fine," Johnson said.

Dick laughed. The laugh trailed off into silence.

Watch his eyes. Watch his eyes.

"Any last requests, Foggy?"

Johnson did not answer. He felt his heart pounding in his chest.

Black Dick threw his cigar away. It sailed through the air, sputtered in the mud.

No matter what he does, never take your eyes off him.

Dick drew.

It happened very fast, Dick's body was obscured by a cloud of dense black smoke, and two bullets whizzed past Johnson before his own gun was out, and he felt the third knock his hat off as he aimed and fired. His gun bucked in his hand. He heard a scream of pain.

"Son of a bitch! I'm hit!"

Johnson peered through the smoke, more confused than anything else. At first he could see nothing; Dick seemed to have disappeared entirely from the street.

Then the smoke cleared and he saw the figure writhing in the mud.

"You shot me! Damn! You shot me!"

Johnson stood and stared. Dick struggled to his feet, clutching his bleeding shoulder, his wounded arm hanging limply. He was covered in mud.

"Damn you!"

Finish him, thought Johnson.

But he had already killed a man and didn't have the heart to shoot again now. He watched as Dick staggered across the street and swung onto his horse. "I'll get you for this! I'll get you," he cried, and he rode out of town.

Johnson watched him go. He heard scattered cheers and applause from the surrounding buildings. He felt dizzy, and his legs went watery.

"You did good," Earp said, "excepting you didn't kill him."

"I'm not a gunman."

"That's fine," Earp said. "But mark, you should have killed him. It didn't look to me his wounds were mortal, and now you have an enemy for life."

"I couldn't kill him, Wyatt."

Earp looked at him for a while. "You're a down-Easter, that's the trouble. Haven't got any common sense. You're gonna have to get out of town pronto, you know."

"Why is that?"

"Because, boy, you have a reputation now."

Johnson laughed. "Everybody in town knows who I am."

"Not anymore," Earp said.

It turned out that Foggy Bill Johnson, the man who gunned down Clem Curry and then went up against his brother Dick, was indeed a notorious celebrity in Deadwood. Every man who fancied himself sharp with a gun was suddenly asking to meet him.

After two days of extricating himself from gun-fights, Johnson realized that Earp was right. He would have to leave Deadwood soon. He had just enough money to buy fare and freight on the express stage, and purchased his ticket for the following day. When the light was low, he took one of the horses and checked to see that Little Wind's grave had not been disturbed. So far, it hadn't. The ground had hardened up in the cold and he had left no tracks. Even so, he forced himself to leave immediately, lest he be noticed.

Earp, meanwhile, had grown tired of gambling and a desultory courting of Miss Emily. He had expected

Deadwood to offer him a position as marshal, but no offer was forthcoming, so he was going to head south for the winter.

"When're you leaving?" Johnson asked.

"What's it to you?"

"Perhaps you could ride with me."

"With you and your bones?" Earp laughed. "Boy, every bandito and desperado from here to Cheyenne is just waiting for you to leave Deadwood with those bones."

"I'd be sure to make it if you rode with me."

"I think I'll wait, to escort Miss Emily."

"Miss Emily might come tomorrow, too, especially if you were riding with us."

Earp fixed him with a steady look. "What's in it for me, boy?"

"I bet the stage would pay you as a messenger." A messenger was a guard; they made good money.

"Can't you do any better than that?"

"I guess not."

There was a silence. Finally, Earp said, "Tell you what. If I get you through to Cheyenne, you give me half your shipment."

"Half my bones?"

"That's right," he said, smiling broadly and winking. "Half your bones. How's that sound?"

306 · MICHAEL CRICHTON

"I realized then," Johnson wrote on the evening of
September 28,

> that Mr. Earp was like all the others, and did
> not believe that these crates contained bones at
> all. I was faced with a moral dilemma. Mr. Earp
> had been friendly to me and helpful more than
> once. I was asking him to face real danger and
> he thought he was risking his life for treasure.
> It was my obligation to disabuse him of his
> greedy misconception. But I had received quite
> an education out West, one that Yale had been
> unable to provide. A man has to look out for
> himself, I'd learned. So all I said to him was,
> "Mr. Earp, you have cut yourself a deal."

The stage would leave Deadwood the following
morning.

He woke a few hours past midnight. It was time to retrieve the crates of bones. By prearrangement he had
hired Kang to help him again, since no white man
would want to dig up a dead Indian. They rode the
wagon out of town, and the first thing they did was

excavate Little Wind, who did not smell quite as bad as he had before, because of the cold air.

One by one the crates went into the wagon. They were dirty and moist from being underground but appeared otherwise fine. This time Johnson filled in most of the grave before returning Little Wind to the earth. He paused at the sight of him. The grotesquery was not Little Wind's rotting, gray visage, Johnson realized; it was that he had now buried this poor man three times. Little Wind had died to protect him, and in return, he had not let him rest in peace.

The Cheyenne Road

O nce in town, he continued to the stagecoach station. The coach was already there. It had started to snow again, and a chill wind moaned through Deadwood Gulch. Johnson was glad to be leaving, and methodically hoisted the crates onto the coach. Despite the assurances of the agent, the bones could not all ride up top with the enormously fat driver, Tiny Tim Edwards. Johnson was obliged to purchase an extra passenger seat and place some of them inside. Fortunately, the only passengers were Miss Emily and himself.

Then they had to wait for Wyatt Earp, who was nowhere to be found. Johnson stood in the snow with Miss Emily, looking up and down the bleak street of Deadwood.

"Maybe he's not coming after all," Johnson said.

"I think he will come," Miss Emily said.

While they waited, a redheaded boy ran up to Johnson. "Mr. Johnson?"

"That's right."

The boy gave Johnson a note, and scampered away. Johnson opened it, read it quickly, and crumpled it.

"What is it?" Miss Emily asked.

"Just a good-bye from Judge Harlan."

Around nine they saw the Earp brothers coming down the street toward them. They both appeared heavily burdened. "When they were closer," Johnson wrote, "I saw that the Earps had obtained a collection of firearms. I had never seen Wyatt Earp wearing a gun before—he seldom went armed in public—but now he carried a veritable arsenal."

Earp was late because he had to wait for Sutter's Dry Goods to open, to obtain guns. He carried two sawed-off shotguns, three Pierce repeating rifles, four Colt revolvers, and a dozen boxes of ammunition.

Johnson said, "It appears you are expecting some warm work."

Earp told Miss Emily to climb into the stage; then he said, "I don't want to alarm her any." And then he told Johnson that he thought they faced "a deal of trouble, and no point in pretending it won't come."

Johnson showed Earp the note, which read:

I PROMIS YOU ARE A DED MAN TO-DAY OR MY
NAME IS NOT DICK CURRY.

"That's fine," Earp said. "We're ready for him."

Wyatt's brother Morgan had made a lucrative deal to haul firewood and was planning to stay in Deadwood for the winter, but said that he would ride with Wyatt and the stage as far as Custer City, fifty miles to the south.

Tiny Tim leaned over the box. "You gents gonna palaver all day, or are you ready to crack leather?"

"We are," Earp said.

"Then climb aboard this item. Can't go nowhere standing in the street, can you?"

Johnson climbed onto the stage with Miss Emily, and for the tenth time that morning attended to his crates, cinching them down tightly. Morgan Earp climbed onto the top of the stage, and Wyatt rode shotgun.

A Chinese boy in cowboy boots came running toward the stagecoach. It was Kang, with a worried look on his face.

Johnson fished in his pocket and found a five-dollar gold piece.

"Kang!"

He leaned out the open door and flipped the glittering coin high into the air. Kang caught it on the run with remarkable grace. Johnson nodded at him, knowing he would never see the boy again.

Tim snapped his whips, the horses snorted, and they galloped out of Deadwood in the swirling snow.

It was a three-day journey to Fort Laramie: one day to Custer City, in the center of the Black Hills; a second day through the treacherous Red Canyon to the Red Canyon stagecoach station at the southern edge of the Black Hills; and the third day across the Wyoming plains to the newly built iron bridge that crossed the Platte River at Laramie.

Earp assured him the trip would get safer as they went, and if they reached Laramie, they would be entirely safe; from then on, the road from Laramie to Cheyenne was patrolled by cavalry.

If they reached Laramie.

"Three obstacles stood between us and our destination," Johnson later wrote in his journal:

The first was Black Dick and his gang of ruffians. We could expect to meet them during the first day. Second was Persimmons Bill and his renegade Indians. We could expect to meet them in Red Canyon on the second day. And the third obstacle was the most dangerous of all—and wholly unanticipated by me.

Johnson had steeled himself for a dangerous journey, but he was unprepared for its sheer physical hazards.

The Black Hills roads were bad, necessitating slow travel. Drop-offs were precipitous, and the fact that the coach swayed ominously near the crumbling edge under its load of bones did not reassure them. Several creeks—the Bear Butte, Elk, and Boxelder—were transformed from the recent snows into swollen, raging rivers. The fact that the coach was so heavily laden made the crossings especially dangerous.

As Tiny explained it, "This item gets stuck in the quicksand, middle of the river, we don't go anywheres less we ride back for an extra team, pull this item out, and that's a fact."

And along with the difficulties, they lived under the continuous threat of attack at any moment. The tension was nerve-racking, for the smallest impediment could be dangerous.

Around noon, the coach stopped. Johnson looked out. "Why are we stopping?"

"Keep your head in," Earp snapped, "if you don't want to lose it. Fallen tree up ahead."

"So?"

Morgan Earp peered over from the top of the coach. "Miss Emily? I'd be much obliged, ma'am, if you would get yourself low and stay there until we're moving again."

"It's just a fallen tree," Johnson said. Soil was thin in many places in the Black Hills, and trees often fell across the road.

"Maybe so," Earp said. "Maybe not." He pointed out that high hills surrounded the road on all sides. The trees came right to the road, providing good close cover. "If they're going for us, this'd be a good place."

Tiny Tim got down off the box and went forward to inspect the fallen tree. Johnson heard the sharp clash-clack of shotguns being cocked.

"Is there really danger?" Miss Emily asked. She did not seem the least anxious.

"I guess there is," Johnson said. He withdrew his pistol, looked down the barrel, spun the chambers.

Beside him, Miss Emily gave a little shiver of excitement.

But the tree was a small one, fallen by natural causes. Tiny moved it, and they drove on. An hour later, near Silver Peak and Pactola, they came upon a rockslide and repeated the procedure, but again, they had no trouble.

"When the attack finally came," Johnson wrote, "it was almost a relief."

Wyatt Earp shouted, "You below! Heads in!" and his shotgun roared.

It was answered by gunfire from behind them.

They were at the bottom of Sand Creek Gulch. The road ran straight here, with room on both sides for horsemen to keep up and discharge their guns into the open coach.

They heard Morgan Earp, directly above them, scraping over the roof of the coach, and they felt it sway as he took a position near the back. There was more firing. Wyatt called distinctly, "Get down, Morg, I'm shooting." There was more firing. Tiny whipped the horses, cursed them.

Bullets thunked into the wood of the coach; Johnson and Emily ducked down, but the crates of fossils, precariously strapped to the seat above, threatened to tumble down on them. Johnson got up on his knees and tried to cinch them tighter. A horseman rode alongside the coach, aimed at Johnson—and in a sudden explosion disappeared from the horse.

Astonished, Johnson looked out.

"Foggy! Get your head in! I'm shooting!"

Johnson ducked back in, and Earp's shotgun blasted past the open window. More gunshots from riders outside splintered the doorposts of the carriage; there was a scream.

Cursing and shouting, Tiny whipped the horses; the coach rocked and jolted over the rough road; inside the carriage, Johnson and Miss Emily collided and bounced against each other "in a manner which would be embarrassing were circumstances not so exigent," Johnson later wrote. "The next period—it seemed hours, though it was probably a minute or two—was a nervous blend of whining bullets, galloping horses, shouts and screams, jolts and gunshots—until finally our coach rounded a bend, and we were out of Sand Creek Gulch, and the shooting died off, and we were safely on our way once more.

"We had survived the attack of the notorious Curry gang!"

Only a damn fool would think so," Wyatt said when they stopped to rest and change horses at the Tigerville coach station.

"Why, wasn't that the Curry gang attacking us? And didn't we get away?"

"Look, boy," Wyatt said. "I know you're from back East, but nobody's that stupid." He reloaded his shotguns as he spoke.

Johnson didn't understand, so Morgan Earp explained. "Black Dick wants you pretty bad, and he wouldn't risk all in such an ill-made attack."

Johnson, who had found the attack terrifying, said, "Why was it ill-made?"

"Riskiest attack there is, on horseback," Morgan said. "Riders can't shoot worth a damn, the coach is always moving, and unless they can shoot one of the horses in the team, it's very likely to get away, just as we did. There's no certainty in a horseback attack."

"Then why'd they try one?"

"To put us at our ease," Wyatt said. "To put us off our guard. You mark my words, they know we have to stop and change teams at Tigerville. Right now they're riding like hell to set up again."

"Set up where?"

"If I knew that," Wyatt said, "I wouldn't be worried. What do you think, Morg?"

"Somewhere between here and Sheridan, I figure," Morgan Earp said.

"That's what I figure, too," Wyatt Earp said, cracking his shotgun closed. "And the next time, they'll really mean business."

The Second Attack

Half an hour farther on, they halted at the edge of the pinewoods, before the sandy banks of Spring Creek. The meandering water was deceptively low, and more than a hundred yards wide. The late-afternoon sun glowed off the slow, peaceful ripples. On the far bank, the pinewoods were thick and dark.

They watched the river silently for several minutes. Finally, Johnson poked his head out to ask why they were waiting. Morgan Earp, on top of the stage, leaned over and tapped him on the head, and held his finger to his lips, to be silent.

Johnson sat back in the coach, rubbed his head, and looked questioningly at Miss Emily.

Miss Emily shrugged, and slapped a mosquito.

Several minutes passed before Wyatt Earp said to Tiny, "How's it look to you?"

"Dunno," Tiny said.

Earp peered at the tracks on the sandy riverbank. "Lot of horses passed here recently."

"That's usual," Tiny said. "Sheridan's just a couple of miles south on the other side."

They fell silent again, waiting, listening to the quiet gurgle of the water, the wind in the pines.

"You know, there's usually birds hereabouts at Spring Creek," Tiny said finally.

"Too quiet?" Earp said.

"I'd say too quiet."

"How's the bottom?" Earp asked, looking at the river.

"Never know till you get there. You want to make a play?"

"I guess I do," Earp said. He swung down off the box, walked back, and looked into the coach at Johnson and Miss Emily.

"We're going to try to cross the creek," he said quietly. "If we get across, fine. If we get trouble, you stay down, no matter what you see or hear. Morg knows what to do. Let him handle things. Okay?"

They nodded. Johnson's throat was dry. "You think it's a trap?"

Earp shrugged. "It's a good place for one."

He climbed back onto the box and cocked his shotgun. Tiny whipped up the horses, and they started across at breakneck speed, the coach lurching as the wheels hit the soft sandy banks, and then splashing and jouncing over rocks in the riverbed.

And then the shooting started. Johnson heard the whinny of the horses, and with a final lurch the coach stopped abruptly, right in the middle of the river, and Tiny shouted, "That tears it!" and Morgan Earp began firing rapidly. "I'll cover you, Wyatt."

Johnson and Miss Emily ducked down. Bullets whined all around them, and the coach rocked as the men moved above them. Johnson peeked over the sill and saw Wyatt Earp running, splashing through the river toward the far shore.

"He's leaving! Wyatt's leaving us!" Johnson cried, and then a fusillade sent him diving for cover again.

"He wouldn't abandon us," Emily said.

"He just did!" Johnson shouted. He was completely panicked. Suddenly the coach door swung open and Johnson screamed as Tiny threw himself in, landing on top of them.

Tiny was gasping and white-faced; he pulled the door shut as a half dozen bullets splintered the wood.

"What's happening?" Johnson asked.

"Ain't no place for me out there," Tiny said.

"But what's happening?"

"We're stuck in the middle of the damn river, that's what's happening," Tiny said. "They killed one of the team, so we ain't going nowhere, and the Earp boys are shooting away like blazes. Wyatt took off."

"They have a plan?"

"I surely hope so," Tiny said. "'Cause I don't." As the gunfire continued, he clasped his hands together and closed his eyes. His lips twitched.

"What're you doing?"

"Praying," Tiny said. "You better, too. 'Cause if Black Dick takes this stage, he'll just naturally kill us all."

In the reddish afternoon light, the stagecoach sat immobile in the middle of Spring Creek. On top of the stage, Morgan Earp lay flat and fired into the trees on the opposite shore. Wyatt made it safely to the far bank, and plunged into the pinewoods opposite.

Almost immediately, the shooting from the far side diminished: the Curry gang had something new to worry about now.

Then from the far shore there was a shotgun blast and a loud scream, agonizing. It trailed away into silence. After a moment, another shotgun blast, and a strangled cry.

The Curry gang stopped firing at the coach.

Then a voice cried, "Don't shoot, Wyatt, please don't—" and another blast.

Suddenly half a dozen voices on the far shore were shouting to each other, and then they heard horses galloping off.

And then nothing.

Morgan Earp knocked on the roof of the coach. "It's finished," he said. "They're gone. You can breathe now."

The passengers inside struggled to their feet, brushed themselves off. Johnson looked out and saw Wyatt Earp standing on the far bank, grinning. His sawed-off shotgun hung loosely in his hand.

He walked slowly back through the stream toward them. "First rule of a bushwhacking," he said. "Always run toward the direction of fire, not away."

"How many'd you kill?" Johnson asked. "All of them?"

Earp grinned again. "None of them."

"None of them?"

"Those woods're thick; you can't see ten feet ahead of you. I'd never find 'em in there. But I knew they were spread out along the bank and probably couldn't see each other directly. So I just shot my gun a few times, and made a few hideous cries."

"Wyatt can really make hideous cries," Morgan said.

"That's so," Wyatt said. "The Curry gang panicked and ran."

"You mean you just tricked them?" Johnson said. In a strange way he felt disappointed.

"Listen," Wyatt Earp said. "One reason I'm still alive is I don't go asking for trouble. These boys are none too quick, and they got an active imagination. Besides, we got a bigger problem than getting rid of the Curry boys."

"We do?"

"Yeah. We got to get this coach out of the river."

"Why is that a problem?"

Earp sighed. "Boy, you ever tried to move a dead horse?"

It took an hour to cut the animal loose, and float it downstream. Johnson watched the dark carcass drift with the current until it had disappeared. With the five remaining horses of the team, they managed to haul the coach out of the sand and onto the far shore. By then it was dark, and they drove quickly to Sheridan, where they obtained a fresh team.

Sheridan was a small town of fifty wooden houses, but it seemed everyone had turned out to greet them; Johnson was surprised to see money changing hands.

Earp collected a lot of it.

"What's going on?"

"They were wagering on whether we'd make it," Earp said. "I had a few bets myself."

"Which way'd you bet?"

Earp just smiled and nodded to a saloon. "You know, it would be sporting for you to go inside with me and buy a round of whiskey."

"You think we should drink at a time like this?"

"We won't see any more trouble until Red Canyon," Earp said, "and I'm thirsty."

Red Canyon

They reached the town of Custer at ten o'clock at night. The night was dark, and Johnson was disappointed; he couldn't see much of the most famous place in the Black Hills, the Gordon Stockade at French Creek.

Just one year before, in 1875, the first miners of the Gordon party had built log cabins surrounded by a wooden fence ten feet high. They had entered the Black Hills in defiance of the Indian treaty, and they intended to pan for gold and hold off the Indians with their stockade. It had taken a cavalry expedition from Fort Laramie to get them out; in those days the army was still enforcing the Indian treaty, and the stockade stood deserted.

Now, everyone at Custer was talking about the

new Indian treaty. Although the government was still fighting the Sioux in the field, the cost of the war was high—already in excess of $15 million—and it was an election year. Both the expense of the fighting and the legitimacy of the government's position were hot campaign issues in Washington. Therefore, the Great White Father preferred to conclude the war peacefully, by negotiating a new treaty, and to this end, government negotiators had arranged to meet with Sioux chieftains in Sheridan.

But even specially picked chiefs were disgusted by the new proposals. Most of the government negotiators agreed with them. One of them, now on his way back to Washington, said to Johnson that it was "the hardest damn thing I ever did in my life. I don't care how many feathers a man wears in his hair, he's still a man. One of them, Red Legs, looked at me and said, 'Do you think this is fair? Would you sign such a paper?' And I could not meet his eyes. It made me sick.

"You know what Thomas Jefferson said?" the man continued. "In 1803, Thomas Jefferson said that it would take a thousand years before the West was fully settled. And it'll be settled in less'n a hundred years. That's progress."

Johnson recorded in his journal that "he seemed an honest man sent to do a dishonest job, and now he could not forgive himself for carrying out the instructions of his government. He was drunk when we arrived, and drinking more when we left."

Morgan Earp left them at Custer, and they went on without him. By midnight, they had passed Fourmile Ranch, and headed into Pleasant Valley. They passed Twelve-mile Ranch, and Eighteenmile Ranch in the darkness.

Shortly before dawn, they reached the entrance to Red Canyon.

The Red Canyon coach station had been burned to the ground. All the horses had been stolen. Flies buzzed around a half dozen scalped bodies, evidence of Persimmons Bill's depredations.

"Guess they didn't hear about the new treaty," Earp said laconically. "I reckon we won't be eating here."

They proceeded immediately through the canyon. It was a tense journey, slow because they had no fresh team, but they made it without incident. At the far end of the canyon they followed Hawk Creek toward Camp Collier, which marked the southern entrance to the Black Hills.

Now, in the morning light, they stopped for an hour to graze the horses, and to breathe a long sigh of relief. "Not long now, Mr. Johnson," Earp said, "and you'll be owing me half those bones."

Johnson decided it was time to tell him the truth. "Mr. Earp," he began.

"Yes?"

"I appreciate everything you have done to help me get out of Deadwood, naturally."

"I'm sure you do."

"But there's something I have to tell you."

Earp frowned. "You're not backing out on your deal?"

"No, no." Johnson shook his head. "But I have to tell you, the crates really are just fossil bones."

"Uh-huh," Wyatt Earp said.

"They are just bones."

"I heard you."

"They are of value only to scientists, to paleontologists."

"That's fine with me."

Johnson smiled wanly. "I only hope you won't be too disappointed."

"I'll try not to be," Earp said, and winked, and punched him on the shoulder. "You just remember, boy. Half those bones are mine."

He had been a strong friend," Johnson wrote, "and I suspected he would make a dangerous enemy. Thus it was with some trepidation that I resumed the journey to Fort Laramie, and the first civilization I had seen in many months."

Fort Laramie

Fort Laramie was an army outpost that had grown into a frontier town, but the army garrison still set the mood, and its mood was now bitter. The army had fought the Indians for more than eight months, and had suffered serious losses, most especially the massacre of Custer's column at the Little Bighorn. There had been other bloody engagements as well, at Powder River and Slim Buttes, and even when they were not fighting, the campaign had been harsh and arduous. But all the news from the East told them that Washington and the rest of the country did not support their efforts; numerous articles criticized the military conduct of the campaign against "the noble and defenseless red man." For young men who had seen their comrades fall, who had returned to a battle scene to bury the scalped and mutilated bodies of friends, who had seen corpses with their genitals cut off and stuffed in their mouths—for these soldiers, the Eastern commentary made for difficult reading.

As far as the army was concerned, they had been ordered to undertake this war, without being asked their opinion of either its feasibility or its morality; they had followed orders as best they could, and with considerable success, and they were angry now to be unsupported, and to be fighting an unpopular war.

The fact that the politicians in Washington had underestimated both the difficulty of a campaign against "mere savages" and the outrage that it would cause among the liberal establishment of the Eastern cities—uninformed writers who had never set eyes on a real Indian, and who had only fantasies of what the Indians were like—was no fault of the army.

As one captain put it, "They want the Indians eliminated, and the lands opened up to white settlers, but they don't want anybody to get hurt in the process. That just ain't possible."

Added to this was the ugly fact that the war had now entered a new phase. The army was engaged in a war of attrition with the Indians, in which they planned to kill all the buffalo and thus starve the Indians into submission. Even so, most military men expected the war to drag on for at least three more years, and to cost another $15 million—although nobody in Washington wanted to hear that.

The arguments, back and forth, raged in the coach station on the outskirts of town. Johnson had an unappetizing lunch of bacon and biscuits, then sat in the sun outside the station. From where he sat, he could see the iron bridge crossing the Platte.

For more than a decade, the Platte River valley had been trumpeted by Union Pacific brochures as "a flowery meadow of great fertility clothed in nutritious grasses, and watered by numerous streams." In fact, it was harsh, god-awful country. Yet the settlers were coming.

From the earliest pioneer days, the Platte River itself was known as especially treacherous and difficult to cross, and this new iron bridge represented one small improvement in a series of changes that were opening the West to settlers, making it more accessible.

Johnson dozed off in the sun and awoke when a voice said, "Hell of a sight, ain't it?"

He opened his eyes. A tall man was smoking a cigar and staring at the bridge.

"That it is," he said.

"I remember last year, that bridge was just talk." The tall man turned. He had a scar running down his cheek. The face was familiar, but the recognition came slowly.

Navy Joe Benedict.

Marsh's right-hand man.

Johnson sat up quickly. He had only a moment to wonder what Navy Joe was doing here before a familiar heavyset figure emerged from the coach house and stood beside Benedict.

Professor Marsh glanced at Johnson and said in his formal way, "Good morning to you, sir." He gave no sign of recognition and immediately turned to Benedict. "What's the delay, Joe?"

"Just hitching up a new team, Professor. We'll be ready to leave in the space of fifteen or twenty minutes."

"See if you can quicken it," Marsh said.

Navy Joe left, and Marsh turned to Johnson. He appeared not to recognize him, for Johnson looked very different from the last time Marsh had seen him. He was leaner and more muscled, with a full beard, and hair that had not seen scissors since leaving Philadelphia more than three months before. It hung down almost to his shoulders. His clothes were rough and dirty, caked in mud.

Marsh said, "Just passing through?"

"That's right."

"Which way you going?"

"To Cheyenne."

"Come from the Hills?"

"Yeah."

"Whereabouts?"

"Deadwood."

"Mining gold?"

"Yeah," Johnson said.

"Strike it rich?"

"Not exactly," Johnson said. "What about you?"

"In point of fact, I myself am going north into the Hills."

"Mining gold?" Johnson asked, to his private amusement.

"Hardly. I am the professor of paleontology at Yale College," Marsh said. "I study fossil bones."

"That right?" Johnson could not believe that Marsh had not recognized him, but it seemed he had not.

"Yes," Marsh said. "And I hear there are some fossil bones to be had in Deadwood."

"In Deadwood? That right?"

"That's what I hear," Marsh said. "Apparently a young man has them in his possession. I hope to obtain them. I am willing to pay well for them."

"Oh?"

"Yes indeed." Marsh took out a fat roll of greenbacks, and inspected them in the sunlight. "I would also pay for information about this young man and his whereabouts." He looked closely at Johnson. "If you take my meaning."

"I don't reckon I do," Johnson said.

"Well, you've just come from Deadwood," Marsh said. "I wonder if you know anything of this young man."

"This man got a name?" Johnson asked.

"His name is Johnson. He's quite an unscrupulous young fellow. He used to work for me."

"That right?"

"Indeed. But he left my company and threw in with a band of thieves and robbers. I believe he's wanted for murder in other territories."

"That right?"

Marsh nodded. "You know anything of him?"

"Never heard of him. How you going to get those bones?"

"Buy them if necessary," Marsh said. "But I intend to have them, by whatever means may be required."

"You want 'em bad, then."

"Yes, I do," Marsh said. "You see," he said, pausing for dramatic effect, "these bones I'm talking about are actually mine. Young Johnson stole them from me."

Johnson felt rage sweep over him. He had been enjoying this charade, but now he was flushed with anger.

It took every bit of self-control he could muster to say laconically, "That right?"

"He's a lying skunk, no doubt of it," Marsh said.

"Sounds a bad one," Johnson said.

At that moment, Wyatt Earp came around the corner and said, "Hey, Johnson! On your pegs! We're moving out."

Marsh smiled at Johnson. "You little son of a bitch," he said.

The Laramie Bone Deal

I t seemed," wrote Johnson in his journal, "that many pigeons had come home to roost in Laramie."

Most of the town was preoccupied with another figure from Johnson's past, Broken Nose Jack McCall. Jack had run from Deadwood and had gotten to Laramie, where he had bragged about killing Wild Bill Hickok. The reason he spoke so freely was that a miners' court in Deadwood had tried him for that murder, and had acquitted him when he claimed that Wild Bill had killed his young brother many years before, and he was just avenging that crime. In Laramie, Jack talked openly of killing Hickok, certain that he could not be tried twice for the same crime.

But Jack didn't realize that the Deadwood miners' court was not legally recognized, and he was promptly thrown into jail in Laramie and formally tried for Hickok's murder. Since Jack had already publicly admitted to it, the trial was short; he was convicted and sentenced to be hanged, a turn of events that "irked him mightily."

While Jack's trial was going on, an episode far more important to William Johnson was occurring down the road in Sutter's Saloon. Wyatt Earp was sitting at a table, drinking whiskey with Othniel C. Marsh and negotiating for the sale of half Johnson's bones.

They were both hard bargainers, and it took most of the day. For his part, Earp appeared amused.

Johnson sat with Miss Emily in the corner and watched the proceedings. "I can't believe this is happening," he said.

"Why does it surprise you?" she asked.

"What were my chances of running into that professor?" He sighed. "One in a million, or less."

"Oh, I don't think so," she said. "Wyatt knew Professor Marsh was in the territory."

A slow creeping sensation moved up Johnson's spine. "He did?"

"Surely."

"How did he know?"

"I was with him in the hotel dining room," she said,

"when he heard the rumor that there was some college teacher in Cheyenne buying up all manner of fossils and asking about some bones in Deadwood. The miners were all laughing about it, but Wyatt's eyes lit up when he heard the story."

Johnson frowned. "So he decided to help me get the bones out of Deadwood to Cheyenne?"

"Yes," she said. "We left the day after he heard that story."

"You mean Wyatt always intended to sell my bones to Marsh, from the beginning?"

"I believe so," she said softly.

Johnson glared across the saloon at Earp. "And I thought he was my friend."

"You thought he was a fool," Emily said. "But he is your friend."

"How can you say that? Look at him bargaining there, haggling over every dollar. At this rate they'll be at it all day."

"Yes," Emily said. "Yet I'm sure Wyatt could conclude the deal in five minutes, if that was what he intended."

Johnson stared at her. "You mean . . ."

She nodded. "I've no doubt he's wondering why you are sitting here while he stalls Professor Marsh for you."

"Oh, Emily," he cried, "I could kiss you!"

"I wish you would," she said softly.

"Too many things were happening at once," wrote Johnson.

> My head was fairly spinning with these developments. I hurried outside with Emily, and postponed kissing her in order to send her off for a hundred-pound sack of rice, a bolt of tarp cloth, and a long-handled shovel. Meanwhile I hastily obtained the requisite large rocks, which fortunately were near at hand, remnants of the blasting that had been done to erect the new Platte bridge.

He found yet another Chinese laundry and paid a small sum to use the fire and iron kettle with which they heated water. He spent three hours boiling fresh rice paste, making sure the concoction was gelatinous enough, and clutching the rocks with bamboo laundry tongs and dipping them into the pasty ooze, coating them. When they were dry, he poured dust over them, to make them suitably grimy. Next to the heat of the fire, they dried quickly. Finally, he removed the precious bones from all ten crates, and placed the new stones in the old crates, closing them carefully so that there would be no marks indicating they had been opened.

By five that afternoon, he was exhausted. But all of Johnson's fossil bones were safely hidden in the back of the stable, wrapped in tarp cloth and buried under a pile of fresh manure, the shovel hidden in the straw with them and the substitutions set out with a tarp covering, as the originals had been. Earp and Marsh arrived soon after. Marsh grinned at Johnson. "I expect this will be our last meeting, Mr. Johnson."

"I hope so," Johnson said, with a sincerity Marsh could not have imagined.

The division was begun. Marsh wanted to open all ten crates and inspect the fossils before dividing, but Johnson steadfastly refused. The division was meant to be between him and Earp, and it would be done randomly. Marsh grumbled but agreed.

Midway through the process, Marsh said, "I think I had better look at one of these crates, to satisfy myself."

"I have no objection," Earp said. He looked directly at Johnson.

"I have plenty of objections," Johnson said.

"Oh? What are they?" Marsh asked.

"I'm in a hurry," Johnson said. "And besides . . ."

"Besides?"

"There's your father," Emily prompted him suddenly.

"Yes, there's my father," Johnson said. "How much did Professor Marsh offer you for these stones, Wyatt?"

"Two hundred dollars," Wyatt said.

"Two hundred dollars? That's an outrage."

"It is two hundred more than you have, I believe," Marsh said.

"Look, Wyatt," said Johnson. "There's a telegraph office here in Laramie. I can cable my father for funds, and by this time tomorrow I can give you five hundred dollars for your share."

Marsh darkened. "Mr. Earp, we have made our deal."

"That's so," Earp said. "But I like the sound of five hundred dollars."

"I'll give you six," Marsh said. "Now."

"Seven fifty," Johnson said. "Tomorrow."

Marsh said, "Mr. Earp, I thought we had a deal."

"It's amazing," Earp said, "how things keep changing in this world."

"But you don't even know if this young man can come up with the money."

"I suspect he can."

"Eight hundred," Johnson said.

Half an hour later, Marsh pronounced himself happy to take Earp's share of the bones, at once and without inspection, for a thousand dollars in cash. "But I want that box," he said suddenly, spying the one with the small X on the side. "That means something."

"No!" yelled Johnson.

Marsh drew his weapon. "It would appear that box has contents that are especially valuable. And if you believe that your life is also especially valuable, Mr. Johnson, which I do not, then I suggest you let me remove this crate without further discussion."

Marsh had the boxes loaded onto a wagon, and he and Navy Joe Benedict headed north, toward Deadwood, to retrieve the rest of the bones.

"What does he mean, the rest of the bones?" Johnson asked, as he saw the wagon drive off into the sunset.

"I told him there was another thousand pounds we left behind in Deadwood, hidden in Chinese Town, only you didn't want him to know about them," Earp said.

"We better get moving," Johnson said. "He won't go far before he cracks open one of those cases and finds he has bought worthless granite. And he'll be back hopping mad."

"I'm ready to go," Earp said, thumbing through the money. "I feel well satisfied with my return on this trip."

"There's one problem, of course."

"You need crates to replace the ones you just lost," said Earp. "I bet the army garrison has some, given their need for provisions."

Within an hour they had procured ten crates of more or less equal size as the ones Marsh had taken. Johnson unearthed the bones from their manure bed, and packed them carefully but quickly. The box containing the dragon teeth received another *X*, which satisfied him more than he could say.

They left, within minutes, for Cheyenne.

Earp was up on the box with Tiny. Inside the coach, Miss Emily stared at him. "Well?"

"Well, what?"

"I think I've been very patient."

"I thought you might be Wyatt's girl," he said.

"Wyatt's girl? Wherever would you get an idea like that?"

"Well, I thought so."

"Wyatt Earp is a scoundrel and a drifter. The man lives for excitement, gambling, shooting, and other pursuits of no substance."

"And me?"

"You're different," she said. "You're brave, but you are also refined. I bet you kiss real refined, too."

She was waiting.

"I learned," Johnson wrote in his journal, "one immediate lesson, which was the unwisdom of kissing aboard a bucking stagecoach. My lip was deeply bitten and the blood flowed freely, which inhibited, but did not stop, further explorations of this nature."

He added, "I hope she did not know I had never kissed a girl before, in the passionate French way which seemed to be to her liking. Except for that one time with Lucienne. But I will say this for Emily. If she did know, she did not say anything, and for that—and for other experiences with her in Cheyenne—I am eternally grateful."

Cheyenne

In the unimaginable splendor of a room at the Inter-Ocean Hotel (which he had previously seen as a roach-infested dump), Johnson took his ease for several days, with Emily. But first, upon arrival and signing the hotel register, he ascertained that the Inter-Ocean maintained a steel-walled strong room, with one of the new combination time locks, developed for banks against would-be bank robbers. The boxes were carried into the room by the porters. He tipped them generously so that they would not resent him and whisper about the boxes to their less friendly colleagues.

The first day, he soaked in four baths in succession, for after each he found his body was still dirty. It seemed as though the dust of the prairie would never leave his skin.

He visited the barber, who trimmed his hair and beard. It was startling to sit in the chair and inspect his own face in the mirror. He could not get used to it; his features were unfamiliar; he had the face of a different person—leaner, harder, determination now in his features. And there was the scar over his upper lip; he rather liked it, and so did Emily. The barber stepped back, scissors in one hand, comb in the other. "How's that look, sir?" Like everyone else in Cheyenne, the barber treated Johnson with respect. It wasn't because he was rich—no one in Cheyenne knew he was rich—but rather because of something in his manner, his bearing. Without meaning to do so, he looked like a man who might shoot another one—because he now had.

"Sir? How does that look?" the barber asked again.

Johnson didn't know. Finally, he said, "I like it fine."

He took Emily to dinner in the best restaurant in town. They dined on oysters from California, and wine from France, and *poulet à l'estragon*. She recognized the name of the wine, he noticed. After dinner they walked arm in arm on the streets of the town. He remembered how dangerous Cheyenne had felt when he had been here before. Now it seemed a sleepy little railway junction, populated by braggarts and gamblers putting on airs. Even the toughest-looking customers stepped aside on the boardwalk when he passed.

"They see you wear a gun," Emily said, "and you know how to use it."

Pleased, Johnson took Emily back to the hotel early, and to bed. They stayed in bed most of the following day. He had a wonderful time, and so did she.

"Where will you go now?" she asked him on the third day.

"Back to Philadelphia," he said.

"I've never been to Philadelphia," she said.

"You'll love it there," he said, smiling.

She smiled back, happily. "You really want me to come?"

"Of course."

"Really?"

"Don't be silly," he said.

But he began to feel that she was always one step ahead of him. She seemed to know the hotel better than he would have expected, and enjoyed an easy overfamiliarity with the men behind the desk and the waiters in the dining room. Some even seemed to recognize her. And when he and Emily strolled the streets and window-shopped, she recognized Eastern fashions readily.

"I think this one's very pretty."

"It seems out of place here, not that I am the expert."

"Well, a Western girl likes to know what's fashionable."

He would have reason to ponder this statement later.

A few steps along the wooden walkway, she said, "What sort of person is your mother?"

Johnson had not thought of his mother for a long time. The very thought was jolting in some way. "Why did you ask that?"

"I was just wondering about meeting her."

"How do you mean?"

"Whether she will like me."

"Ah, of course."

"Do you think she'll like me, Bill?"

"Oh, she'll like you fine," Johnson said.

"You don't sound convinced." She pouted prettily.

"Don't be silly," he said, and squeezed her arm.

"Let's go back to the hotel," she said. And quickly, she licked his ear.

"Stop it, Emily."

"What's the matter? I thought you liked that."

"I do, but not here. Not in public."

"Why? Nobody's looking at us."

"I know, but it's not proper."

"What difference does it make?" She was frowning. "If nobody is looking at us, what possible difference could it make?"

"I don't know, it just does."

"You're back in Philadelphia already," she said, stepping away and staring at him.

"Now, Emily . . ."

"You are."

But all he said was, "Don't be silly."

"I'm not being silly," she said. "And I'm not going to Philadelphia."

He did not know what to say.

"I just wouldn't fit in," she said, wiping a tear from her cheek.

"Emily . . ."

She cried openly. "I know what you are thinking, Bill. I've known for days now."

"Emily, please . . ." He had no idea what she meant, for the last three days had been the most deliriously pleasurable of his life.

"It's no good—don't touch me, please—it's no good, that's all."

They walked back to the hotel, side by side, not speaking. She held her head high and sniffled occasionally. He was uncomfortable, clumsy, not knowing what to do.

After a time, he glanced at her and saw that she was no longer crying. She was furious. "After all I did for you," she said. "Why, you'd be long dead from Dick if

I hadn't helped you, and you'd never have gotten out of Deadwood if I hadn't talked Wyatt into helping you, and you'd have lost your bones in Laramie if I hadn't helped you see a plan . . ."

"That's true, Emily."

"And this is the thanks I get! You cast me aside like an old rag."

She was really angry. Yet somehow he realized it was he who was being cast aside. "Emily . . ."

"I said don't touch me!"

It was a relief when the sheriff came up to them, tipped his hat politely to Emily, and said, "You William Johnson of Philadelphia?"

"I am."

"You the one staying at the Inter-Ocean?"

"I am."

"You have some identification of who you are?"

"Of course."

"That's fine," the sheriff said, taking out his gun. "You're under arrest. For the murder of William Johnson."

"But I am William Johnson."

"I can't see how. William Johnson is dead. So whoever you are, you're surely not him, are you?"

Handcuffs were snapped on his wrists. He looked at her. "Emily, tell him."

Emily turned on her heel and walked away without a word.

"Emily!"

"Let's go, mister," the sheriff said, and pushed Johnson toward the jail.

It took a while for the details to come out. His first day in Cheyenne, Johnson had cabled his father in Philadelphia, asking him to send $500. His father had immediately cabled the sheriff's office to report that someone in Cheyenne was impersonating his dead son.

Everything Johnson produced—his Yale class ring, some crumpled correspondence, a newspaper clipping from the Deadwood *Black Hills Weekly Pioneer*—was taken as proof that he had robbed a dead man and probably killed him as well.

"This fellow Johnson's a college man from back East," the sheriff said, squinting judiciously at Johnson. "Now that couldn't be you, could it."

"But it is," Johnson insisted.

"He's rich, too."

"I am."

The sheriff laughed. "That's a good one," he said. "You're a rich college man from back East, and I'm Santa Claus."

"Ask the girl. Ask Emily."

"Oh, I did," the sheriff said. "She said she's real disappointed in you, you gave her a big story about yourself and now she sees you for what you are. She's living it up in your hotel room and selling off those crates of whatever it is you brought with you to town."

"What?"

"She's no friend of yours, mister," the sheriff said.

"She can't sell those crates!"

"I don't see why not. She says they're hers."

"They're mine!"

"It's no good getting all hot like this," the sheriff said. "I checked with some folks come down from Deadwood. Seems you showed up there with a dead Indian and a dead white man. I'll lay you a hundred to one that white man was William Johnson."

Johnson started to explain, but the sheriff held up his hand. "I'm sure you got a story to explain it," he said. "Your type always does."

The sheriff went out of the jail. Johnson heard the deputy say, "Who is that fella?"

"Some desperado, putting on airs," the sheriff said, and he went out for a drink.

The deputy was a boy of sixteen. Johnson traded him his boots to send a second telegram to Philadelphia.

"Sheriff'll be mighty angry if he finds out," the

deputy said. "He wants you to go to Yankton to be tried for murder."

"Just send it," Johnson said, writing quickly.

DEAR FATHER:

SORRY I WRECKED YACHT. REMEMBER PET SQUIRREL SUM-MER 71. MOTHER'S FEVER AFTER EDWARD BORN. HEAD-MASTER ELLIS WARNING AT EXETER. I AM TRULY ALIVE AND YOU ARE CAUSING GREAT TROUBLE. SEND MONEY AND INFORM SHERIFF.

YOUR LOVING SON PINKY.

The deputy read the telegram slowly, mouthing the words. He looked up. "Pinky?"

"Just send it," Johnson said.

"Pinky?"

"That was my name as a baby."

The deputy shook his head. But he sent the telegram.

"**Now look** here, Mr. Johnson," the sheriff said, unlocking the cell a few hours later. "It was an honest mistake. I was only doing my duty."

"You got the telegram?" Johnson said.

"I got three telegrams," the sheriff said. "One from your father, one from Senator Cameron of Pennsylvania, and one from Mr. Hayden at the Geological Survey in Washington. For all I know there are more coming. I'm telling you it was an honest mistake."

"That's fine," Johnson said.

"No hard feelings?"

But Johnson had other things on his mind. "Where's my gun?"

He found Emily in the lobby of the Inter-Ocean Hotel. She was drinking wine.

"Where are my crates?"

"I have nothing to say to you."

"What have you done with my crates, Emily?"

"Nothing." She shook her head. "They are just old bones. Nobody wants 'em."

Relieved, Johnson collapsed in a chair beside her.

"I can't see why they are so important to you," she said.

"They are, that's all."

"Well, I hope you got some money because the hotel is asking for the bill and my smiling at the desk man is wearing thin."

"I have money. My father sent—"

She wasn't listening, however, but staring across the room past him. Her eyes lit up: "Collis!"

Johnson turned to look. Behind him, a heavyset, dour

man in a dark suit was checking into the hotel at the front desk. The man looked over. He had the mournful expression of a basset hound. "Miranda? Miranda Lapham?"

Johnson frowned. "Miranda?"

Emily was standing, beaming. "Collis Huntington, whatever are you doing in Cheyenne?"

"Bless me, it's Miranda Lapham!"

"Miranda? Lapham?" Johnson said, not only confused by Emily's new name but by the sudden idea that he might not have known her real identity at all. And why had she lied to him?

The heavyset man embraced Emily with warm and lingering familiarity. "Why, Miranda, you look wonderful, simply wonderful."

"It's delightful to see you, Collis."

"Let me look at you," he said, stepping back, beaming. "You haven't changed a bit, Miranda. I don't mind telling you I've missed you, Miranda."

"And I you, Collis."

The heavy man turned to Johnson. "This beautiful young lady is the best lobbyist the railroads ever had in Washington."

Johnson said nothing. He was still trying to put it together. Collis Huntington, Washington, railroads . . . *My God—Collis Huntington!* One of the Big Four of the Central Pacific in California. Collis Huntington, the blatant corruptionist who traveled each year to Washington with a suitcase full of money for the congressmen, the man once described as "scrupulously dishonest."

"Everyone misses you, Miranda," Huntington went on. "They all ask for you still. Bob Arthur—"

"Dear Senator Arthur—"

"And Jack Kearns—"

"Commissioner Kearns, what a dear man—"

"And even the general—"

"The general? He still asks for me?"

"He does," Huntington said sadly, shaking his head. "Why don't you come back, Miranda? Washington was always your first love."

"All right," she said suddenly. "You've convinced me."

Huntington turned to Johnson. "Aren't you going to introduce me to your companion?"

"He's nobody," Miranda Lapham said, shaking her head so her curls moved prettily. She took Huntington's arm. "Come, Collis, we'll have a delicious lunch and you can tell me the news of Washington. And there is so much to do, you will have to find me a house, of course, and I will need some setting up . . ."

They moved away, arm in arm, to the dining room.

Johnson sat there, stunned.

At eight the next morning, feeling he had lived a decade in a few months, he took the Union Pacific train east, all ten crates stored in the rattling luggage car. The monotony of the voyage was most enjoyable, and he marked the greening of the landscape. The arrival of autumn could be seen in the top leaves of the oaks and maples and apple trees. At each stop, he would get off and buy the local newspapers, noticing an Eastern point of view creeping into the editorials about the Indian Wars—and various other topics.

On the morning of the fourth day, in Pittsburgh, he telegraphed Cope to say he had survived and would like to come speak with him; he said nothing about the crates of bones. Then he telegraphed his parents and asked that they have an extra place set for dinner that night.

He arrived in Philadelphia on October 8.

Four Meetings

At the train station, Johnson hired a man with an empty greengrocer's wagon to take him to Cope's house on Pine Street in Philadelphia. It wasn't a long trip, and he arrived to find that Cope owned two matching three-story stone row houses, one a residence and the other a private museum and offices. Most surprising was that Cope lived perhaps only seven or eight blocks from Rittenhouse Square, where Johnson's mother was even now preparing for his arrival.

"Which house is the residence?" he asked the wagon owner.

"I do not know, but I think that fellow will tell you," the man said, pointing.

It was Cope himself, bouncing down the steps. "Johnson!"

"Professor!"

He gave Johnson a firm handshake and a decisively strong hug.

"You're alive and—" He spied the tarp over the back of the wagon. "Is it possible?"

Johnson nodded. "It wasn't impossible, is perhaps my best answer."

The crates were taken directly into the museum half of Cope's property. Mrs. Cope came in with lemonade and wafers, and they sat down; they oohed over his stories, fussed over his appearance, exclaimed over his crates of bones.

"I will want to have a secretary transcribe an entire account of your adventure," said Cope. "We need to be able to prove that the bones we excavated in Montana are the bones that sit now in Philadelphia."

"A few may have broken from the way the wagon and stages bounced around," Johnson said. "Plus there may be a few bullet holes or bone chips, but mostly they're all here."

"The *Brontosaurus* teeth?" Cope asked, his hands twitching in excitement. "Do you still have the teeth? It may not reflect well on me, but I have been worrying about this since the day we thought you had been killed."

"It's this crate here, Professor," Johnson said, finding the box with the X.

Cope unpacked it on the spot, lifted the teeth one by one, and stared at them for a very long time, transfixed. He set them down in a row, much as he had done on the shale cliff many weeks earlier, nearly two thousand miles to the west. "This is extraordinary," he said. "Quite extraordinary. Marsh will be hard put to match it for many years."

"Edward," said Mrs. Cope, "hadn't we better send Mr. Johnson home to his family?"

"Yes, of course," Cope said. "They must be eager to see you."

His father embraced him warmly. "I thank God for your return, son."

His mother stood at the top of the stairs and said weepily, "The beard makes you look frightfully common, William. Get rid of it at once."

"What's happened to your lip?" his father said. "Are you wounded?"

"Indians," Johnson said.

"Looks like teeth marks to me," Edward, his brother, said.

"That's so," Johnson said. "This Indian climbed aboard the wagon and bit me. Wanted to see what I would taste like."

"Bit you on the lip? What, was he trying to kiss you?"

"They are savages," Johnson said. "And unpredictable."

"Kissed by an Indian!" Edward said, clapping his hands. "Kissed by an Indian!"

Johnson rolled up his trousers and showed everyone the scar where the arrow had pierced his leg. He produced the stump of the arrow. He chose not to tell them many details, and said nothing of Emily Williams or Miranda Lapham or whatever her true name was. He did tell them about burying Toad and Little Wind.

Edward burst into tears and ran upstairs to his room.

"We're just glad to have you back, son," his father said, looking suddenly much older.

The fall term was already under way, but the dean of Yale College permitted him to enroll anyway. Johnson was not above the dramatic effect of putting on his Western clothes and his gun and striding into the dining room.

The entire room fell silent. Then someone said, "It's Johnson! Willy Johnson!"

Johnson strode over to Marlin's table. Marlin was eating with friends.

"I believe you owe me money," Johnson said, in his best tough voice.

"How colorful you look," Marlin said, laughing. "You must introduce me to your tailor, William."

Johnson said nothing.

"Should I presume you had many dime Western adventures and killed men in actual gunfights?" Marlin said, hamming it up for their listeners.

"Yes," Johnson said. "That would be correct."

Marlin's antic smile dropped, unsure of Johnson's meaning.

"I believe you owe me money," Johnson said again.

"My dear fellow, I owe you nothing at all! If you remember, the terms of our bet were that you would accompany Professor Marsh, and the entire school knows you did not get far with him before he cast you aside as a rogue and scoundrel."

In a single swift movement, Johnson grabbed Marlin by the collar, effortlessly hoisted him to his feet, and slammed him against the wall. "You snotty little bastard, you give me that thousand dollars or I'll break your head open."

Marlin was gasping, and noticed Johnson's scar. "I don't know you."

"No, but you owe me. Now tell everybody what you are going to do."

"I'm going to pay you a thousand dollars."

"Louder."

Marlin repeated it loudly. The room laughed. Johnson dropped him in a crumpled heap to the floor and walked out of the dining room.

Othniel Marsh lived alone in a mansion he had built on a hill outside New Haven. As he walked up the hill, Johnson had a sense of the loneliness and isolation of Marsh's life, his need for approval, for status and acceptance. He was shown to the drawing room; Marsh was working there alone, and looked up from a manuscript he was preparing.

"You sent for me, Professor Marsh?"

Marsh glared at him. "Where are they?"

"You mean the bones?"

"Of course I mean the bones! Where are they?"

Johnson held Marsh's gaze. He realized he was no longer afraid of the man, in any way. "Professor Cope has the bones, in Philadelphia. All of them."

"Is it true you have found the remains of a hitherto unknown dinosaur of great size?"

"I am not at liberty to say, Professor."

"You are a fatuous fool," Marsh said. "You have squandered your own opportunity for greatness. Cope will never publish, and if he does, his report will be so hasty, so filled with inaccuracies, that it will never attain the recognition of the scientific community. You should have brought them to Yale, where they could be properly studied. You are a fool and a traitor to your college, Johnson."

"Is that all, Professor?"

"Yes, that's all." Johnson turned to leave. "One more thing," Marsh said.

"Yes, Professor?"

"I don't suppose you can get the bones back?"

"No, Professor."

"Then it's gone," Marsh said wistfully. "All gone." He returned to his manuscript. His pen scratched on the paper.

Johnson left the room. On his way out, he passed a small skeleton of the miniature Cretaceous horse *Eohippus*. It was beautifully formed, beautifully assembled, this pale skeleton from the distant past. Somehow it made Johnson sad. He turned away, and hurried down the hill toward the College.

Postscript

COPE

Edward Drinker Cope died penniless in 1897 in Philadelphia, having exhausted his family fortune and his energy battling Marsh. He was relatively young still, only fifty-six years old. But he had seen the first *Brontosaurus* skeleton assembled at the Yale Peabody Museum and more than fourteen hundred papers published. He is credited with the discovery and naming of more than one thousand vertebrate species and more than fifty kinds of dinosaurs. One, *Anisonchus cophater*, he said he named "in honor of the number of Cope haters who surround me!" He donated his body to science and instructed that after death his brain size be compared with Marsh's, it being commonly believed at the time that brain size determined intelligence. Marsh declined to accept the challenge.

MARSH

Othniel Charles Marsh died two years after Cope, alone and embittered in the house he had built for himself. He was buried in the Grove Street Cemetery in New Haven, Connecticut. He and his fossil hunters discovered five-hundred-odd different fossilized animals, including some eighty dinosaurs; he named them all himself.

EARP

Wyatt Earp died on January 13, 1929, in a rented bungalow near the intersection of Venice and Crenshaw Boulevards in Los Angeles, after acting in silent movies and then selling the rights to his life story to Columbia Pictures. In later years he was strongly influenced by the wishes of his wife, Josie. He told his life story as he remembered it, or chose to remember it, to Stuart N. Lake, a Pasadena writer, two years before his death. When published as *Wyatt Earp, Frontier Marshal*, it made a terrific impression, and established his fame enduringly.

STERNBERG

Charles Hazelius Sternberg became a celebrated American fossil collector and amateur paleontologist who wrote about his time with Cope. He was in fact working for Cope when Cope died, and learned of his death three days later, wired directly by his wife. Sternberg wrote two books: *The Life of a Fossil Hunter* (1909) and *Hunting Dinosaurs in the Badlands of the Red Deer River, Alberta, Canada* (1917). He was responsible for finding the *Monoclonius*, or, as it is commonly known, the horned dinosaur. He quoted Cope as saying, "No man can say he loves us, when he wantonly destroys our work; no man loves God who wantonly destroys his creatures." Fossils collected by Sternberg are displayed in museums around the world.

Author's Note

"Biography," observed Oscar Wilde, "lends to death a new terror." Even in a work of fiction about individuals long dead, there is reason to consider his sentiment.

Readers unfamiliar with this period of American history may be interested to know that Professors Marsh and Cope were real people, their rivalry and antagonism depicted here without exaggeration—in fact, it has been toned down, since the nineteenth century promoted a degree of ad hominem excess that is hard to believe now.

Cope did go to the Montana badlands in 1876, and discovered the teeth of *Brontosaurus*, essentially as recounted here.*

---

* Editor's note: Charles H. Sternberg attributed this discovery to Cope in his 1909 memoir, *The Life of a Fossil Hunter*. Others have credited the discovery of the *Brontosaurus* to Marsh.

The antagonism between Cope and Marsh that played out over ten years is compressed here into a single summer, with some changes. Thus, it was Marsh who made the false skull for Cope to find, and so on. However, it is true that on many occasions the workers of Cope and Marsh fired on one another—with much more serious intent than suggested here.

The character of William Johnson is entirely fictitious. I would not read this novel as history. For history, read Charles Sternberg's detailed account of Cope's trip to the Montana badlands in *The Life of a Fossil Hunter.*

I am indebted to E. H. Colbert, the eminent paleontologist and curator of the American Museum of Natural History, for first bringing the story of Marsh and Cope to my attention; in his kind correspondence he suggested a novel about them; he also provided me with my first leads in his books.

Finally, readers who inspect photographic books, as I have done, should be extremely careful about the captions. There has emerged a new breed of photo book in which authentic pictures of the West are accompanied by bleak, elegiac prose. The captions may seem to fit the pictures, but they do not fit the facts—this sad, melancholy attitude is a complete anachronism. Towns such as Deadwood may look depressing to us now, but they were exciting places then, and the people who inhabited them were excited to be there. Too often, the people who write captions to photographs indulge their own uninformed fantasies about the pictures and what they mean.

All the events of 1876 occurred as reported here, except that Marsh did not lead a party of students west that year (he had gone every year for the previous six, but remained in New Haven in 1876 to meet the English biologist T. H. Huxley); that all of Cope's bones traveled safely on the Missouri steamer, and no one continued on to Deadwood; and that Robert Louis Stevenson did not go west until 1879. The descriptions of the Indian Wars are accurate, sadly so, and from a vantage of some hundred-plus years later, it seems safe to say that the American West described in these pages, like the world of the dinosaurs long before, was soon to be forever lost.

Afterword

Michael's dedication to his craft was endless: over the course of his forty-plus-year career, he wrote thirty-two books; his work inspired many films, and as a director, screenwriter, and producer himself, he created iconic movies and television programs. Not only was he always working on his next project, he was always working on his "next *projects*." Michael was constantly reading, clipping interesting articles, amassing research for new work by looking to the past, observing the present, and thinking about our future. He loved to tell stories that blurred the lines between facts and what-if scenarios. You always came out of a Crichton novel, film, or television event smarter and wanting more. Because his work was so densely researched, you couldn't help but believe that, yes, perhaps dinosaurs could be brought back to life through DNA found in a well-preserved mosquito or that nanobots could operate intelligently and independently and wreak havoc on their human creators and the environment.

His work is as relevant and engaging as ever, as demonstrated by the gigantic success of the *Jurassic Park* franchise, and in HBO's reimagining of his classic film *Westworld*.

Honoring Michael's legacy has been my mission ever since he passed away. Through the creation of his archives, I quickly realized that it was possible to trace the birth of *Dragon Teeth* to a 1974 letter to the curator of vertebrate paleontology of the American Museum of Natural Histroy. After reading the manuscript, I could only describe *Dragon Teeth* as "pure Crichton." It has Michael's voice, and his love of history, research, and science all dynamically woven into this epic tale. Nearly forty years after Michael first hatched the idea for a novel about the excitement and the dangers of early paleontology, the story feels as fresh and fun today as it was to him then. *Dragon Teeth* was a very important book for Michael—it was a forerunner of his "other dinosaur story." Its publication is a wonderful way to introduce Michael to new generations of readers around the world and is an absolute treat for longtime Crichton fans everywhere.

Publishing *Dragon Teeth* has been a labor of love, and I want to thank the following people for their assistance in this endeavor: my creative partner, Laurent Bouzereau; Jonathan Burnham, Jennifer Barth, and the team at Harper; Jennifer Joel and Sloan Harris of ICM Partners; the remarkable team at the Michael Crichton Archives; Michael S. Sherman and Page Jenkins; and, of course, our beloved son, John Michael Crichton (Jr.).

—SHERRI CRICHTON

Bibliography

Barnett, Leroy. "Ghastly Harvest: Montana's Trade in Buffalo Bones." *Montana: The Magazine of Western History*, vol. 25, no. 3 (Summer 1975): 2–13.

Barton, D. R. "Middlemen of the Dinosaur Resurrection: The 'Jimmy Valentines' of Science." *Natural History* (May 1938): 385–87.

———. "The Story of a Pioneer 'Bone-Setter.'" *Natural History* (March 1938): 224–27.

Colbert, Edwin H. "Battle of the Bones. Cope & Marsh, the Paleontological Antagonists." *Geo Times*, vol. 2, no. 4 (October 1957): 6–7, 14.

———. Men and Dinosaurs: The Search in Field and Laboratory. Dutton: New York, 1968.

———. Their Discovery and Their World. Dutton: New York, 1961.

Connell, Evan. *Son of the Morning Star: Custer and the Little Big Horn.* Berkeley, California: North Point Press, 1984.

Dippie, Brian W. "Bold but Wasting Race: Stereotypes and American Indian Policy." *Montana: The Magazine of Western History,* vol. 25, no. 3 (Summer 1975): 2–13.

Eiseley, Loren. The Immense Journey: An Imaginative Naturalist Explores the Mysteries of Man and Nature. New York: Vintage Books, 1959.

Fisher, David. "The Time They Postponed Doomsday." *New Scientist* (June 1985): 39–43.

Grinnell, George Bird. "An Old-Time Bone Hunt." *Natural History* (July–August 1923): 329–36.

Hanson, Stephen and Patricia Hanson. "The Last Days of Wyatt Earp." *Los Angeles Magazine* (March 1985): 118–26.

Howard, Robert West. *The Dawnseekers: The First History of American Paleontology.* New York: Harcourt Brace Jovanovich, 1975.

Jeffery, David. "Fossils: Annals of Life Written in Rock." *National Geographic,* vol. 168, no. 2 (August 1985): 182–91.

Josephson, Matthew. *The Robber Barons: The Great American Capitalists 1861–1901.* New York: Harcourt Brace Jovanovich, 1934.

Lake, Stuart. *Wyatt Earp: Frontier Marshal.* New York: Houghton Mifflin Company, 1931.

Lanham, Url. *The Bone Hunters.* New York: Columbia University Press, 1973.

Marsh, Othniel Charles. "The Dinosaurs of North America." *Annual Report of US Geological Survey* (January 1896).

Matthew, W. D. "Early Days of Fossil Hunting in the High Plains." *Natural History* (September–October 1926): 449–54.

Mountfield, David. *The Railway Barons.* New York: W. W. Norton, 1979.

Nield, Ted. "Sticks, Stones and Broken Bones." *New Scientist* (December 1985): 64–67.

O'Connor, Richard. *Iron Wheels and Broken Men.* New York: Putnam's, 1973.

Osborn, Henry Fairfield. *Cope: Master Naturalist: The Life and Letters of Edward Drinker Cope.* Princeton, New Jersey: Princeton University Press, 1931.

Ostrom, John H. and J. S. McIntosh. *Marsh's Dinosaurs.* New Haven, Connecticut: Yale University Press, 1966.

Parker, Watson. *Gold in the Black Hills.* Norman: University of Oklahoma Press, 1966.

Plate, Robert. Dinosaur Hunters Othniel C. Marsh and Edward D. Cope. New York: D. McKay Co., 1964.

Reinhardt, Richard. *Out West on the Overland Train.* New Jersey: Castle Books, 1967.

Rice, Larry. "Badlands." *Adventure Travel* (July–August 1981): 38–44.

————. "The Great Northern Plains." *Backpacker* (May 1986): 48–52.

Romer, A. S. "Cope Versus Marsh." *Systemic Zoology,* vol. 13, no. 4 (1964): 201–7.

Scott, Douglas D. and Melissa A. Connor. "Post-mortem at the Little Bighorn." *Natural History* (June 1986): 46–55.

Shor, Betty. *The Fossil Feud Between E. D. Cope and O. C. Marsh.* Hicksville, New York: Exposition Press, 1974.

Stein, Ross S. and Robert C. Bucknam. "Quake Replay in the Great Basin." *Natural History* (June 1986): 28–36.

Sternberg, Charles H. *The Life of a Fossil Hunter.* New York: Henry Holt and Company, 1909.

Taft, Robert. *Photography and the American Scene.* New York: Dover Publications Inc., 1964.

West, Linda and Dan Chure. *Dinosaur: The Dinosaur National Monument Quarry.* Jensen, Utah: Dinosaur Nature Association, 1984.

Wolf, Daniel. *The American Space.* Middletown, Connecticut: Wesleyan University Press, 1983.

About the Author

MICHAEL CRICHTON (1942–2008) was the author of the groundbreaking novels *The Andromeda Strain*, *The Great Train Robbery*, *Jurassic Park*, *Disclosure*, *Prey*, *State of Fear*, and *Next*, among many others. His books have sold more than 200 million copies worldwide, have been translated into thirty-eight languages, and have provided the basis for fifteen feature films. He was the director of *Westworld*, *Coma*, *The Great Train Robbery*, and *Looker*, as well as the creator of *ER*. Crichton remains the only writer to have a number one book, movie, and TV show in the same year.